RETURN

A FOR THE STARS NOVEL

RETURN

O McCARTHY

ISBN (paperback): 979-8-9908446-4-3
ISBN (ebook): 979-8-9908446-5-0

Editing & proofreading by Caitlin Miller
Cover design & typesetting by Benita Thompson

*For Gabriella, you've been with me and these characters
since the very beginning—all those years ago in Texas.
I love you beyond the stars.*

*Lily S, thank you for pushing me to finish this series.
Reach is better because of you.*

When facing monsters, man must remember,
The worst monsters have always been made by man.

PART 1

1

Home is a strange word. It's even stranger when the exact place you call home can only be pinpointed on a universal scale. I can call Earth home, but I can't tell you a country that is my home, and I certainly can't break it down into a city or an exact address. There are no geographical coordinates to pair with a specific place. That isn't how my life has panned out.

I stare out of the round ball that I'm maneuvering across the barren surface of Mars. The clear Martian glass compound keeps me separated from the harsh elements of a planet that would just as soon freeze me to death.

Earth is nothing more than a bright star in the sky, but I know the truth—that out there, in the vast cosmos, is a planet whose surface sustains life. It is diametrically opposed to the planet I'm currently on.

"Reach?" Llama's voice sounds throughout the *traverse-ball* thanks to the interconnected communication systems. "What's it like up there right now?"

I grimace as I survey the endless miles of iron-oxidized dust. "Red," I reply. "And dusty."

There's a beat of silence, and I can picture Llama's face as she responds, "I suppose it's also rusting."

I laugh. Llama's dry humor is a brand that many people don't understand, but it's one of the things I love about her. "Definitely. I think Mars might have a vendetta against life, because everywhere I look, I see things that would kill me."

"Reach." Llama's voice is stern now. She's entered into *Princess Llama of Souterraine* mode. "Seriously, we need a report on the surface conditions. When will you be returning to the training base?"

I release the joy sticks to stop the ball, then swipe the glass from left to right. An operating system appears, showing the charts and graphs of different surface conditions that I'm currently measuring through the traverse-ball's sensors. I quickly scan the computer projections.

"I'm at sixty-four percent completion with the data compilations. That's an hour more, at least, to finish the observations and get back to the surface portal airlock."

"Hmm," she hums. A low voice sounds, but I can't make out the words. "I don't like it," Llama whispers.

"You don't like what?" I ask, alarm building in my chest.

Her breath hitches. "There's a dust storm fifteen miles behind you. Its trajectory isn't yet known."

I twist around on the uncomfortable seat to look out the ball's rear wall. A haze is barely present, but still visible in the distance.

"I see it. But it's still far off." My hands manipulate the controls of the traverse-ball again, and I begin moving forward.

A low rumble of voices sounds.

"Reach." Llama's commanding voice is back. "You need to return to Souterraine. Immediately."

I swivel around to check on the haze. It's still in the distance, and there's nothing but the smooth track of the traverse-ball cut into the dust behind me for miles.

"Why?" I ask. "I have enough time to finish the data collection and return."

"As the Princess of Souterraine, I am ordering you to return immediately."

I hear the panic in her voice, but there's nothing to worry about up here. "Princess Llama"—I exaggerate the honorific—"you do know that you can't order your husband around, right?" I tease, hoping to break the tension.

"You're not my husband yet. Now, get back to the colony."

I smile at her tone and think of our upcoming marriage. If you'd asked me a year ago, when Llama and I first landed on Mars, if I was in love with the woman who betrayed me, my answer would have been a firm and irrefutable no. It also would have been a lie. I've always loved her.

"Reach, you have to come back," she says, softer this time, and it's the quiet plea that does it. Maybe we'll have an incomplete data set that will set our travel plans back a bit, and I strongly suspect some technological glitch in her monitoring systems of the surface, based on what I am seeing and reading, but I would rather soothe her anxiety than stay and complete this mission.

"Ok. I'm on my way."

A whoosh of air sounds as she blows a breath and whispers, "I love you, Reach."

I turn the controls and head west back to the airlock that will take me to the underground colony of Souterraine.

And that is when I see it. The reason Llama insists I return to the colony with an incomplete data set is clear.

It's not one dust storm fifteen miles south.

There's a second dust storm to the west—and this one is much closer.

I'm in real danger. A surface dust storm can last forever, and there will be no way of knowing which way I'm going once I'm in the thick of it.

I urge the ball to roll faster across the desert, but I'm already at top speed, and the dust storm is quickly gaining on me. The red cloud rolls and roils toward me like a wave of rusty fury.

I'm not at the surface portal to get back underground when the first grains of fine red sand strike the glass of the traverse-ball and the wind buffets me.

I don't want to die on Mars.

2

Traverse-balls have a homing system that functions like the old NASA-era Mars Rovers. The system points me in the direction of the surface portal, but there's a risk: once the particles of Martian grit become too dense, the homing system will be completely ineffective. And what does a ball do when exposed to significant winds? *It rolls.*

That is the point of the traverse-ball. It's an efficient way to cover long distances on the surface without utilizing the challenging resource of rubber. That is saved for underground use, and recycled diligently by the people of Souterraine Colony. But in a dust storm, a ball is subject to the whims of crosswinds and the overall freakish nature of weather in thin atmospheric conditions. In a dust storm, I will first get lost on the surface of the planet, then die from starvation, if not from the only slightly-more-pleasant-to-imagine internal injuries of being *inside* a ball when it's being tossed around like a children's toy.

I manipulate the screen in front of me to show the homing device beacon on a contour map of Mars' surface. One mile. *I can make it one mile.* A green pinprick of light on the map flashes to show where I'm headed, while a red dot reveals my location. Traverse-balls move efficiently, but efficient doesn't always mean *fast*.

I have maybe ten minutes if I don't encounter any unexpected obstacles before I'll reach the surface portal and dock into the port. The fragments of ancient rock that have been ground into such fine particles that they now sift and change and fly through the air plink against the glass surrounding me. The homing signal should be emitting a longer flash the closer I get to it, but instead, the green flashes become more erratic.

While a traverse-ball technically has only one speed, I don't have time. What I do have is physics. I know it's going to hurt, but I'm going to have to help the rotating exterior pick up velocity by slamming my body at the forward point of rotation—repeatedly.

I place my feet on the seat, which is attached to a frame inside the ball, keeping it stationary as the outer ball rolls, and push up to a crouch before I throw my weight to the front of the orb, making it rotate faster. I do this three times before I realize that I could push against my feet and, hand over hand, help the ball roll.

My shoulder is bruised, my head hurts, but the homing signal is beeping even less frequently than before, and the red dust swirling around the ball might be thicker. It's hard to tell with my eyes burning from pain.

Suddenly, the red dot and the green flash on the contour map screen connect. There's a grinding of gears, and, after a moment of stillness, a vertical drop into the bowels of Mars.

I'm sweaty from the ordeal, but after nearly dying yet again on this planet, I can't help it. When Llama runs to me in the dimly lit hallway that connects the traverse-ball garage to the rest of Souterraine I put out both arms to catch her in a tight embrace. It doesn't matter how much it hurts; what matters is that I'm where I need to be. I'm alive.

"Reach." Llama breathes out a sigh. "You listened."

"I try," I say before dropping my arms and rubbing my right shoulder. It doesn't massage the pain away.

"Are you hurt?" Llama asks.

"Not much," I lie, but she fixes me with a stern look.

"Then you'll be seeing Dr. Harold as soon as you're back at the castle."

"Bossy much?" I tease.

"No, I'm just in charge here."

"True," I whisper as I plant a kiss on the top of her head. I'm rewarded with a look of adoration in her blue eyes and contemplate a longer kiss when more people appear around the bend in the hallway.

"Reach!" Queen Eleanore cries. "That was harrowing."

"Glad you're back," Phil says in a much calmer voice.

"Is the incomplete data set still something that can be used?" I ask Phil.

He nods.

"Yes, it's helpful," a new, deep voice cuts in. "But would you mind explaining to me how you were able to get the traverse-ball up to 10.84 miles per hour? It's not designed to go that fast." The King of Souterraine fixes me with a stern glare. I glare back, because my future grandfather-in-law is all bark and no bite.

"Alfred," Queen Eleanore chides. "That was terrifying. Whatever Reach did, I'm so glad he did it. No technology is worth 'saving' at the expense of a human life." Her warm brown eyes sit above prominent cheekbones and regard me with affection.

Llama slips her hand into mine and squeezes tightly. "Surface missions are the worst part of this," she whispers, but the king and queen overhear.

"I strongly suspect that the surface missions on Mars are easy compared to what will await you back in Nation," King Alfred drawls as he meets my gaze and runs a hand down the short gray beard covering his chin.

I'm inclined to agree.

I know Nation. And while Mars is an unforgiving, inhospitable geographical location that will kill indiscriminately, Nation is an unforgiving, inhospitable social structure specially designed to ensure that people like me and Llama don't have a chance at a good life.

If I had to choose, I'd take geography every time.

DEBRIEFING AFTER A surface mission has become standard in Souter-raine's Preparation Sector. The entourage leaves me when we arrive at the locker room. Llama hangs back for a moment after the king, queen, and Phil disappear around the bend. She stands on her tiptoes and places a firm kiss on my lips before she whispers, "You didn't forget," and then walks away, leaving me staring at her retreating form and listening to the swish-swish of the stiff fiber fabric that makes up her long red dress.

No, I didn't.

Just under a year ago, when Jezero Colony suffered the fate of extinction from an airlock malfunction and collapse, I promised her I wouldn't leave her again. I knew I couldn't really promise that, but I recklessly did it anyway. Her words are a reminder of a promise I can't fulfill, but will die trying to. Ironically, she was asking me to promise *not* to die.

I duck into the locker room and change out of my traverse-ball mission clothing. The spacesuit is flexible, shiny like tin foil, and able to withstand short excursions onto the surface proper. Although the traverse-ball is a barrier between the actual surface of Mars and the human body, no one wants to take any chances, so anytime a traverse-ball is used, the user wears a spacesuit. It is completely redundant, because the only way to escape a traverse-ball without a port is if the glass compound cracks. If the glass compound cracks, you'd need to place a helmet on your head immediately, and even then, you'd probably experience your veins boiling from the rapid drop in temperature and atmosphere. So, yes, we wear them in case we have to evacuate the ball, and if we evacuate the ball, we will die.

Back in the twentieth century, the world was worried about something called *nuclear war*. In the event of a nuclear attack, schools told students to hide under their classroom desks. It was completely unreasonable advice, and yet it was something they were instructed to do. It gave people a sense of power, of control. The spacesuit issue is the same. They are comfortable, so no one on a surface mission minds.

As I slip into the tan-colored pants and the dark green button-up shirt that make up the common clothing of Souterraine colonists, I marvel at the underground world that has thrived for centuries on Mars. Yes, it's coming to a close, and yes, its resources will have been thoroughly depleted in the next few years. And yet, it's here. An entire colony of people that escaped Nation before the Scientific Revolution and built a place that not only valued human life, but culture and art, in addition to technology.

Llama's connection to the King and Queen of Souterraine as their granddaughter was shocking when we arrived on Mars, but she was born to lead. The way she stepped into her role as Princess of Souterraine and embraced her people here only serves to heighten her beauty. And make no mistake, my fiancée is beautiful.

But more than beautiful, she's smart. She's cunning. She's a survivor. And she's determined to right wrongs. Vengeance isn't something I find attractive, but there's an iron cord in her will that isn't about getting even. At first, maybe that's what it was, but now, it's not about payback. Llama wants *justice*. And I want it too.

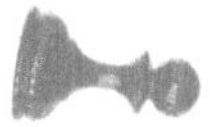

I rotate my shoulder to work out the tension when I walk into the debriefing room. Instead of the few people who usually handle the debriefing, this time, the auditorium-like space nestled into a border of giant willow trees is full.

Llama sits next to her grandparents, a crown of white flowers twisted together atop her light brown hair. Her blue eyes meet my own and widen for a moment before she raises one eyebrow delicately and tips her head to the side while staring at my shirt buttons.

I look down and discover that, in my musings about Souterraine and Llama herself, I missed a few. My shirt is a haphazardly buttoned mess. There's no way for me to fix this without completely starting over, and I'm in a room full of people.

"Reach," King Alfred says. "Sit." He's stern, and his eyes take in my disheveled appearance and don't even blink as I follow his command. This is the first clue that something important is happening. The second clue is when Queen Eleanore waves her hand and Margot, the Intergalactic Technological Communications manager originally from Jezero, stands and walks to the front of the room. Margot *never* comes to anything except advisory council meetings.

"Your Majesties," she begins as she meets the king, queen, and Llama's eyes. Then she turns her gaze on me as her hair, which has become more gray with each passing day she's been head of the COMS Department, reflects the soft glow of the light above. "President Reach."

"We have a message that is of interest to everyone in this room." Her jaw tightens. "I actually have *two*. One message from Sigma, and one from…Leader."

I start at the mention of Leader. Sigma, my mother, has sent several messages to the colony. But *Leader*? She's never contacted Souterraine or Jezero.

"It appears that Leader is unaware of Jezero's demise. And she believes she is communicating with Percy." She looks at me. I grimace. "This is a delicate situation, and I'm not certain how to handle it. On the one hand, do I tell her Percy is a criminal who lost his post? Or do I gather information by not telling her? It's a ruse I'm not entirely comfortable with, but it may matter significantly for your lives."

Game theory.

I push off the wooden bench where I've been sitting next to Llama. "What does the message say, Margot?"

Margot holds out her palm, places a triangular stand on it, and a round disc on top. The contraption makes a tablet that she spins counter-clockwise for a moment. She reads:

"LDR: Jezero COMS, you've been communicating with government entity Enforce, but now this is Leader. There is suspected extreme unrest at latitude 46.871068 and longitude -89.31414. Surveillance requested."

Something about those coordinates feels off, but if Leader is requesting Jezero's help in surveilling outside the Wards, that's an indication that things are falling apart, at least somewhere.

Llama slips her hand into mine and gently tugs me back into the seat. "What does the message from Sigma say?" she asks in a calm, collected voice.

Margot nods and spins her tablet again before reading. "Sigma: A hero has freedom to marry. Reach, rise, return before the sun sets."

Llama's eyes track to mine. She grins before hopping off the wooden bench.

"She did it!" she exclaims. "She escaped, and she got to them!"

"Perhaps, my dear," Queen Eleanore inserts, "you could fill us in? Those messages from Sigma are often rather cryptic."

Llama looks out at the room. "There is definitely unrest happening in Nation, and it must be significant if Leader is requesting help from Jezero with surveillance. Although Nation has a robust surveillance system in place for the Citizens, they never kept up with surveilling the Wards beyond a certain point. Since Sigma—Reach's mother—is outside of the Wards, there is presumably no structure for surveillance in her location. Nation senses something is happening and wants to know about it."

"Yes, dear, that part makes sense," Queen Eleanore says with a frown. "What doesn't make sense is that phrase 'a hero has freedom to marry.'"

Llama's smile can't help but widen. "It means that Hero, our friend from Hub, escaped, went off-grid, and found Freedom. They were going to be unionized in Nation, but Freedom had to disappear to prevent..." She trails off and looks at me. I give her an encouraging nod. "To prevent himself from having to sign the death papers for his own parents, who were tried as traitors to the government." There's a gasp as the people in the room all inhale in shock. Her slender throat cords. "It's a barbaric place, really. Masquerading as scientifically efficient." She composes herself. "But Sigma is telling us that things must have unraveled at Hub if Hero found her way to Freedom. And she's also telling us the good news, too."

King Alfred stands, the vines that make up his crown not floral, but woody and green atop his gray hair. "Ah, but what do *we* do about all this? The game theory is murky here, is it not?"

Without any hesitation, every single eye in the room turns toward me.

4

I'm used to being under scrutiny. It hasn't happened nearly as often on Mars as it did in my childhood, but in a strange way, I'm grateful for the practice that weaving a twisted lie of me being half-Martian to the government and manipulating data on all the human experiments waged on me gave me in moments like this.

Ironically, the lie was nearly true. I am of Martian descent, but not *alien* Martian. Underground *human* Martian colonists. That legacy is gone now that my father, Greg, perished in the collapse of Jezero Colony. Thoughts flood my brain as I try to make sense of the metaphorical chessboard with three players, with one player who doesn't realize she's playing with a second opponent.

The advantage is that Nation does not know we have teamed up with my mother and the Resistance. The disadvantage is that we're here on Mars, and they're all back on Earth.

"I think," I say, trying to buy some time. "I think it might be best to continue the conversation with Nation. Perhaps appear as if we're entertaining the idea of helping, but at a cost. That would tell us what the situation is better than guessing." I look to Llama, who nods in agreement.

"And I also think—" I blow out a breath. "I think Sigma was asking us to give an update on when we will return to Earth."

Queen Eleanore's face sets into hard lines, while King Alfred's jaw tightens. We might be preparing to return to Earth and overthrow Nation with the Resistance, led by my mother, but it's something neither royal is particularly pleased about.

Fortunately—or unfortunately—resources on Mars have become scarce. The colony will die out in years unless a large group evacuates. This room is full of the one hundred plus people training to be a Souterraine army, allies with the Resistance against Nation.

"Yes, well," Queen Eleanore says in a brisk fashion, "your training is progressing, but it's still too soon—"

"Your Highness," Margot interrupts, "with all due respect, there are more messages."

"Why didn't you say so?" Queen Eleanore asks.

"It doesn't make much sense."

"What is it, Margot?" King Alfred growls.

Margot responds with three words: "Sigma: Benko Gambit."

My eyes go wide, my mouth drops open, and my hand runs through my unruly hair.

"What on earth does that mean?" King Alfred throws his hands in the air in frustration.

"It's her move," I say. She's telling me her opening move. And she's using chess terms to do it. Sudden inspiration strikes me. "Who here knows how to play chess?" I ask as I look around the room.

Llama shyly raises her hand, and I understand why, because although she technically knows how to play, she's definitely not skilled at it.

Two hands in the back slowly rise. I gesture for them to stand so I can see who it is.

Beatriz and Cait.

I scrub a hand down my face, because although I knew they

were part of this cohort, the women standing are females I'd rather not deal with again. Women who were field operatives for Jezero, and while I act as the President of Jezero here in Souterraine, I'd just as soon burn the sash they revere.

I groan and let my shoulders slouch, but Llama kicks my calf, and when I turn to see why, I'm met with a stony gaze and a barely perceptible shake of the head.

I square my shoulders against the rising tension in my body. The dull ache of the bruise there turns into a throbbing pain. I bite the pain down because that's what's expected of me as a leader here.

"I think," I say, and though I speak quietly, there isn't any ambient noise in the room, so my voice sounds louder than normal, "that we all need to learn to play chess." My eyes track to Queen Eleanore and King Alfred. They frown, but each of them nods.

Queen Eleanore stands and begins counting the number of people in the room. She whispers, "112. That's fifty-six sets needed. It will take some time."

Beatriz and Cait still stand in the back. I look at them and realize what needs to happen next.

There might not be a chess set for each pair of colonists preparing to return to Nation in the first wave of the Souterraine evacuation schedule, but there is at least one chess set in the castle library. Sometimes, watching is equally as valuable as doing.

"Cait, Beatriz," I call. "Would you please come up here?"

As the two women make their way to the front of the debriefing space, I turn to Queen Eleanore. "Could we get the chess set from the library brought here?" I ask in a low voice.

Queen Eleanore nods, and with a look of pain in her eyes, leaves the room.

Queen Eleanore returns minutes later with the chess set. She must have taken a MUV—Martian Ultralite Vehicle—and floored it.

When she brushes aside the curtain of willow branches and steps through, chess set in her hands, she looks regal. She *is* regal, but there is a resoluteness about her leadership in this moment that says she doesn't like what's happening, but she's doing it because she must. She is choosing to set her own prejudices aside and do what is right for her people—even the people of Jezero Colony, who have been absorbed by Souterraine.

Beatriz and Cait wait quietly next to me. I close my eyes for a brief moment, then turn to face the room again. "It will take time before everyone has access to a chessboard and pieces. In the meantime, let's watch a match."

Llama brings a small wooden table over from the side of the space, while King Alfred produces two small wooden stools. Queen Eleanore places the board on top of the table, removing the top to reveal the pieces stored inside.

Cait and Beatriz stare at the table and the set, then look at me.

"Which one of us is playing you?" Cait asks.

I open my mouth and close it again. I had thought they'd play each other, but I don't know how to say that when the expectation that *I* play is suddenly palpable in the minds of everyone in the room.

I blow out a breath. I didn't intend to play a match today after my ordeal on the surface of Mars, but I guess I will be.

Llama speaks up. "Which of you is better?"

Beatriz raises her hand shyly. "I beat Cait last time…in…field training."

My fingers find their way to my temple, and I massage the pressure there. These women, who were field operatives, keep reminding me of Jezero and their services to that colony.

"Then Reach will play you, Beatriz," Llama says it dismissively, as if Beatriz is beneath her, but I see what's really happening. Llama hasn't forgiven Beatriz for her attempts to use me.

One large exhale, and then I'm ready. "Ok, then. Let's begin."

Cait disappears back into the edge of the crowd, and Beatriz begins setting up the board.

"White or black?" Beatriz asks.

"Black," I say, knowing it gives Beatriz a slight advantage.

She studies the board for a moment, and then makes her opening move—the Meadow Hay Opening.

This match is going to take all my wit.

5

Beatriz is good at chess.

But I'm better.

I'm able to take a pawn *en passant* on the fourth move, and Beatriz's whole strategy unravels. I'm honestly not sure if she had a strategy. Perhaps it was to not have a strategy and merely respond to my moves. It resulted in a chaotic board and a smothered mate, where my knight trapped her king, who was prevented from escaping by his own pieces.

Beatriz smiles at me, her long blonde braid looking out of place on the shoulder of Souterraine clothing. "Congratulations. You played well."

I scratch my head in response and stare at the board for a moment. There's a metaphor here, and I'm trying to find it. "Thank you," I grind out between my clenched teeth, because while Beatriz isn't tempting to me in any way anymore, and I know that her agency has been decommissioned, I hate *what* she was.

Llama stands and asks, "Who has questions?"

Every single hand rises in the air.

I try not to grimace, but clearly I'm going to have to be the one who answers all these questions. My shoulder burns, and I'm exhausted. All I want is to fall into my bed and nap. And then eat a hunk of Bernard's bread.

King Alfred narrows his eyes at me, and I drop my hand away from my shoulder, where I was massaging the pain away. His deep voice fills the space. "That was an exposition. We will be having teaching matches in the future, but will be adjourning this debriefing. You are dismissed and required to report to your regular colony duties for the rest of the day." He turns to me. "Reach, you are dismissed to see Doctor Harold."

Llama stands and moves next to me. "Good match," she whispers in my ear before gently touching my forehead. Her brow creases. "You're warm."

"It was rather disconcerting to have all those people watching my every move," I quip.

"Still, I'll feel better once the doctor sees you. Your right shoulder is what's bothering you?" I nod, too exhausted for words. "Come on, let's take the MUV back to the castle." She tips her head back to indicate her grandparents. "They won't mind."

In a haze, I follow her and climb into the MUV parked outside the willow training base. It's strange that so much of Souterraine is open air and out of doors. The castle doesn't have a large enough space to contain the one hundred twelve colonists who are actively preparing for war against Nation, so the willow grove became the makeshift training base.

Llama slides into the driver's seat and begins maneuvering the vehicle back to the castle. My head hurts, and my throat is dry, but the pain in my shoulder is the most unbearable it's been. Still, I don't want to look weak, so I clench my jaw and look ahead where the large wooden doors of the castle gleam.

When I exit the MUV, I have the brief thought that only responding to my moves on the chessboard was Beatriz's downfall.

Without a strategy, a player is doomed. We're only responding to Nation right now. Our strategy isn't fleshed out.

Understanding encompasses me like I've been thrown into a pool and am swimming in it. And then the ground slaps my face.

Doctor Harold glares at me as I sit up in my bed and feel the tight bandages wrapped over my right shoulder.

"No," I say, running my fingers over the fabric. "No, no, no, no."

"Yes," Dr. Harold says in response. "Why is it that you dislike my orders so much?"

"Why is it that you made it so I can't move my right arm at all? It's in a sling!" I retort. "I'm *right*-handed."

"Guess you'll be ambidextrous by the end of next week, then." He stands. "Oh, and Reach."

"Yes?" I scowl at him.

"You really should rest."

I groan and start to move my right hand to my face in irritation, but am stopped by the twinge of pain and the doctor's reproving glare. I switch to my other hand, letting my left palm hit my cheek and scrubbing it down my face.

Dr. Harold nods in approval. "Very good, then," he says. "Princess Llama is waiting. Shall I send her in?"

I nod.

He leaves, pushing the door wide, and Llama enters. My breath catches, the way it always does when I see her in her rightful place here in Souterraine.

She surveys me as I recline, propped up on pillows in my bed. She sets the vase of flowers from my dresser against the door, keeping it ajar. When she stands again, I smile at the concern in her gaze.

"What happened?"

"Well…" I start. "It was the dust storm, and I knew how to make physics work, but I didn't know how to make it work as well as it could have at first."

She raises one eyebrow. "As well as it could?"

I shake my head, but even that causes pain to pulse through my shoulder, so I stop. "I'm here. I survived. I came back."

Llama's face softens, and she sits in the chair next to my bed. "You remembered," she whispers.

I reach out my left hand and cup her cheek with it as she leans into my touch. We take a moment, revelling in the closeness of being quiet together. The moment doesn't last.

The pattering of feet reverberates down the hall, echoing off the wooden floor, walls, and ceiling. Pippa and Ethan slide around the corner and into my room. Queen Eleanore follows, a bemused tight-lipped smile on her face. "Ethan, Pippa," she chides. "We do not run around corners."

"Yes, Mama," Pippa says at the exact same time Ethan says, "Yes, 'mere." The two hang their heads, but somehow don't look sorry at all.

"What's the prognosis?" Queen Eleanore asks as she moves around the room and tidies things up. I'm not messy by nature, but this was an extenuating circumstance, and now I can't use my arm for at least two weeks.

"Dislocated shoulder," I say as the queen picks up a shirt from the ground, folds it, and places it in the wooden dresser. "I can't use my right arm at all for two weeks."

She stops and turns, facing me. Pippa and Ethan stare at my shoulder. "But can you play chess still?"

I think for a moment. "Yes. I'll be slower to move the pieces, but yes."

"Good." She frowns as if she's being forced to swallow something distasteful. "Because you were right. Everyone in Wave Cohort 1 needs to have a rudimentary understanding of the game."

I blink.

"Yes, Reach," Queen Eleanore says. "On Souterraine, we haven't prioritized thinking like our opponents, because there was no need. Now, I fear that is going to be to our detriment. Nation will not accept a Souterraine way of life, and I'm not willing to accept Nation's."

Llama looks at me, then back at Queen Eleanore. "Has the set-making begun?"

Pippa laughs, then reaches into the pocket of her dress and holds out a crudely carved white wooden pawn. "I made it," she proudly declares.

Ethan produces a similarly carved black pawn. "We're going to learn to play. Right? Present Reach?"

I bite my lip to keep from laughing at Ethan's inability to say *President*. "It's Reach, Ethan. Unless I'm wearing the sash."

Ethan's big eyes widen even more. "But you'll teach us, right, Reach?"

Llama tips her head to the side, watching me. Ethan and Pippa are undoubtedly my soft spots and she knows it.

"Yes," I say. "Yes, I'll teach you to play chess."

Pippa claps her hands in delight, and Ethan bounces up and down before he flings his tiny body at me and hugs me.

The sudden impact jostles my shoulder, and I stifle a cry of pain.

"Ethan," Queen Eleanore scolds.

"Sorry," he says, sticking out his bottom lip.

I take my left hand and ruffle his hair. "It's ok. I'm excited about chess too."

"Can we learn now?" Ethan asks, looking from me to Queen Eleanore and back again.

"I think, dear," Queen Eleanore says in response, "that Reach needs to rest. But perhaps tomorrow you and Pippa could spend some time with him and start to learn."

I smile, but all I can think is that between Ethan and Pippa and the one hundred twelve members of Wave Cohort 1, I'm going to be playing a lot of chess.

6

Mornings on Souterraine are always perfect. Everything about it is idyllic. Everything except for the people grumbling about hosting the remnants of Jezero Colony and now having to provide for extra people on an already dwindling supply chain.

Today, I'm walking through the agricultural sector of Souterraine that produces peas. The plants climb trellises, creating tunnels of white flowers interspersed with the green leaves and vines. My shoulder healed enough that I can manage some normal duties, but I certainly won't be returning to the surface for data sets anytime soon. Edith, a middle-aged woman in tan-colored overalls, meticulously checks the plants as we walk together. "So," she says. "You're the Jezero President."

"Acting Jezero President only during matters of state."

"It's convenient, don't you think?"

The sweet perfume of the plants gives me a bit of a headache. "What is convenient?"

"You," she says simply. "You're the president of the remnant of a colony on Mars, and you want to return to Earth, and *you* are getting what you want."

I stop and frown. She's implying something, but I can't figure out what. "What does that mean?" I ask.

She looks me over from head to toe, her eyes snagging on my sling. "It means that your arrival here, when things are breaking down, is suspicious."

"Suspicious to whom, exactly?" I grit out. "I don't think you were present at all the meetings Princess Llama and I had with leadership upon our arrival."

She hums in response.

I shake my head. I'm the acting President of Jezero Colony, but this is a matter of Souterraine state. I'm literally walking through a giant garden of peas.

"What are the latest updates on the blight?" I ask, point-blank. I might as well *not* beat around the bush with her. She certainly isn't.

"Contained." She frowns. "For now."

"And what about the food storage plans?"

She grimaces. "Stable at a five-year hold with a rationing plan of eighty-two percent typical rations."

"What was it last time?"

"Ninety percent rations."

I blink. "Why the change?"

"Unexpected surplus of population."

Suddenly, it makes sense. The Jezero colonists aren't taking more than their fair share, but they are an extra burden on the resources of Souterraine, including food, and it's the workers who are feeling it most acutely when they dole out the rations to the different sectors, or harvest and store them.

We reach an intersection in the tunnels of pea plants.

"Declan!" Edith calls as she looks down a different tunnel. "Deck! Come on over."

A young man with sandy blond hair, blue eyes, and massive muscles jogs down the row. "Yes, ma'am?" he says, tucking a pair of gardening gloves into the back pocket of his own tan-colored overalls. I haven't seen him at the school, so he must be close to my age. Or maybe a bit older than twenty.

"This is Reach," she says simply.

He nods along. "Yes, I know who he is."

"Good, then you'll be pleased to know that he's picking with you for the rest of the day in the rows that are ready for harvesting."

Declan blinks in surprise, but not before I do. I was unaware I was picking peas today. But I have the time, so I might as well contribute.

"Just show me where," I say, smiling at both Edith and Declan.

"Uh." Declan scratches at the back of his neck. "It's this way." He swallows. "Sir."

"Reach is fine," I reply. I know Souterraine stands on their honorifics, but I never understood it. I'm not a prince, or a king, or a royal. I'm a reluctant figurehead for a colony that's been forced to find refuge in Souterraine. And by *reluctant,* I don't mean 'accepted it willingly because I was the best person for the job in a humble-brag way.' I mean 'accepted it because it was thrust upon me in the midst of a very challenging transition period.'

"See you later, Reach," Edith says as Declan and I start off down the rows of peas. "Deck, have Reach report to the drying racks in three hours."

Declan gives a single head bob before picking up the pace. He's fast, and I have to nearly jog to keep up with him as he navigates a veritable maze of pea plant tunnels. My shoulder throbs from the motion, but speedwalking isn't better. I bite the inside of my cheek to keep from groaning.

It feels like forever before Declan stops beside plants bulging with green pea pods. He looks at me as if he forgot I was still here, or he expected me to conveniently disappear along the way.

"What do we do?" I ask, breaking the awkward silence as he stares at me.

"Uh." He swallows. "We pick them." He points to the pea pods. "We put them in a bucket and then take them to the drying racks."

"Where are the buckets?" I ask, looking around.

Declan reaches under the trellises at the intersection of two rows and produces two stacks of silver buckets. He looks at the plants, then the buckets, and nods. "This should be enough for this row."

He pulls one bucket out of the stack and hands it to me. I take the handle with my left hand. He turns and begins snapping pea pods off the plants and tossing them into his own bucket. He's meticulous and fast.

I watch for a moment before I begin my own harvest.

The problem: I'm not left-handed. And I can't use my right hand to snap the pods off. I break open several of the pods as I try to twist them off the stems with my non-dominant hand.

"Try not to break the pods open if you can help it. It's more fiber if we store and distribute peas in the pods," Declan instructs over his shoulder.

I blow out a frustrated breath. I'm already going slower than Declan, and I'm going to have to slow down even more in order to keep the peas in their shells.

I finally get the hang of it, and we fall into a sort of rhythm. "So, Declan," I say to break the silence. "How long have you worked in this sector?"

"Two years. I always wanted to grow things, so I studied anything related to agriculture in school. But that's not looking like it's worth knowing much anymore."

"What do you mean?" I ask, something about that comment not sitting right.

"You and Wave Cohort 1 are off to Earth, and I guess the plan is for everyone to leave Mars and return to Earth eventually. I suspect that Martian agriculture and Earth Ag are very different."

I consider his words. "Yeah, probably. But there's always a need for food, right?"

"Definitely."

"And if you can grow things on Mars, surely you can grow things on Earth."

"The variables," Declan says, "are intensely different."

"True, but people have done it for centuries there."

He shrugs. "Oh good, your bucket's full. We'll leave these full buckets at the intersection and grab wagons before we take the buckets to the drying racks."

I nod, and we continue picking, this time throwing the pods into new buckets. Even with my left-hand issue, I'm getting better and faster.

"So, sir," Declan says, breaking the silence.

"It's Reach, really," I say. "Unless I'm wearing that ridiculous sash. Then I get to be called president."

Declan's eyebrow arches at my tone. "I would have thought you'd liked being president."

"Not particularly," I respond.

"Hm." He looks at the ground, at my shoes, then up at my face. "You're different than I thought you'd be."

"Is that good?" I ask.

"Might be." He shrugs. "What do you like to do for fun?"

"When I'm not trying to escape hostile governments?" I consider that for a moment. "I play chess."

"I've always wanted to learn."

"We're teaching Wave Cohort 1 now. You should come to the seminars and learn."

Declan's eyes widen. "I can do that? I'm not in Wave Cohort 1." He looks at the ground, and I am suddenly privy to the shame he feels at *not* being in Wave 1. "I...uh...I wanted to join, but my mother and Edith said they needed me here."

"Declan," I say, letting my voice sound commanding. "You are doing more in these fields than you can imagine for the future of Souterraine."

"Souterraine won't exist in five years," he murmurs.

"Souterraine might all be able to make it back to Earth with enough preparation and careful planning and attention to resources. Trust me, what you are doing here today, it matters. And yes, you are welcome to come to learn to play chess at the seminars if you can get time off from your duties here."

Declan meets my eyes, and a moment of understanding passes between us. I see the moment he believes me to be sincere. "When are the seminars?"

I grin as I tell him.

7

Evening meals on Souterraine have become more chaotic since Ethan joined the royal family. He has questions about everything, and while Queen Eleanore and King Alfred always answer him kindly, lately the bulk of his questions have been directed at me.

Bernard prepared a delicious stew, crusty bread, and a heaping of vegetables. On any other day, my mouth would water. But today, after seeing the peas and learning about the true reality of the rations shortage, any attempt to enjoy the food makes it taste like sawdust.

"Reach?" Queen Eleanore asks, setting her wooden spoon aside the wooden bowl.

My eyes snap to hers.

"What's wrong?"

I force a bite down and swallow. "I was at the agriculture sector for peas today."

"Yes?" King Alfred interjects.

"They said that the ration plans had to be adjusted. Mars has five years *if* harvest projections are on target, and *if* we hold steady at eighty percent of the original ration plan."

Llama tenses in the chair next to me. She calmly sets down her soup spoon and reaches under the table, squeezing my hand with her own.

"Yes," King Alfred confirms. "That's true. We've been monitoring the agriculture sections. So far, blight has been contained. That is really the crux of the matter though. If we can contain the blight, we can maintain the ration schedule."

"But Edith blamed the Jezero colonists."

Queen Eleanore closes her eyes and then looks directly at Ethan. "Isn't life worth a little sacrifice?"

"Yes, but twenty percent of the original ration plan…it's too much."

"It's how we can provide for everyone. Especially those who didn't have proper nutrition in the first place." She looks away from me and then slides her gaze over to Ethan again. "The children from Jezero did not have the same access to fresh food that we have. We are asking the Souterraine adults to reduce their intake of agricultural products so that the children from Jezero can experience proper nutrition during this time."

Ethan takes a huge bite of his bread, crumbs flying everywhere.

Guilt and frustration work their way down my limbs. "Shouldn't you explain that to the people?" I press. "Shouldn't they be made aware?"

King Alfred sets a cloth napkin on the side of his wooden tray. "The queen and I have made decisions with our advisors that are in the best interest of the future. Your experience with the rations is very different as a member of Wave Cohort 1 than someone who will be here until Wave Cohort 3. Once you return to Earth, you will no longer require Souterraine rations. Therefore, you don't have the full picture. We are trying to help the children from Jezero survive to make it to Wave Cohort 3. I think you would know that a long-term space mission isn't easy on the body."

I frown. The king has a point, but shouldn't he still explain it to everyone?

"Reach," Queen Eleanore says. "It's been a very long few days for you. Bernard made dessert. You and Princess Llama must have yours in the thinking garden."

Llama startles at her name, but looks at me and smiles.

The queen has decreed that Llama and I are going on a date.

Bernard packed our dessert in a wicker picnic basket and tossed a red-and-white checked blanket in as well. I hold the basket on my left arm, while Llama opens the door out of the castle and into the thinking gardens. She marches across the clover field and into the cacophony of vibrant flowers. When she reaches a wooden bench with orange and yellow flowers behind it, she spreads the blanket on the ground and sits.

She arranges her burgundy-colored dress around her legs, and the Souterraine shoes are all I can see of her feet. I sit next to her, crossing my own legs and marveling at the reddish undertone of everything.

Even though Souterraine is a vastly accomplished agricultural society, we're still on Mars.

"Reach?" Llama asks as she reaches into the basket and pulls out a large bowl. "What do you think happens now?"

My brow creases. "I think we continue training Wave Cohort 1."

"No," Llama responds. "About Hero, and Freedom, and Earth?"

"Oh," I breathe. "I don't know."

"But the game theory. You always know the game theory." She waits expectantly for my response.

"Llama," I say, meeting her piercing blue eyes with my own hazel ones. "There's too many variables. I can't possibly have any theory about this game until we know more."

Her eyes lower, and her nails pick at her cuticles. I sense her apprehension; her nerves are palpable.

"Llama," I repeat as I place my hand over hers. "We're in this together."

She bites her lip, and when she turns her face toward mine, the sheen of tears mists her eyes.

"We'll figure it out, Llama. I promise," I whisper before pressing a sweet kiss to her lips.

She pulls away, her eyes liquid pools. "Could you please talk me through it? I don't feel like I understand it. And I ..." She trails off, looking up at the blue dome that functions as Souterraine's sky. "I'm supposed to understand it. They count on me to understand this."

The weight of what she's carrying crashes down on my shoulders. It's her burden to bear as the princess, but it's my burden to share as her betrothed. I haven't been talking with her much lately. I've been focused on surface missions, on chess, on preparing for Wave Cohort 1 to return to Earth.

"Llama." I trail my thumb over her cheekbone. "I'm sorry. I know game theory isn't how you think about things."

"It's how you *do*, and I wish I understood it."

"I think what happens next is that we go to Earth. And we meet up with the Resistance at those coordinates. There must be a plan from the Resistance that we can join with. But also, we have something Nation will desperately want."

"What's that?"

"Data. From the surface missions on Mars." I see the moment the wheels click into place for her.

"And data from an extremely successful colonization period on Mars."

I nod. "Science is progress. But it might be their downfall."

Llama leans her head against my shoulder. "I hope you're right."

After a moment of sitting together, Llama straightens and positions the dessert bowl in front of us. Bernard packed a chocolate pudding and two spoons. We take turns taking a bite, and as the pudding diminishes, the blue color of the sky turns a hazy, inky dark. Llama settles closer to me, and I wrap my arm around her.

We sit, staring at the false sky of Souterraine, and I have never wanted anything in that moment as much as I want to see the real night sky from Earth again.

"It needs to be sooner," I whisper against Llama's hair.

"Hm?" she hums sleepily in response, her head back on my shoulder.

"We need to leave Souterraine and return to Nation sooner than we thought."

"That's nice," she murmurs and yawns.

We sit together, wrapped in the darkness of a Souterraine night, until King Alfred appears.

8

Wave Cohort 1 training isn't easy. It's a week later, and I've been able to lose my sling, thanks to the medical care of Doctor Harold. I can exercise again, but there are still twinges of pain. The one hundred twelve of us selected to be part of this group have certain skills, aptitudes, or traits that make military-style training logical. Technically, Llama and I are the leaders of the group, but we're also not in charge of training. King Alfred and Queen Eleanore brought both Souterraine and Jezero scientists to the cohort to create a comprehensive education plan for our training. For a group of unassuming colonists who mostly studied plants in their careers, they've taken their directives very seriously. A few studied kinesiology, and some are engineers, but most of the scientists have given their lives and studies to food production.

Today, it's the kinesiologists Nick and Paul who are in charge of the training. The two men are as different as night and day. Nick with translucent skin, blue eyes, and short blond hair, and Paul with dark skin, narrow brown eyes, and long black hair secured from his face with a thin net. Despite their opposite appearances, Nick and

Paul are clearly having the time of their lives directing the members of Wave Cohort 1 in physical fitness.

Llama and I have an advantage because we've trained this way before. After a series of exercises that Nick and Paul call a circuit, it's obvious that though Llama and I experienced weakness from our space sojourn and extended time in zero-g, we're still one of the four people who's the most prepared for our mission.

The other two people are Cait and Beatriz, former field operatives for Jezero.

Llama wipes her brow with a towel and lowers her canteen into the river. She drinks deeply before turning to me, running her hands over her wide-legged, shin-length training uniform pants. "Lift would love them," she mutters.

I laugh, remembering her attitude toward our trainer on Earth. "Yeah," I say. "They'd be best friends."

"A total bromance," Llama quips, and I laugh even harder.

Cait and Beatriz stand off to the side, filling their own wooden canteens from the river before they drink deeply. We're the only ones on the riverbank as the rest of our cohort tries to finish their circuits.

Llama closes her eyes for a moment and then walks over to the other women. "You two finished fast," she says, forcing a smile.

"We've trained like that before," Cait responds, but she doesn't smile. Her pale eyes and blonde hair have the reddish tint peculiar to everything on Mars, and it stands out on her fair coloring more than on others.

"But still," Llama says with a tight jaw. "Good job."

"Thanks," Beatriz responds. Her blonde hair is tucked behind her back in a braid, and she smiles, but it's a blank mask over a bland face. I scrub my hand across my brow. I can't believe I once thought she was beautiful. She wasn't. Here, devoid of artifice and trickery, she's about as alluring as a blank piece of paper.

"You finished quickly." Paul walks backward from the exercise area as he keeps an eye on the rest of the cohort.

"Yeah," Llama responds. "We've all trained before."

"Good," Paul says before barking, "Silas! Activate your core, *then* lift." He frowns at the people still on the field. "It's going to take a miracle to get you ready for space."

"I'm not so worried about space," I mutter. "I'm worried about returning to Nation and having to fight."

Paul tips his head slightly toward me. "Fighting. Hmm. Our instructions were space travel prep. Should we be teaching hand-to-hand combat?"

I blow out a breath. "Yes," I say through clenched teeth.

"That's never been a Souterraine way of things. I don't expect it would go well with this group," he responds.

Llama scrunches her eyes shut. The two of us are the only people who hold the true depth of understanding of what we're facing when we return to Nation.

Surprisingly, it's Cait who speaks. "It wasn't something unheard of in Jezero. We can teach everyone basic hand-to-hand combat in a week. Right, Beatriz?"

Beatriz beams. "Absolutely."

"How would you know that?" Paul asks, his arms crossed over his chest and his biceps flexing impressively.

Cait zeroes in on him. "Special operatives from Jezero, you know."

Paul blinks as he turns to survey the two women from Jezero. "It's true?"

"It doesn't matter now," I say, breaking between them.

"President Reach could reinstate us at any time." Cait smirks.

Paul frowns and stares at me.

"I'm not. I haven't. I have no plans to reinstate anything from Jezero."

"But you could," Beatriz supplies in an overly sweet voice.

Llama steps forward to break the tension. "I think they're done," she says to Paul as she gestures at the group on the lawn.

"TIME!" Paul calls, and the group stops. The only sound for the next minute is the heavy breathing of one hundred eight people collectively trying to catch their breath.

Nick jogs over to Paul. The two confer for a moment before they stand and address the group.

Nick calls out to the cohort. "You need more training. Take a break for your chess seminar, and then return here after. From now on, we're doing physical exercises three times daily."

Groans sound from the group, and I can't tell if it's because of the chess seminar or the prospect of another exercise session.

SINCE THERE ARE more exercise sessions after the chess seminar, no one bothers cleaning up. Instead, we trek to the debriefing 'room' tucked into the copse of willows.

When I push aside the branches to enter the space, I find that there are sixty small tables made from tree stumps placed strategically around the clearing inside. Next to each table are two stools, and on each table is a roughly carved wooden chess set.

Llama pulls back willow branches on the other side, and together we create a sort of door for our fellow Wave 1 members. They file in through the gap in the branches. I smile, nod, bob my head, and greet the ones I know by name.

"Please take a seat with a partner at one of the tables," I direct. I catch a whiff of my own body odor after a session of hard exercising, and I'm glad that I'm not the only one who smells. I'm also glad that we're in the willows and the soft fragrance of the plants covers up some of the stench.

I begin to drop the willow branches, when a tall form ducks

through. He scrunches his nose and pulls back before he pushes a hand over his mouth.

"Declan?" I say in surprise at his appearance.

"Sorry, but *what* is that smell?" he asks, swallowing.

Apparently the odor is worse than I thought.

"We have another workout after this seminar," Llama supplies. "No one bothered getting cleaned up after our first one."

"Oh." Declan moves closer to Llama and lowers his hand from his mouth. "I'm here for the chess seminar."

"Great," I respond, and I genuinely mean it. "Take a seat at one of the tables."

He nods and walks to the single empty table left in the room. Llama looks at me and shrugs. "I guess I'm learning along with him."

I take the next twenty minutes to describe how each of the pieces moves and then tell each table to play. I circulate as they play, ready to answer questions and help as needed.

Declan raises his hand.

"Yes?" I say, stopping by his and Llama's board.

"I don't think there's another move on the board," Declan says, scratching behind his ear.

I take in the board. Llama's been checkmated.

"How many moves?" I ask Declan, my jaw dropping.

"Two each," Llama confirms.

"Fool's Mate." I blink. "Llama? Did you really not think that through?" I'm incredulous.

"I'm not a chess prodigy, Reach," she grinds through her teeth and I know I've offended her.

"Sorry, Llama, it's…I thought you'd have known…"

She bristles. "I was trying something different."

A hand waving at the back of the space catches my attention. "I'm going to go help some others, but I think you should play again."

I've just finished explaining how the "horse" is actually called a "knight" and how it moves, when I catch Declan's hand in the air. Llama slumps on her stool and places her palm on her face before sliding it down, giving her the appearance of melting.

I leave the group I'm with and return to Declan and Llama's table. It doesn't take me long to see that Declan has forced Llama into checkmate again.

"How many moves?" I ask him.

"Ten," he replies, looking bashful.

Llama snorts. "Reach, I think you need to play him."

At Llama's words, every head in the room turns to me.

"Play him? Could we watch? Will you? Is he that good?" The questions assault my ears.

I don't want to play a total beginner, but it will be a learning opportunity for the group. "Sure. Declan? You up for it?"

Declan shrugs noncommittally, but I sense that he wants to compete against someone harder to beat than Llama. I feel for her. I love her, but she's awful at chess.

"Ok." I blow out a breath, then address the rest of the cohort. "If you'd all gather around. Maybe one partner on the grass and one on a stool?"

One partner from each pairing brings a stool over while the other partner sits in a circle on the clover. "You be white," I say to Declan, handing him the slight advantage that comes with being the first player to make a move.

"Ok." He begins setting up the board. I set my pieces, and when I look up, Declan's pieces are arranged perfectly. I'm impressed.

Declan makes the first move. I counter. He loses a piece first, but on the next turn, takes my piece.

The game goes on, and I'm finding that I have to think a lot harder than I expected.

Finally, there are only two logical moves left I could make. One will leave me vulnerable, but he might decide to protect his remaining bishop instead of attacking me. The other will result in a stale-mate *if* he sees it.

I consider the board for a moment before opting for the more dangerous attack. Declan slides his bishop to a different square. In one move, I'll have him at checkmate.

I move my knight and say, "Checkmate."

The crowd around us erupts in cheers, clapping, and whistling.

Declan's eyebrows squish together. I see the moment he realizes what he did.

"Good job, Declan," I say. "You were hard to beat."

Declan scowls at the board before looking back to me with pale green eyes. "Good job, Reach." He extends a hand and I grasp it, shaking it heartily.

"How many times have you played?" I ask, because I can't imagine he's a total beginner after that performance.

"Three, including this."

I blink. He's never played until today.

I've met someone who's naturally better at chess than I am.

Llama slips her hand into mine and tugs. I turn to her as she stands on her tiptoes and whispers in my ear, "He needs to be here; he knows game theory the same way you do. We need to get him on Wave Cohort 1. He'd be an excellent strategist."

I swallow. My pride is slightly wounded from how difficult that match was, but I know she's right.

"You're the princess here," I remind her.

Llama turns to Declan and surveys him. She doesn't wear a floral crown since we came from exercising, but everyone knows who she is.

"Declan," Llama says in her official, commanding tone. "You are ordered to join us as a member of Wave Cohort 1."

Declan reels back. "But I can't. Edith said I couldn't. I have to help with the peas."

"You wanted to join?" I ask.

Declan flushes bright red. "Uh…" he stammers. "I'm helping ensure no one on Mars starves."

"But when we asked for applications, did you submit one?" Llama asks.

"No."

"Why not?" she presses.

"I didn't want to lose my job if I wasn't chosen, and Edith said that's what would happen."

Llama's eyes blaze as she turns to me, seething with rage. Somehow, she keeps her voice cool. "We will be going to see Edith now." Llama then addresses the rest of the group. "You will be returning to physical fitness training. President Reach, Declan, and I have important business to attend to."

And then Llama, in her smelly, sweaty training clothing, with her hair an unruly mess due to the exercise, turns and marches out of the willows.

Declan meets my gaze for a moment, his mouth open. I raise my brows at him before I turn.

We have no choice but to follow Princess Llama of Souterraine.

10

Llama marches with purposeful steps across the clover field, down the hill, away from the river, and to the castle. It gleams in the light of the artificial Souterraine sun, the polished wood standing strong above the greenery.

Llama passes by the red rock cairn at the front door, seven red rocks stacked neatly, balanced on each other to depict the family that lives inside. One for Ethan, Pippa, Llama, me, the queen, and king, and one for each of Ethan's parents. The cairn always makes my throat tighten. Llama always pauses by it, but today she passes by without slowing.

I look at Declan, who's shoved his hands deep into the pockets of the reddish tan colored overalls the Ag workers wear. His face is set in a blank mask, and I don't know what he's thinking, or feeling, or anything. I don't know what Llama's aim is, but she's on a mission, and I know enough to know not to trifle with her.

She opens the heavy front doors of the castle and, with her head held high, marches imperiously down the hall. She doesn't seem to have any specific destination in mind, because we pass all the ones that would make sense. Instead, she leads us to a door tucked into the corner of a supply room. She knocks twice, then yanks on the handle.

A soft light emanates from below, and Llama peers over the edge of a hole in the floor. "Urgent!" She squats down onto her heels and calls down, "We have something to discuss immediately."

The unmistakable sound of giggles draws closer. Ethan's head pops up from the hole in the floor, followed by Pippa's.

"Hi, Princess Llama," Ethan says. His eyes are wide, but his smile is wider.

Llama nods her head at him. "I need to speak to—"

"Yes?" King Alfred's head appears. He places his arms on the floor, crosses them, and peers at Llama.

Llama draws a deep breath. "This gentleman"—she hooks a thumb behind her to where Declan stands—"is part of the Ag sector, growing peas."

King Alfred tips his head and studies Declan for a moment. I move out of the way to allow him a better look.

"Yes?" he questions, quirking a brow.

"He's extremely adept at game theory," Llama continues.

The king's lips firm.

"And he's not in Wave Cohort 1." Llama looks at Declan. "Edith wouldn't allow him to join."

The king hisses, a sharp puff of breath escaping his otherwise stoic face. "Did you want to apply?" he asks Declan directly.

Declan nods.

"And did you?"

Declan shakes his head.

"Why not?"

Declan scratches the back of his neck and shifts from side to side. "My supervisor… recommended that I not."

"What did Edith say exactly?"

"That I wouldn't be accepted," Declan mumbles to the floor. "And that without peas, we'd all starve to death."

King Alfred tenses. He leans down, placing his weight on his forearms, and then in one smooth move, slides his legs up and over the edge of the hole in the floor. He must be close to seventy Earth years, but he moves with the agility of someone who never stopped moving, and wouldn't allow something like age to prevent him from living his life.

He stands, then stoops and extends a hand to Ethan, who can't quite manage to pull himself out. Pippa slithers out on her own, standing and brushing non-existent dirt and dust from the front of her dark red dress.

"Hi, Reach," she says, tugging my hand into her own and squeezing it tightly. Pippa is older than me, but her genetic disability has given her a childlike approach to life. I squeeze back and she grins.

Ethan comes and grabs my other hand. "Reach!" he exclaims. "Pippa and I were in her playroom. She has slides, books, and a whole wall of keys."

I blink. *A wall of keys? There's a playroom in the castle floor?*

The king and Llama start walking away, Declan following behind. "I think I need to follow them," I say to Ethan and Pippa, who are still clutching my hands.

"Ok," Ethan says, bouncing on his toes a little.

Pippa pulls on my hand and then takes off running down the hall. Mercifully, she lets my hand drop instead of dragging me along.

King Alfred, Llama, and Declan disappear around a turn in the hallway, so I lengthen my strides to keep up. Ethan's tiny legs shuffle along, but before long, I have to slow down. When I shorten my strides, Ethan turns to me and grins, revealing a missing tooth and a dusting of freckles on his nose. Souterraine Colony has been good for him.

We arrive at the library ten minutes after everyone else.

"—doing what's best," Queen Eleanore says.

I step through the cracked door to the library. Ethan sees Queen Eleanore sitting on the window seat. He runs right over to her and climbs onto her lap. She takes a moment and looks down at him, smiling gently. Ethan's adoption by the monarchs of Souterraine is something truly beautiful.

"But still," Llama presses. "It *wasn't* what's best. He..." she hisses. "He nearly beat Reach, and it was his third time playing chess."

Queen Eleanore shrinks back as if she's been struck. "Really?" she asks, surveying Declan up and down.

"Yes, Your Highness," Declan murmurs at the floor, a faint blush on his cheeks. "I didn't mean to cause any disruptions."

"No," Queen Eleanore says sternly. She deposits Ethan to the ground and stands. "None of that. Your name is Declan, right?"

"Y-yes," he stammers.

"And your tree?" King Alfred asks.

"Oak," Declan responds, still focusing on the polished wood planks.

"Edith will need to be informed," King Alfred says to Queen Eleanore.

Llama looks from both her grandparents to Declan and back again. "He's been given override orders to join Wave Cohort 1, then?"

"Yes," the monarchs of Souterraine affirm in unison.

"Reach?" Queen Eleanore looks at me. "Would you agree with Llama that this Declan of Oak will be an asset to Wave Cohort 1? Especially in regard to strategy and game theory?"

Declan scrunches his eyes closed and keeps his face tipped toward the floor, as if he can't bear to hear the answer.

"Yes," I answer immediately.

Declan raises his gaze from the floor for a moment, and I catch the relief in his pale green eyes.

"Declan of Oak," Queen Eleanore says in her commanding 'ruler voice.' "You are to report to Wave Cohort 1 for training from tomorrow onward. You are dismissed from your duties in the Ag sector, with the exception of the next week, where you will be harvesting every afternoon."

Declan nods in acknowledgment. "Thank you," he whispers.

"You're welcome," Queen Eleanore says, swooshing her gray-colored dress around her legs as she starts to walk toward the library door. She murmurs the next part: "Now to go tell Edith."

11

Queen Eleanore swishes down the hallway, her shoes flapping on the wood. Declan and I stand there, unsure of what to do. King Alfred stands with his arms crossed and a scowl painted on his face.

"Pippa?" King Alfred says to his daughter.

Pippa pops out from behind a stack of books. "You take Ethan and yourself to Bernard. You will be helping in the kitchen. Reach, Llama, and I are going to attend to business in the Ag sector."

Pippa tips her head to the side for a moment, then says, "Yes!" She gallops over to Ethan, grabs his hand, and then takes off at a run down the hallway. Ethan's Souterraine shoes fly off in the commotion, and he's half running, half being dragged by Pippa.

"Pippa!" King Alfred scolds. "Slow down! Ethan's legs aren't as long as yours!"

Pippa slows marginally, but then the two of them disappear around a corner, and there's no way of knowing if she continued to stay at a slower speed.

"Well, you three," King Alfred directs at us. "We need to grab a MUV and head to the Ag sector."

"Isn't that where…" Declan starts, but bites his lip and looks at the ground instead.

"Yes, but I suspect she'll need backup."

Ag sectors are massive, formed in lava tubes, and can take days to traverse if you don't know where you're going. King Alfred knows where he's going, but Declan is even more self-assured.

"She's meant to be in row Q at the intersection of Q and seven," he supplies. That means nothing to Llama, whose brow furrows, but since I harvested here, I do have an idea of the grid pattern that the Ag sector is arranged in.

The king pilots the MUV down some rows before pulling to a stop at the junction of P and five. "Which way?" he asks Declan.

Declan looks around for a moment, spies the signs, and says, "Left."

King Alfred pulls the small vehicle to the left and continues driving down the lengthy rows.

"Declan," Llama starts. "Would you mind explaining to me how you know which way to go?" She gazes out at the trellised pea plants, which all look alike, and which block the distance.

"Oh, yes." Declan swallows. "Princess Llama."

Declan does not have the same easy nature he had when it was only me and him picking peas. He's tense, like an overwrapped coil.

"And?" Llama presses.

Declan crams his eyes shut, then opens them again. "This sector is laid out using a grid method. The rows that run North–South are lettered, and the rows that run East–West are numbered. A is the easternmost North–South row in the grid, and 1 is the northernmost East–West row. When you know how the grid works, you can find anyone at an intersection as long as you know which way is north."

"You just explained…GPS coordinates," I say, after picking my jaw up off the floor of the MUV.

I don't know what I expected of Declan, but he's breaking all the conventional molds I'd tried to push him into.

"That's how all the Ag sectors work." He shrugs. "Some of them are flipped, though; it depends on the crop. Beans are a mirror image of this, so you start at the southernmost point with A."

Llama meets my eyes, and I can see her shock.

"There they are," Declan says, pointing.

Queen Eleanore stands, her hands on her hips, while Edith gesticulates wildly. Her hands draw circles as she speaks. King Alfred stops the MUV and hops out of the door.

Without the roar of the MUV engine, I can hear the last part of what she's saying.

"—harvest all this when I lose my best picker?"

"Edith," he warns, breaking her tirade. King Alfred steps next to Queen Eleanore and wraps a strong arm around her waist. He fixes Edith with a stern glare before continuing to speak. "We will ensure that the harvest is picked on time."

"How?" Edith snaps, her pale blonde braid swinging like a lariat as she spins in a circle and indicates the rows of pea plants. "How is that supposed to happen? I'm already short harvesters. Declan is the *best* Ag hand I have. He's supposed to manage this section next year. And with the blight, we don't have time to waste. Every worker has already been assigned max capacity duties."

Inspiration strikes me like lightning would a tall tree back on Earth.

I walk closer to the king and queen, leaving Declan and Llama looking on from the side. "I know someone who doesn't have any assigned duties."

All the eyes turn toward me. I swallow, because this idea might be great. It also might be terrible.

Instead of letting him sit in jail for his crimes against Martian humanity as he awaits justice to be served by a trial according to the Martian charters, why *not* put him to work?

"Percy," I say simply.

Five voices respond in unison, "NO."

12

"PERCY?" Llama questions, her blue eyes blazing. "Percy, who..." She stops and draws in a breath. "Percy, who single-handedly almost killed an entire colony of people and then showed no remorse for his actions?"

I nod.

"But, Reach," Queen Eleanore butts in. "He's not...trustworthy."

"Isn't it better to have him be useful than have him sitting idle? You once told me that when people wanted power, you found a way for them to have it, in a limited capacity. You could make Percy in charge of rows two to four, and he'd jump at the chance."

"Yes, but plants don't respond to power tactics the way people do," Edith says dryly.

"True. But in this case, that's a good thing."

Llama's eyes flash fire, but it's Declan who speaks.

"You propose to put the man awaiting trial for his part in Jezero Colony's demise to work?" he clarifies.

"Yes, that's exactly what he's proposing," Llama hisses. "A man who can't be trusted. A man who, for all we know, would sabotage the plants and cause our ruin."

"But isn't Souterraine already ruined?" Declan replies, rubbing the back of his neck.

Llama gapes.

"It's an interesting game theory," Declan adds. "I think it will work."

King Alfred scowls, but Queen Eleanore steps forward. "What rows need harvesting the most?" she asks Edith.

"We're on rows eight and twelve tomorrow," Edith replies.

"He'll be here in Declan's place."

"I can't keep an eye on him."

"You won't have to." Queen Eleanore smirks. "Reach will. Reach, you'll need to collect Percy from house arrest and also inform the Jezero leaders of this change in Percy's status."

The sash of Jezero leadership is my least favorite item I own. The navy-blue fabric sash crisscrosses my body, creating an X from hip to shoulder. The white stars have a thin red line between them, and for some reason, the person wearing this sash is given the power of the Presidency in Jezero Colony.

Never mind the fact that Jezero Colony is gone. Never mind the fact that my father who wore it before me was simultaneously a coward and a hero. Never mind the fact that the man I'm about to see is the worst kind of criminal—the kind with a thirst for power, and no remorse.

I draw in a breath, trying to find the courage to be a leader for the remainder of Jezero Colony, and when it doesn't come, I yank the sash over my head in frustration.

What good is a stupid symbol if it doesn't mean anything to the person who wears it?

I brush a lock of my wayward hair off my forehead before I look in the standing mirror placed in the corner of my room. Framed in willow wood, the glass creates sunspots on the shining floor that sparkle and move. A soft pressure pushes against my shins. I look down and discover Shadow, the queen's black cat, has pressed through the crack in the door. Shadow hisses at the spot, then reaches out his front paw before swiping at the glimmer. He gives up quickly and returns to rubbing his sides against my legs, meowing. Absent-mindedly, I reach down and stroke his silky fur.

"I don't know, Shadow," I whisper. "I thought it was a good idea, but what if it isn't? What if he sabotages the peas? They're the best source of protein to grow on a large scale. Am I being reckless?"

Shadow meows, but I can't tell if it's a positive or negative sound.

"I know," I say. "I know. I have to man up and be a leader, but I didn't ask to be acting President of Jezero Colony. I didn't ask to be a leader. I never asked for any of the things that happened to me in Nation, or on Jezero, or even the things here on Souterraine—"

"Is Souterraine so bad?" Llama's voice sounds from directly behind me, and I startle. I didn't hear her come in. I was distracted by the cat.

I turn to her, catching the amusement in her eyes as she surveys my pants legs. They are covered in cat hair. I shrug before pulling her into a hug. "No," I whisper against her hair. "Souterraine has been the best." I place a kiss on her brow, accidentally knocking her crown of flowers askew. "I got to find out the truth about who you were born to be, and I'm the luckiest man in the world."

Llama's eyes sparkle as she pulls back from the hug and laughs. "You should probably kiss me, then." She arches one brow delicately. "You know, for courage."

My lips meet hers, and I'm safe, happy, full, complete.

"Reach!" Queen Eleanore calls, knocking on the solid wooden door. "It's time to go to the Jezero section." She steps through the door and cocks a brow at Llama, who is trying to straighten her crown without drawing attention. It's obvious we were kissing, and it's obvious that Queen Eleanore doesn't hate it as much as King Alfred does. In fact, the gentle smile that crosses her face makes me think she's pleased to have caught us in a rare moment of connection. Ever since training began, the upcoming mission has been our priority.

"Would you like me or Princess Llama to accompany you?" she asks.

I frown. I don't want Llama to be dragged into Jezero politics any more than she already was. I look to Llama, but I can't read her stony expression.

"I'm going to have to talk to Percy, aren't I?" I ask, thinking through what Llama must be feeling.

Queen Eleanore nods. "And you'll need to bring him to the Ag sector tomorrow."

"Llama, do you want to come today?"

Llama steps toward me and slips her hand into mine. "I want to go with you wherever you go, Reach."

The calmness and sincerity of her words soothe me in a way the Presidential sash of Jezero and all its associated power never could.

13

Queen Eleanore drives along the winding river path. Llama and I sit together in the back seat. Both of us are quiet. Llama's knee bounces. She may be a princess here, but in Jezero, her life was worth less than a pound of Martian rock. It's not easy to face down a den of lions, no matter how courageous you are.

Llama's courage is an iron rod in her core, but that doesn't mean she isn't anxious. Truthfully, I'm anxious too. I may be the acting President of the defunct colony, but I don't look forward to telling them that I've found suitable employment for Percy as he awaits trial. If the Jezero colonists had their way, many of them would have simply shoved him outside the surface airlock and washed their hands clean of him.

It was only the consistent reminder of the Martian Charters that kept *that* from happening. As it is, Percy has been under guard by both Jezero and Souterraine since arriving here after Jezero's demise.

Queen Eleanore parks at a copse of tall trees. This particular stand is maple, and she places her palm gently on the bark before she inhales sharply. When she drops her hand, she rolls her shoulders back. Then, she straightens her crown and walks into the Jezero section, her head held high.

Llama's hand squeezes mine before she drops it to her side. "The sash, Reach," she murmurs before she places her hand on my chest and untwists the fabric that has bunched and displaced the stars-and-stripes pattern. I catch one of her hands with my own, trapping it against my heart for a moment.

"Llama," I whisper as her eyes meet mine. "I don't want to do this."

Her lips quirk down in a small, sad smile. "I know. But you must." She pulls her hand away, and in a near replica of her grandmother, straightens her crown, then passes to the maples, where she also places a palm on the trunk.

I watch her go. I know she's right.

I must.

Queen Eleanore leads Llama and me up a path to the wood and stone cottages of the Jezero colonists. She stops before we enter the village proper and gestures that I should take the lead. As the President of this strange pocket of displaced people, I suppose she's right.

I step in front of the procession and pass through the gate. At the first home, a cairn of rocks stands outside the door. I count them—five rocks, balanced perfectly on top of each other—to note how many people reside in that structure. The next home has three, then six, then two, then three. Most of the homes have three. I knew the population of Jezero was a closely guarded secret, but taking my time to count the cairns, the bleak future Jezero was destined for is obvious. Their leadership was not strong, even if their President was my father.

My throat tightens as my hands clench at my sides. Thinking of Greg makes tears well, but I shove them down. Yes, he was my father, but I didn't truly know him—not really.

I close my eyes, trapping the hot wetness gathered there and blinking it away. I think of Ethan, of the life that he gets to have now, and how Greg gave his own life for the boy's sake.

I don't want to be the President of this defunct colony, but I will, because I can make a difference for children like Ethan.

I march to the center of the circle of homes, standing in the middle of the clearing in total silence. No one is out, no one sees me, and I don't know how to summon the people of Jezero.

Llama steps next to me. She closes her eyes and draws a sharp breath before she begins to sing. It's a haunting sound, more hums than words, and it's surprisingly close to what the Jezero colonists did to welcome us when we first arrived on Mars.

Doors to each of the cottage homes creak open and people look around. When they see me and the sash, they join the lament. By some unseen signal, they stop in unison, and the people file into an orderly circle around me.

I swallow, gulping down my nerves. "Citizens of Jezero," I orate. "I come to you today with news you need to hear. The man named Percy McAllistair will be given a duty to assist Souterraine Colony while he awaits his trial by peers."

An angry thrum reverberates through the crowd, shock waves of sound spread out, and sudden tension vibrates through the ground into my own chest.

"President," a man says, stepping forward. He wears his own sash, a navy blue one with three gold five-pointed stars interspersed along it. "Surely you must know that this is not advisable."

I frown. I expected some pushback, but not outright scorn from the section leaders.

"It *is* advisable." I spin around slowly as I talk, making eye contact with each of the leaders. "Percy McAllistair is here, and we require his services to contribute to the community while Wave Cohort 1 is training."

"So this is about your little war, then?" a female voice shouts.

"Little war?" I rear back for a moment as if I've been slapped, but then anger bubbles up and spills out. "There is no such thing as a little war. And if you would prefer to die on Mars, there's no need for you to return to Earth. As it is, you'll need a group of people to overthrow the corrupt leaders first. That does mean, as you so eloquently put it, war."

"That's enough!" A woman shoulders her way to the front of the circle. She has a white sash with six navy five-pointed stars along the fabric. "This is our President." She points at me. "He says he has a need for Percy McAllistair. I personally think cleaning toilets is too good for him, but what do I know? We're here because *they* let us be here." She points at Llama and Queen Eleanore, who stands at the back, surrounded by the Jezero colonists. "She clearly wants Percy for something, so let her have him. It's no burden to us."

"But the law says…"

"The law!" Choruses of objection all citing the law sound from around the circle.

"The law says Percy McAllistair will be tried for his crimes against Martian humanity by a group of his peers," I shout. "In the meantime, he will be picking peas to augment the protein portions of each person within Souterraine's borders."

"But don't they have machines for that?" a man calls. This one does not wear a sash.

I shake my head. "No. The pea plants are too delicate. They can't be harvested by machine. In fact, all the food you eat here is harvested by human hands. The Ag sector needs every hand it can get with the influx of extra mouths to feed. I would think you would be grateful for Percy to contribute meaningfully to society instead of sitting in a house and doing nothing to help anyone."

A murmur of agreement zings through the crowd. Finally, another voice calls out, "But when will his trial be?"

I look to Queen Eleanore, who nods. "When we're ready for it." I exhale sharply before I say the next words. "I need to speak to Percy McAllistair now."

The crowd is shocked into silence, and they part, splitting the circle and creating a path through the throng. The path leads to a single building set apart from the others.

Percy's prison.

14

Llama's eyes meet mine with trepidation. I shake my head. This is a meeting between me and my father's former best friend. There's a score to settle here, but even as the urge to be violent roars through my veins, the other part of me—the part of me raised by my mother—remembers no one is outside of redemption. Bad people can change, but it's choices that ultimately prove who someone *is*.

Llama gives one tiny nod, and I start down the path to Percy's prison, alone.

When I pass the guards stationed outside the door, they move aside and let me through. The interior of the house is dim, curtains drawn. The slight breeze of Souterraine makes the curtains flutter, and the whistle of a kettle rings out from the small kitchen. I pass through the main room and duck through the doorway, down a step, and into the wooden kitchen.

Percy sits, his back ramrod straight in a wooden chair. The kettle sings. Two cups are placed on the table, a selection of tea leaves laid out around the cups.

"Reach," Percy says, not looking at me, but continuing to focus directly ahead of him.

"Percy," I respond before grabbing the towel and sliding the kettle off the flame. With a flick of my wrist, I turn off the stove knob.

"Sit," Percy instructs.

"Bold words to say to the man holding a kettle of boiling water," I retort.

"You won't hurt me."

My eyebrows arch. "Can you be sure?"

Percy snorts. "Absolutely." He doesn't look back, but he gestures to the table. "Sit down. You came all this way from your comfortable position of power. You need something from me."

I sit in the chair across from Percy, placing the kettle on the table. The smell of scorched wood assaults my nose. A pang of guilt at burning a perfectly good table flits across my skin, but the moment Percy opens his mouth again, it leaves.

"What do you need from me? I doubt you're here for vengeance." His blue eyes narrow, and he glowers at me as he leans forward. He sits back suddenly. "Tea?" Deftly, he grabs the towel and wraps it around the handle, pouring the water into each of the cups. "I'm partial to oolong myself." He scoops up leaves and drops them into the tendrils of steam. I watch him with narrowed eyes. I do not trust this man's hospitality.

He picks up a cup and thrusts it at me, hot liquid sloshing out over the sides of the cup. It burns the skin on my knuckles, and though a hiss of breath escapes my teeth, I do not cry out.

"Thank you," I bite through the pain.

Percy surveys me. His head tips to the side, and the gleam of pleasure at my pain can't be suppressed.

My eyes lock on his as I take a sip, blowing on the hot liquid before the drops sting my tongue. I set the cup down, and Percy shifts in his chair.

"Surely you didn't poison it," I say, and tip my head toward his own cup. "I have that much faith in you at least."

Percy swallows, his Adam's apple bobbing in his thin throat. He lifts the steaming mug to his own lips and sips, and I get a look at his neat, clean cuticles.

"What do you want, Reach?" he says as he slams the cup on the table. Liquid sloshes out of the rim and over down the sides.

"To tell you that you have a job."

Percy scoffs. "I hardly think sitting here inside a hut and awaiting my trial is a job."

"I thought so too." I meet his hard gaze with my own stony one. The briefest moment of confusion flits across his brow. "You've been assigned to the Ag sector. Harvest time."

"Mm," Percy hums noncommittally. "I'm sure I have been. What will I be doing there?"

"Harvesting," I reply.

"Yes, but what?"

I shrug. "Something that you can't ruin. You're not trustworthy enough for anything of more importance. You'll be picked up tomorrow, and I'll be escorting you to the fields."

"You think I don't know about you, don't you?"

"I know you know about me."

"You think that your little woman friend makes you a man. You think that returning to Earth will solve all the problems on Mars. You think that *you* can save everyone. Perhaps your biology studies weren't as robust as the ones on Jezero, but survival of the fittest matters. That's how people are saved. When the weak die. Weak, like your—"

"Enough!" I roar, slamming my hand on the table. "You will *not* insult him, or her, or anyone who has the decency to think of a future with hope!"

Percy leans back against the chair and smirks. "I believe, Reach," he examines his nails, "I just did. And it's not my problem if you're too pigheaded to realize what you are, and what you must be to survive this place."

Anger courses through my veins as I stand, palms on the rough wooden table, with a snarl carved onto my face. The burn from the kettle makes a dark ring that perfectly matches my mood.

"You will not survive this. You can't. You love too many people. Ultimately, it's love that's the weakness. Your father's demise was *love*. Your little lady friend that you think you *love*—that's not love. It's a biological urge. You're better off without those. You could be great, you know. You really could."

I straighten, turn my back on this man who used my father for power and nearly killed an entire colony of people. "That's too bad, Percy," I whisper as I walk away from the table. As I step through the main room, I have one final thought. I turn and, in a clear voice, loudly pronounce, "I'm glad you've chosen not to procreate. When you die—and you will die one day—the stains of your own choices will not be passed onto the next generation. Survival of the fittest, and all that."

I take a moment to let the words land—to let him think about his choices, his weakness, and the hypocrisy of his own message.

And then I slam the door.

15

I STRIDE DOWN the path, leaving befuddled guards in my wake. They jumped when I slammed the door, but didn't say anything. Perhaps the storm clouds on my face gave away that the meeting with Percy did not go well.

My long legs eat up the red gravel as I stalk toward the Jezero colonists. Llama stands talking to a group of advisors, gesturing with her hands. I do not care that I have an audience. I do not care that Percy is the bane of my existence. All I care about in this moment is telling Llama that I need her, that I love her, and that a future with her is a future worth hoping for. The opposite of everything Percy said.

The advisors silently part as Llama stops talking, her blue eyes locked on mine. Every step of the Souterraine shoes makes a resounding flop in the sudden silence.

I reach her, wrap my arm around her waist, and tug her to me as I lean in to kiss the woman I love deeply. As if kissing her can take the coating of disgust left in the wake of my interaction with Percy away.

It doesn't, but that doesn't stop me.

It is the Queen of Souterraine who does. She clears her throat loudly.

I don't stop. Llama does. She pulls back, her crown askew as she searches my eyes with her own gaze. It's as if she's forgotten where we are, because she places one finger on her lips, feeling them, before she shakes her head and blinks.

She turns to the queen and sees the children of Jezero staring. The adults mostly have their gazes averted, but the advisor with the six stars smirks at me. I smirk back and tighten my arm around Llama's waist, which knocks her crown even more crooked.

A slight pink tinges her cheeks as she looks up at me and deliberately adjusts her crown to be straight.

"Now that *that's* been taken care of," Queen Eleanore says as she steps forward. "I would like to inform you that the mandatory workloads for everyone in the Ag sector have increased by ten percent."

A small grumble of discontent growls through the group. Queen Eleanore holds up both hands, palms out. "This is because we did not have the additional population added into our food projections when you entered into Souterraine."

The grumble gets louder.

"You're saying we have to work harder, because we're here?"

"We almost died, lady! And you're saying we need to add ten percent to our workloads?"

"We lost everything!"

Queen Eleanore looks at me, then calmly untwists the furled sash at my shoulders. "And Souterraine is supporting a logistical load that we were not prepared for in our calculations. Would you like to send your representatives to the Ag and food store sectors to see?" She pats the Presidential sash before she turns to the crowd. "Well?" she questions, placing one hand on her hip and cocking a brow.

No one says anything, and the tension mounts to an unbearable level. I take charge.

"Yes," I speak up. "Tomorrow, all the section leaders will report to the Ag and food storage sectors. You can see for yourselves that what Queen Eleanore says is true."

The Jezero advisors bob their heads. I gave them a direct order while wearing the Presidential sash, which means that I overrode Queen Eleanore's invitation. For half a moment, I worry that I overstepped, but then I remember they had their opportunity to protest the idea before I spoke.

"Is there anything else you need from me?" I ask the Jezero colonists.

They shake their heads, clearly not used to being asked about *their* needs by their President.

"Good." I slip my hand into Llama's and stride away from the village, not waiting to see if Queen Eleanore is following, because I know she will—she has the keys to the MUV.

Llama quirks her eyebrow and asks, "What was that?"

"What was what?" I smirk, knowing what she's asking about, but wanting her to say it.

"That…" She closes her eyes for a moment. "Kiss."

"I can't kiss my betrothed?"

"I have *no* idea if you can do that when you're wearing that stupid sash, Reach."

"Oh." As usual, Llama is a step ahead of me. While I was focused on the physical, she was focused on the repercussions of the action.

"Well," Queen Eleanore drawls as she passes the front of the MUV. "That was quite a surprise for everyone, I think."

Llama turns to her grandmother. "What was?"

"All of it," Queen Eleanore responds with a knowing glint in her eye. "But I don't think the Jezero colonists are used to seeing public displays of affection. And especially not from someone who's wearing the Presidential sash."

My cheeks heat, but Llama whispers, "Reach, you get to do things your own way. Not whatever *they* say. You get to be *who* you *are*." She leans into me and rests her cheek on my shoulder.

Queen Eleanore climbs into the vehicle and starts it. "Are you two coming?" she calls over the dull hum of the engine. "Or would you prefer to walk to the castle?"

Llama smiles at me before she answers her grandmother in French. "We'll walk."

Walking back to the castle means we follow the river. Llama hikes her dress up to her knees, slips off her shoes, and carries them as she steps into the shallow current.

"Ahhh, that feels so nice," she says as the cool water laps at her ankles. The Souterraine clothes are comfortable, but I have never understood the appeal of these shoes. I slide them off and roll the cuffs of my pants to my shins before I step into the water. Something about the water makes me relax, but then again, it might be the fact that I'm here, with Llama.

I glance at the water, but my gaze snags on the Presidential sash of Jezero. The fabric binds me like a chain, and my fingers toy with the sash while my thoughts run amok. It's not the first time I wish my father hadn't perished in the collapse. And yet, if he hadn't, what would have happened? Was it worth sacrificing his life for Ethan's? Was it worth letting Percy serve justice instead of leaving him there?

"Reach." Llama waded over to me while I was thinking. She gently takes my hand and pulls it away from the sash, then she slips one of the loops back over my head before drawing the other away from my body. "That better?" she asks as she holds the sash in her hand.

Free from the constraining weight of symbolic garments, I grin at her. "You have no idea."

"I think," she says as she meets my eyes and lets her gaze linger, "I think that I do."

Llama was born to be a princess, but maybe she feels the weight of leadership too. Maybe she's struggling under the decisions and the expectations we were never prepared for, and the fact that everyone in Wave Cohort 1 is going to be depending on *us* for their survival when we return to Earth and attempt to overthrow Nation.

"What happens when we die?" Llama murmurs as she looks away at the opposite bank where the willow branches dip and sway, making patterns on the surface of the water.

I swallow. I have *no* idea what happens when we die, but she wants hope.

"I think," I say, catching the sheen of a tear rolling down her cheek as I look at the idyllic scene before us, "I think it's a lot like here."

"I hope so."

I lift her hand to my lips and press a kiss there before we begin splashing toward the castle in a soft, gentle silence.

16

When the light changes from night to morning, I blink open my eyes. The wooden shutters let the soft breeze flow through, and since there are no insects on Souterraine, I enjoy the melded divide between indoors and outdoors, even if it means I'm up early. I sit up, accidentally dislodging the black ball of warmth that tends to seek refuge on my chest while I sleep.

"Sorry, Shadow," I murmur as the cat hisses in rebuttal. But honestly, the cat sleeps there so often that I don't even register its presence anymore.

Shadow slinks toward the door, where he waits for me to crack it open. When I do, he slithers through, his tail waving haughtily in dismissal. *Cats.*

I scrub a hand down my face, the soft stubble of morning on my cheeks. A trip to the bathroom and a shave later, I'm ready to get dressed for the day. I shrug on light brown pants before turning to the top drawer. The Presidential sash of Jezero catches my eye from where it sits on the dresser, and I glare at it as I pull open the shirt drawer and select a light tan color. I shrug it on over the soft under-clothes. Everything here is tinged red, which means the tan color looks slightly pink as I stare at my reflection in the mirror.

My hazel eyes have a hardness to them now, something I didn't have when I arrived on Mars but inherited along with the figurehead role of President. My hair is unruly, the brown waves a shaggy mess of partially tangled curls. The rosy undertones of the fiber make my tanned skin more prominent. I would not have thought that Souterraine's underground sun would produce coloring on my skin, but after all that time locked in Hub, my previously translucent skin looks healthy. The gravity situation on Mars is strange, since we're underground, but I haven't shrunk. If anything, I may have grown taller. I'll chalk it up to Souterraine's diet and the fact that I haven't seen a single scientifically prepackaged calorie sluice in months.

It's the calorie sluices that bring back to mind what I have to do today. Instead of training with Wave Cohort 1 this morning, I'll be accompanying Percy to the pea fields and supervising him. The whole reason we need him to contribute to the colony is so Declan can join Wave Cohort 1 and Souterraine can stay at least in the *range* of food production needed to support the people of both Souterraine and Jezero.

The problems of leadership are heavy.

A knock sounds on my door. I open it to find Llama, a twisted flower crown of red peonies on her head, standing on the landing between the three room suites that make up this turret. She looks me up and down, and her blue eyes twinkle. Does my chest puff up a little knowing she finds me attractive? Yes, yes, it does.

"Good morning," I say.

"Morning," she responds. "Are you ready for today?"

"As ready as I can be."

"Do you know what you'll do if Percy…" She rolls her bottom lip under her top teeth. "If he causes trouble?"

I roll my shoulders against the discomfort of that thought. Dr.

Harold's medical salves helped my shoulder heal remarkably fast, but it's still tight. "I guess I could overpower him."

"Hopefully it won't come to that."

I grasp her hand and pull her to me, placing my palms on her shoulders. She looks up into my eyes. They remind me of the sky on Earth. I miss the sky. "I promise, Llama," I whisper before I cup her chin in my palm and lower my lips toward hers. "I'll be careful."

She presses her lips against mine before stepping away, straightening her crown, and placing her palm in my own. "Breakfast?"

"Always."

Bernard hands me keys to a MUV as I hand him my oatmeal bowl after breakfast. Llama holds a jug of maple syrup in her hand and helps him clean. Bernard didn't like us helping when we first arrived, but then seemed to slowly accept that we weren't going to let him do all the work while we were in the castle. Truthfully, I *like* feeling like I helped. After years of being caged up, doing something feels like freedom.

"Good luck today," Bernard murmurs, his rough palm pressing the keys into my palm. "I'd be more worried about the Souterraine harvesters than about Percy himself."

I loop the key around my pointer finger. "What do you mean?"

"Percy is an unpopular man here."

I snort. I knew that.

"I'm saying, Reach," Bernard warns sternly, "that you need to keep an eye on him, not for fear of him, but for fear *for* him."

"I thought violence wasn't a concern here," Llama interjects.

"Have you ever studied what happens to societies when food scarcity occurs?"

Llama huffs. "My whole life was food scarcity."

Bernard turns to her, his brown eyes shining with fatherly compassion. "You're stronger than you know. Sadly, when people haven't experienced hunger, they don't know their own strength. And when people *worry* about hunger, they do very strange things."

"I can see that," I mutter.

"Princess Llama," Bernard says. "Really. You have more mental fortitude because of your struggles than you could ever imagine."

"I don't think being hungry is a good thing, Bernard," Llama replies. "It mostly just…hollows you out from the inside until there's nothing left but a shell."

"That's true." He nods. "But Llama—" He shakes his head and tries again. "Princess Llama"—this time he remembers the honorific that matters so much to the people of Souterraine—"you are equipped to lead people because of your experiences. You have experienced things people here have never felt—that they will be feeling for the first time. You, Princess Llama, have lived through pain. And that's not something many people *here* have lived through. They need someone to show them how. You don't think that Wave Cohort 1 will feel pain when you return to Earth? You don't think that they will face hunger confined on a spaceship? Princess Llama, your role here isn't ornamental. It's true leadership."

I gape at Bernard. He's never said this many words. Llama's jaw hangs open, but then she snaps it shut and slowly places the maple syrup jug back onto the table with a thud before she barrels into Bernard for a hug.

Bernard's words rattle me. All along, I thought I was the leader. I'm not. Sure, I was a human experiment on Earth, and sure I was locked up inside a science center for years of training, but it is *Llama*, who endured a horrific childhood in Ward Eleven, who has the most need to fight Nation. It's Llama who has the skills to lead Wave Cohort 1.

The game theory here is fascinating. Nation used me as a pawn. I thought I was the most powerful piece—the queen—but ultimately it was Llama, whom they saw as their own pawn, who holds the power. When we return to Earth, will Nation see me as a pawn, or will they see me as a more powerful piece? Will they get it right? Will they see that I'm predictable, that I move in patterns, that I support Llama?

I don't know the answer to these questions, but I do know that here, on Souterraine, everything is more complicated than it seems.

17

Percy pulls a harvest vest over his Souterraine-issued clothes. His are clearly cast-offs from when the laundry attendants made a mistake because they aren't red-tinged, but vibrant pink. I stand, watching him from a bit of a distance, but something about watching him and not participating feels wrong. I'm not a warden. Yes, I'm watching him, but he's here because we have a quota to make up, and I have two fully capable hands.

"Edith!" I call.

She turns from halfway down the row. "What?" she yells back as she starts jogging toward me.

"Can I get a harvest vest too?"

She's closer now, but she stops, her eyes wide and her mouth opening and closing like a fish. "You. Want. A. Harvest. Vest?"

I nod. That *is* what I said.

Edith lets out a low whistle.

"Well?" I say as she continues blinking at me. "Can I get one?"

"Uh. Sure." She scratches her head. "I didn't think you'd want to pick. You being all…royal…kind of…and all."

"I'm not royal."

"I meant…important, President, and living in the castle."

"Edith." I put my hand out to stop her. "I'm here. I'll help."

She blows out a breath, trying to get over her shock that some-one in a position of authority would ask to help. I'm not sure what that says about her interpretation of leadership, but Bernard's commentary about Llama today has me thinking deeply on the topic. Standing there, watching a prisoner do hard labor, that's something Enforce would do, a behavior that would be sanctioned and expected by the leaders of Nation. I don't want to be like Enforce. I don't want to be like Nation.

Edith breaks me from my thoughts. "We'll have to drive to go get you one."

"Ok," I say. "Let's go."

She sighs. "We'll have to leave Percy here. There are only two seats."

I frown. "Or you could get a vest and bring it back? I'll help fill Percy's harvest vest pockets while we wait for you to return."

Edith nods. "That's a good plan. Why didn't I think of that?"

Percy stands off to the side, methodically picking the pea pods and placing them in the canvas fabric vest pockets. The vest slides over the head, with five deep pockets along the front and back. The thought is that when the front is full, you can slide it around and wear the produce on the back, continuing to fill the front, then dump the rest into buckets.

Edith takes off at a jog down the row, disappearing into the plants, back to the MUV.

I stand next to Percy and begin picking pea pods off the plants.

"May I?" I ask, indicating Percy's vest once I have a handful of peas.

Percy shrugs.

"I wonder why they use these vests?" I muse.

Percy hasn't said a word to me this entire morning, but he turns toward me. "Because, Reach, the distance from the pea pod to a basket or satchel would require the same repetitive motion, with the same distance between the motions over and over again. By varying the distance of the action, you prevent mental fatigue. Plus, you have the advantage of filling a quota in manageable chunks instead of in a denomination that's simply too large to comprehend. You can fill your vest multiple times, but you mentally break the vest into pockets. While the outcome is the same as if you filled your basket twice, the reality is, the psychological aspect makes the vest easier."

I blink. His wheedling voice is condescending, but he's right. I shrug, then drop another handful of pea pods into his pocket. "Are you a psychologist?" I ask.

"I dabbled in it." He snaps a pea pod off the plant and pops it into his smug mouth.

I wish we were on Earth and there were bugs here so I could hope he was eating one. There are no bugs here, and he is not eating one, but it doesn't stop the thought.

What would that say about my psychology?

"For instance," Percy's nasally voice cuts in, "I know that you hate me."

I don't look at him. Instead, I continue methodically snapping pods off the plants. Still, the weight of Percy's words is heavy.

Hate.

Isn't *hate* what brought us from Earth to Mars? Isn't *hate* what built Nation into the system it uses now?

"I don't hate you," I say calmly, but loud enough that I'm sure he hears it. My ears burn with heat, but I don't look at Percy. I can't show him any reaction beyond this one.

Percy stops picking pea pods. I can see him from my periphery. "That makes you an interesting case study," he quips. "Very noble. Probably thinking you're doing something for the common good. A hero complex."

I don't respond to his barbs. I simply snap another pea pod off the plant and move down the row.

Edith's MUV roars into range. She thrusts the lever into park and hops out of the vehicle. "Here, Reach," she calls, disheveled. Her hair has escaped her braid, and her overalls' strap falls off her shoulder as she offers me a harvest vest.

Grateful to escape from Percy's musings, I walk to her and accept it. As I shrug it over my head, Edith smiles.

"How's it going?" she asks.

"Fine." I glance down the row. It looks like an eternity. "We've got a lot of ground to get to today though."

Edith nods. "It's ok. It will go faster than you think. Also, when you get to the intersection, change directions and go down P-2. No one's been down there in a while. Those should be ready based on when we planted."

I nod. "We can do that."

Edith begins to walk away before stopping abruptly and turning around. "Oh, and Reach." She shoves her hands into her pockets and extracts a rectangular device with several buttons. "Use this to call if you have any problems or need any backup. I'm on channel one."

I nod at the odd comms device. It's simple—almost too simple. I could probably take it apart and reassemble it in less than five minutes. "Thank you, Edith."

She drives away, leaving Percy and me to pick the peas in an awkward silence.

We work our way down the row, filling our pockets in silence. When we reach the intersection, Percy starts to continue straight, but I stop him, placing a hand on his shoulder. "We're supposed to move into this row."

Percy looks down the row with narrowed eyes. "Why?"

I look.

The pea plants nearest the intersection are a bright, verdant green, but a few feet down the row, the plants are yellow, brown, shriveled, and mottled with blackish spots. Flowers hang on limply, drooping from the stems. A few pea pods dangle from the plants that are struggling to stay upright.

The wood of the trellises is visible, standing out against the sickly plants. The stench of rot meets my nose as I walk farther down the row, taking it all in. Percy walks by my side.

"What does it mean?" I whisper, the gears in my mind turning, but not connecting the living, thriving rows of plants with the death surrounding me.

Percy swallows and meets my gaze, his sallow face grave, and the bun at the nape of his neck coming undone. "It means that you're going to go to Earth. Sooner than you'd planned."

Percy's words sink in, searing themselves into my mind.

I extract the radio from my pocket and press channel one. A green light pops on before Edith's voice cackles through the radio. "This is Edith, over."

I shake my head at the strange wording. "This is Reach. In P-2." I gulp. "We have a problem." I blow out a breath. "A really *big* problem."

"P-2? I'll be there asap."

I pocket the radio and turn around to find Percy slumped on the ground, his head between his hands.

"Death is coming," he says. He shakes his head, then looks up and says, with no emotion in his gaze, "Death came for Jezero, and now it's here for Souterraine."

18

EDITH ARRIVES MOMENTS later to find Percy on the ground, still shaking his head, and me staring at the withered, rotting plants with no idea what to do.

"Surface," she whispers as her jaw clenches. Her long braids swing as she walks down the row. "By the surface." She starts to reach out a finger to touch the plants, but then pulls it back and jams her hands in her overalls' pockets. "What happened?" she asks me, her eyes huge.

I shrug. "We turned down this row like you said, and it looked like…*this*."

"Surface…" she hisses.

I remember that *surface* is a swear word here, but to me, it means the top of Mars, a place I've been multiple times since arriving.

"We need to inform the queen and the king and the advisors."

I nod, mute as I stare at the row of destruction.

Edith punches a button on her radio and whispers the words, "Code green".

"What does it mean?" I ask. "What happened here?"

Percy continues rocking back and forth on the ground. I can't tell if he's lost his mind, is genuinely upset, or is weirdly excited. Then, without warning, he stops his rocking and shaking and stands. His cold, calculating eyes pierce my own as he slides his gaze from me to Edith to the plants. "It's *blight*, Reach. The utopia has been infiltrated by parasitic spores, and now…the peas will all die."

I look to Edith, whose mouth sets into a hard line. She nods. "It's blight." She walks a little way down the row, then turns. "We have to get to the castle." She pushes a button on her radio and says, "I need a four-seat MUV." Then she turns to Percy. "You, keep picking."

Percy rolls his eyes, but snaps another pod off the stem and deposits it into his vest.

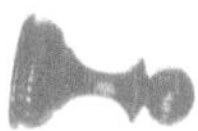

Fifteen minutes later, we arrive at the front doors of the castle. The dark, polished wood gleams in the Souterraine version of the sun, and the clover smells sweet. I stare at the meadow, letting my heart bear the weight of the next moments. The idyllic utopia before me is about to be shattered.

Edith strides to the doors and pulls them open. She marches through the castle to the wooden paneled library, where she sinks onto the window seat and stares unblinking out the window. I stand alone, leaning my back against a tall shelf. The soft breeze lifts the scent of books to my nose. I inhale. The smell of pages, paper, and ink soothes. I asked once how these books came to be on Mars. Queen Eleanore smiled and showed me the digital database that allowed for books to be printed once the colony was established and the people stopped worrying about dying every two seconds. It's not a great feeling to know that the people are a sentence away from that same worry.

Llama and Queen Eleanore round the corner into the library, swishing dresses announcing their arrival. "Edith," Queen Eleanore states. "What do you need?"

Edith sighs, then stands and walks closer to the queen.

Llama walks over to me. "How was prisoner duty?" she asks.

I shake my head. I can't talk right now. I know what she doesn't. I know what *they* all don't. It's too heavy, too hard, too painful.

"What's wrong, Reach?" Llama grasps my hand in her own soft, cool palm.

"Blight," I whisper, looking at the delicate hand in my own large one.

"B…blight?" Llama replies. "In what crop?"

"Peas."

Llama's eyes bug out. "How bad?"

I shrug. I don't understand the full implication of losing a row of peas.

King Alfred's shoes flap against the wooden floor and announce his presence in the library. "Code *green*?" he asks Edith.

Edith's head rests on her palms while she sits on the window seat, and Queen Eleanore sits beside her. The queen's arms wrap around Edith's shoulders as Edith shakes.

"Alfred, dear," Queen Eleanore chides gently. "Edith has informed me that we have lost an entire row of peas to blight."

"Peas? The protein plants?"

"Yes."

"An entire row?"

"Yes."

"And what does that mean for Souterraine?"

Edith picks her head up and blows out a breath. One of her braids has come loose, and the blonde strands whip in her stream of air. "It means that we don't have enough food. And it means that breeze pollination that has worked for three centuries is now a liability, not an advantage."

"What is breeze pollination?" Llama asks, her face a stony mask.

"It means that on Earth, there are multiple ways to pollinate—bees, bugs, birds, wind—but on Souterraine, there are no insects. So, we rely on the breeze to pollinate, *or* we hand pollinate. It takes time, and so, over the years, we've developed plants that breeze pollinate. But blight is parasitic spores that can be carried *on* the breeze. So now, every plant is at risk."

"What about the lava tubes?" I ask. "Can't you cordon off the field that we were in?"

Queen Eleanore's face falls. "We are already in a food shortage situation. Every acre of production lost significantly diminishes Souterraine's time."

I frown, and my hand comes up to my chin, my thumb catching on the deep curve of my mouth as I digest the implication of these words, and do the math. "We have to go. Don't we? Wave Cohort 1. We have to leave, now."

King Alfred's short gray beard bobs as he shakes his head. "No. You can't leave. You're not ready. The *group* isn't ready."

"But Alfred." Queen Eleanore gently places her palm on his forearm. "It's the only way to extend our colony's lifespan back to…what it needs to be. And, if it wasn't for Reach and Llama coming here when they did, we'd be having this same conversation, but with extremely different circumstances. Wave Cohort 1 is training; they have agreed to this mission. It's the only way. Wouldn't you agree, Reach?"

All the eyes in the room meet mine as the silence builds into palpable tension.

With nothing more to say, armed with data, facts, and the game theory of this multifaceted game I've been playing with Nation, now coupled with the game theory of a starving colony, all I can do is nod.

19

"Then we'd better go prepare," Queen Eleanore states. "Edith, can you please supervise the harvest of peas that are not impacted? We'll have to store them separately to prevent contamination, but we don't want to lose potential calories and protein. Has anyone checked on the other crops in the different sectors?"

Edith murmurs something unintelligible.

"I didn't catch that, Edith," King Alfred says dryly.

"I said, I need full power to harvest the peas at the rate you request. And we'll have to check in with beans, squash, and the other vegetable sectors."

"Please do that," Queen Eleanore replies. "And you'll have full power."

"You'll leave the lights on? Constantly?"

"Yes," the queen assures her. "It will be like the midnight sun on Earth."

Llama and I stare at the queen blankly. "You are unaware of the midnight sun?" she asks, then shakes her head. "Another time. We have work to do. Reach, Llama, we need to go to Wave Cohort 1 and interrupt the physical training. We also need to—"

"And you'll give me back my crews?" Edith interrupts. "The ones who went to Wave Cohort 1?"

"In some capacity, yes."

"Then we can have the peas harvested in one week. Maybe sooner. We'll have to work around the clock."

"Good." King Alfred nods. Then he strides to the door and opens it, pulling the heavy door into the room. "Let's get started. We have a week."

Edith and King Alfred leave the room.

Queen Eleanore chews on her lip, then stretches up and adjusts her flower crown. Today, the flowers are roses. She hisses and pulls her thumb away, a bead of red blood on her thumb.

"When will we launch?" Llama whispers.

I close my eyes, squinting against the emotion of everything threatening to press me to the floor. My mind runs calculations rapidly, thinking of all the pieces of information I know, the food storage issue, the physical and mental readiness of the Cohort, the way the transport ships need to be prepared for a journey to Earth, the communication we need to have with Sigma… It's too much. It won't ever happen. It can't ever happen. And yet, we have to make it happen.

My mind lands on a solid number. "Ninety days."

Queen Eleanore meets my gaze with her piercing brown ones. "We need to tell the trainees, and after that, we'll have to make an announcement to all of Souterraine. Reach, you'll need to tell Jezero's remaining colonists before the Souterraine announcement. I think it would be courteous to tell them in their village."

I resist the urge to shudder. I hate having to lead the dysfunctional colony. "Won't they have to get used to hearing everything from *you* when I'm gone?"

Queen Eleanore cocks her head to the side. "Y-yes," she stammers.

"Then what's the point?" I whisper. "I'm leaving. I never meant to be Jezero's President. It's time to let that go."

"Shouldn't it be their choice?" Llama butts in.

My brow furrows. "Like they should choose a replacement for me?"

Llama nods. "At least let them have that sense of control."

Queen Eleanore ticks off her fingers as if she's thinking of a to-do list. "Head to the Jezero Village and let everyone who's there know you have immediate Jezero Presidential business. I'll have the children sent back from experiential learning and let the adults know to report back from their job sectors through the intercolony sector communication system. Everyone should be there in two hours. Then, in three hours, we'll do the full colony announcement."

She leaves the room in a swoosh of skirts and a flip-flop-flap of shoes. Llama and I stand alone in the library. As the queen's footsteps grow fainter, Llama's usually bright eyes dull. "Reach," she says, her voice breaking. "I don't want to…"

"I know," I say, opening my arms for a hug. She steps into my embrace, and the wetness of her tears seeps through the shoulder of my shirt.

"We have to, though, don't we?" Llama hiccups as she steps away.

"Yeah," I whisper. "We do. We have a mission, remember? It was always to go back, to return to Earth and take down Nation."

"Yes, but…" she pauses, and leaves her thought open-ended.

"Llama, Nation is the enemy, and if we stay here, we're playing into their hand. What's an enemy if you're on the same team?"

Llama blinks. "Then I guess we need to go to Jezero Village."

"You're telling me that you're leaving? That you're going back to Earth, and that you don't want to be the Jezero President any longer? And that we have to go take orders from these people again?" The angry hum of the circle of Jezero colonists surrounds me from where I stand in the middle of their village.

"Yes," I confirm. "But, I wanted to propose an option to you."

"What could you possibly have for an option? The only other person in line is Percy!" a colonist cries.

"Not, Percy!" cries someone else.

"No," I cut in. "I propose an ancient system. It's called an election."

"What's that?" calls a woman.

I explain as succinctly as I can the way an election works. The Jezero colonists listen with rapt attention. "It would need to happen immediately. This is an emergency use of the process. Anyone in favor of an election taking place now, please step forward."

Two people step forward, then two more, until only a handful of people remain in their positions. It's clear that the majority is in favor.

"Since a majority is in favor, and since I am abdicating, who would like to run for the role of Jezero President?"

Three women and two men raise their hands. They're all leaders, and all qualified. I breathe a little easier seeing who nominates themselves. "Good." I lead the colonists through the process of voting *one* time for *one* candidate. It's not scientific, but when a clear majority elects Benjamin, a shorter man with graying hair, a ramrod straight spine, and a kind smile, I let out a sigh.

"Benjamin Tusaw," I say as I remove the Presidential sash. "I abdicate my position as President of the remains of Jezero Colony, and through democratic election, pass the position to you." I pass him the sash, and he stares at it with reverence before draping it over his shoulders.

"Thank you," he breathes before he turns to address his people. "Jezero, we have been welcomed here on Souterraine. We will need to work together with the Souterraine leadership to overcome the obstacles former President Reach has mentioned. We come from a place of ingenuity, of technological advancement. If you have *any* knowledge to share—" His eyes touch briefly on a few of the colonists before he continues. "Even if it's not particularly legal…If you have *any* thoughts that could assist Wave Cohort 1 and the colony of Souterraine, it is expected that you will come forward with that information. We may be displaced, but we will always be Jezero at heart."

The crowd roars its approval, and I marvel at Benjamin's oratory prowess. Before I turn to leave, I offer Benjamin the official Jezero salute. To my surprise, he does it in return, and all the Jezero colonists follow suit. Emotion clogs my throat.

Yes, I am relieved to no longer be leading a colony of people I'm connected to only by the strange circumstances of my birth, but as I walk away from the village, a sense of loss hits me too. Tears threaten, but I know I can't dwell on it. I can't dwell on loss, on pain, on finding family only to be disappointed, and then…losing family. Coward, hero—was Greg one or the other? Truthfully, he was *both*.

I need to tell Mom about this. The thought crossing my mind is enough to jar me from the moment and focus me on what's ahead.

I have no choice but to turn my sights to the next phase of the mission that began years ago in a desert compound on Earth: preparing for our return.

As I'm leaving the Jezero Village in Souterraine, an announcement sounds throughout the colony. King Alfred's voice booms, "This is an emergency alert. It is not a drill. All able-bodied members of Souterraine Colony are to report to the meadow in one hour."

The words hang in the air, along with a sense of ominousness. Even the trees, which are always whispering, their branches creating a slight breeze that never ceases, have stilled. The air sits heavy on my shoulders, and I have a headache. My injury from the traverse-ball tenses up, but I massage it as I walk. I'm going to face worse than a Martian dust storm soon.

An hour later, a rectangular platform stands in the meadow. The clover is soft underfoot, with little white flowers interspersed in the deep green. It would be beautiful, except for the sense of dire urgency in the air.

King Alfred, Queen Eleanore, Llama, Pippa, and Ethan sit on the platform, two other chairs remain empty. One between the king and queen, and one between Llama and Pippa. The extra chair throws me for a moment, but then I see Benjamin Tusaw arrive, wearing the Presidential sash of Jezero. He climbs up the stairs to the platform, his graying head bobbing as he ascends. King Alfred greets him with a handshake and a smile, and Queen Eleanore does the same. The entire interaction is so cordial and out of character with previous Jezero-Souterraine relationships that, when I look at Llama, I find her jaw dropped open. I'm tempted to laugh, but I hold it in. This situation is too serious for laughter.

"Hi," I whisper as I take my seat between her and Pippa.

"Hi, Reach!" Pippa says as she shifts in her wooden chair.

"Reach!" Ethan echoes. There's always a bit of melancholy in his eyes, but today it seems painfully obvious. He might be five years old, but he's smart enough to know that *this* is a big deal. *This* is an indication that things are about to change. For Jezero colonists who lived through the collapse of their colony, this must be like living in a recurring nightmare.

"Hi." I give Pippa a wave and flash Ethan a smile.

Llama slips her hand in mine. "It went ok?" she whispers.

"Mhmm," I hum. "I'm no longer President."

"That's a relief."

I stare at her, a question in my gaze. Llama was the one who encouraged me to be the acting President of Jezero. "I thought you wanted me to be…to do…the Presidency?"

She sighs. "You were clouded by what happened, and the trauma, and they were all traumatized. You were what they knew, and some semblance of their normal, even if it was *not* actually normal. It was psychological for everyone, Reach."

"It wasn't psychological for me," I mutter.

"It was," Llama insists, but then stops short as King Alfred, Queen Eleanore, and President Benjamin Tusaw approach a microphone at the front of the stand.

"Souterraine and Jezero," King Alfred begins in his deep, booming voice. "We have an emergency, and it will require your full cooperation to survive. Please keep in mind that we have been a successful colony for over three hundred years. The emergencies we've faced in the past century have been few and far between, although lately it has become apparent that our time on Mars is limited at best. Mars is the only home we have ever known. This news is being shared not to shock, not to cause chaos, not to cause fear, but to communicate honestly."

The crowd standing in the meadow is completely silent.

Queen Eleanore shuffles to the mic. "We discovered today that a critical crop has suffered blight."

A sharp intake of breath sounds collectively throughout the crowd.

"Peas are an important source of protein, and unfortunately, our pea fields have been contaminated. Not all of the crop is lost, but we must rush to harvest, and will need to cordon off that lava tube. We will not be able to grow there again."

Worry, like the first long, deep note of a piano song, reverberates through the crowd. It's not words; it's the intake of breath, it's the turning of heads, the tensing of muscles, clenching of jaws. There's a strange music to the symphony of fear.

"At this time, no other crops have been affected, and we have ample stores of dried food. In addition, we have our animal products, though those have always been used for special occasions. However, due to the dire situation with the pea fields, we will be changing the timeline for Wave Cohort 1. In order to make our time on Mars last longer, reducing the load of the colony is the most efficient and prudent way to move forward. I would now like to introduce to you the new President of Jezero Colony, President Tusaw."

The Souterraine colonists look like they've been run over by a traverse-ball, or a MUV, while the Jezero Villagers clap politely. The Souterraine colonists join in half-heartedly.

"Thank you," Benjamin says. His voice is strong, but soothing. He's a commanding presence, even with his shorter stature. The way the sash stands out on his cream-colored Souterraine shirt draws the eye. He *knows* what he's doing. "After discussion with Their Majesties, we have decided that the Souterraine light will be left on at all hours to allow for rapid harvesting. We will need multiple crews from other Ag sectors, and those with limited responsibilities in their positions, to contribute to the harvest efforts. Wave Cohort 1 is expected to participate in harvesting during the morning session. We will also have a crew responsible for afternoon, evening, and night sessions."

He nods to Queen Eleanore, and she steps forward again.

"Thank you, President Tusaw." From where I sit, I can't see her face, only the ramrod straight posture of her spine. "We will need to work together for this to be successful. As President Tusaw mentioned, Wave Cohort 1 is expected to participate in harvesting and will continue training in the afternoons and evenings. We all must work together to make this a success. However, there are two brave souls from Wave Cohort 1 who have volunteered to embark on a mission before any other."

Her words don't sound right. I haven't volunteered for anything. *Have I?* Has Llama? I look to Llama, only to find her staring at me as if I had betrayed her.

"I didn't," I say, but then stop when Queen Eleanore continues speaking.

"These two brave Jezero colonists have volunteered their unique skill sets for a dangerous mission. It is the mission of Wave Cohort 1 to return to Earth, to assist in the restructuring of the government known as Nation. However, it cannot be done alone. These two Jezero colonists will attempt the dangerous mission of risking contact with other population centers on Earth. Perhaps they will not be as hostile as Nation. Thank you, brave Jezero colonists, for your willingness to embark on this dangerous mission. If we could all acknowledge…" Queen Eleanore points to the center of the crowd, and a separation between the two Jezero colonists and the rest of the crowd forms.

At the center stand the two volunteer Jezero colonists.

My heart jumps to my throat.

It's Beatriz and Cait.

PART 2

21

2 months, 1 week later

I MEET LLAMA in the changing rooms by the traverse-ball ports. This is part of Souterraine and attached to the air cycler, but rarely visited. Ports are too cold, too dark, and too close to the surface for most Souterraine colonists. She brushes her surface spacesuit off with a gloved hand before using her teeth to detach it from her sleeve. Once her gloves are off, she crashes into me in a hug that's so tight, my ribs cut into my lungs from her pressure. She loosens her grip.

"I got it, Reach," she says quickly. "I got the full samples for the tests."

"That's great." I grin. I'm happy she's back below the surface of Mars, where she's safer.

The past few months have involved multiple trips for both of us in traverse-balls. Each time one of us goes to the surface, the other one stays below and monitors the progress. It's hard to navigate watching the woman I love do something dangerous while still overseeing the project from a scientific standpoint. We're collecting sediment to run tests on, specifically tests that Nation's government will want. Having data they'll want is a critical part of our game plan.

Although we're limited in our payload for the return to Earth, samples are being bagged and logged carefully, and a small amount of Martian sediment will come with us.

Our launch is scheduled for three weeks from today. The engineers have been busy assembling the pieces of our transport ship. The space shuttle design is based on the design of the original colonists, but with technological innovations of the past three hundred years. The premise is simple: a spherical design. The force of gravity inside will cause the sphere to roll. It's important that it rolls through the atmospheres of both Mars and Earth, because it reduces the friction on a single part of the equipment, which means it's less likely we'll die a fiery death.

I'm still concerned we might die a fiery death.

Llama steps onto her tiptoes and presses a kiss to my lips, breaking my thoughts from our potential end. Morbid though it may be, if we do die, then at least I'll die with her.

That's not something I could say about the traverse-ball experiments of the past few months. The fact that it's over, that we have the final samples we need, and that neither of us has to endure the gut-wrenching, fear-inducing stress of watching your loved one embark on a mission where survival isn't guaranteed, that's enough to make me forget where I am.

I tighten my arms around Llama and kiss her, long, lingering, slow. After minutes, or maybe hours, she pushes lightly away from me. Her eyes shine. "Miss me?" she whispers.

I nod, too caught up in emotion to speak.

"Llama?" A buzz sounds in Llama's spacesuit. She's still hooked up to COMs, and our friend Phil was manning that station in my absence.

"Yes?" Llama answers, a little sheepish because we didn't immediately return to the colony.

"Could you please report to the COMs station? Margot is requesting you, Reach, and the Jezero President to join her and the king and queen as soon as possible."

Llama's eyes meet mine with confusion.

I shrug.

"Yes," I say. "We'll be there as soon as we can."

A crackle of static, and then a dry voice cuts back in. "Maybe next time don't forget you're still hooked up to COMs."

I bite back a laugh at the dry tone. Poor Phil, forced to listen to us kissing.

Llama shrugs out of her surface spacesuit and hangs it in the locker marked Princess Llama. Since the intensive phase for Wave Cohort 1 began, our clothing has changed. Instead of the natural fibers, loose dresses, shirts and pants, we now wear scientifically-created athletic suits. These suits are flexible, shiny, and a deep inky black. They hug each muscle tightly, but allow for airflow through strategic ventilation pockets. The best part of the entire get-up is that we no longer wear the Souterraine shoes. Now, we wear shoes similar to the ones we had in Nation, with fiber completely covering the heel, the toe, the top of the foot, and a cushion below the sole for comfort. Not flapping as we walk along is a welcome change.

Llama shuts the door and looks fondly at the locker for a moment. We both know next time we wear those suits, we won't be returning to Souterraine again.

Hand in hand, Llama and I leave the locker room and head to the COMs station. I consider apologizing to Phil when we get there, but then again, I'm not really sorry.

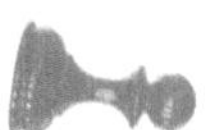

Llama and I duck into the COMs station. Margot has refurbished it from the tiny, dingy office it once was to a hustling and bustling building. Part of Wave Cohort 1's prep has been building a network of robust communication between the spaceship and Souterraine. Since Beatriz and Cait left, regular communication has been in place with their small-scale space shuttle. So far, no problems have been reported.

Margot looks up from her tablet, the triangular spinning technology that somehow holds yottabytes of data in the palm of your hand. "Oh good, you're here," she says. She doesn't smile. I can't decide if her face is neutral because it's always neutral or because something bad is about to happen. Anxiety isn't a constant companion the way it once was for me, but it still flares occasionally. I'd be more worried if it didn't, considering that we're about to embark on yet another space mission, this time to a known hostile planet.

Llama tightens her grip on my hand, and I take comfort in the fact that she knows me, knows my anxieties, knows my fears, knows how my thoughts progress.

"This way, please," Margot says, bobbing her gray head. She walks up a staircase, her shoes flapping with each step.

"I hated those shoes," I whisper to Llama.

She looks down at her own feet and shrugs. "I kind of liked them. But the noise reduction is an improvement."

Margot leads us down a hall and into a conference room. A larger version of the spinning top tablet sits on a wooden table, and wooden high-back chairs surround it. A small spinning tablet is set at each chair. The king and queen stand when we arrive.

"Good, you're here. Was the mission successful?" Queen Eleanore asks as her eyes rove over Llama. In the past weeks, Queen Eleanore's intensity has ratcheted up. Her golden bronze skin seems more easily flushed, and her warm eyes hold a new sadness. It's not hard to figure out why. She loves Llama, has fully embraced her as her granddaughter, and now is sending her away, forever.

"Yes," Llama says, looking around the room. "Phil, all the samples have been taken to the labs, and that completes the samples required for the experiments."

Phil brightens. "Excellent."

Margot coughs subtly, and all eyes turn to her. "Ahem." She clears her throat before spinning the large tablet in the center of the table backward one rotation. Her thumb and forefinger pinch together, and an image appears on the wooden wall. "We have news."

A message appears on the screen.

Key to everything isn't here. Return to the old ways, days, and Earth to unlock the future. -Sigma

Eyes turn to me, but even if it was my mom who wrote that, I have no idea what she means.

"Key?" I ask, thinking of an answer key, or a puzzle key, something logical.

Queen Eleanore crinkles her brow. King Alfred strokes his beard and closes his eyes.

"I don't understand what she means by *key*."

Llama stands. "Does she mean an *actual* key, or a metaphorical one?"

Everyone in the room shrugs.

22

WHAT KEY COULD unlock the future from the past? It's a riddle that I can't solve, and it's keeping me up all night. It doesn't help that the Souterraine light is shining as brightly as if it were day.

For the first time since my arrival, I closed the wooden shutters over my window to block out the light. Unfortunately, that also blocks the gentle breeze that's stirred my very soul to comfort.

Unable to stop the thoughts cycling around my mind like the engines of a spaceship, I slide into my shoes and leave the bedroom. I leave the door cracked on my way out because if Shadow wants to come, he's welcome to. I don't know *where* the cat is right now, but he always finds his way to me. The brightness of the middle of the night is jarring, but I'm not the only one who can't sleep. Llama opens the door to her room and steps onto the landing.

"I thought I heard you," she whispers.

"I'm sorry if I woke you."

"It's the sun, or the…sun here." She grimaces. "I can't sleep with it *on* like this."

I nod my head. "Want to go for a walk with me?"

It's her turn to nod.

She slips her palm into mine, and we walk through the castle to the clover fields. We leave by a side door, Llama leading me toward the queen's thinking gardens. Scents of honeysuckle, the fragrance of roses, and the earthy smell of this garden are all tinged by the slightly metallic undertone of Mars.

"I can't stop thinking about keys," I say.

She situates herself on a bench. "From the *Sigma* message?"

I nod.

"Hmm."

"All I can think of are the keys that we use, like key codes. And I can't imagine that there would be digital key codes we couldn't hack with enough time and patience."

"What about real keys?" Llama asks.

"I've considered those, but we haven't used them in so long…in Nation—"

"In the Wards, people use *real* keys all the time."

"Llama," I start, but she keeps going.

"I wonder…if there are any physical keys, relics from Nation, that made it here. I don't know if that would be possible, but maybe?"

"That would be such a long shot." I wrap my arm around Llama's shoulders and pull her to me. "But I think I know who might know if there were."

"Phil?" Llama questions.

I bob my head.

"Seems like he knows all about the history of Souterraine." I shrug. "And I trust him. I wish he was in Wave Cohort 1, but I know he's needed here."

"Reach, he can't be in Wave Cohort 1. He's not…medically…"

"What?"

"He doesn't hear quite typically."

"What?"

"He's deaf. Haven't you noticed the cochlear implant?"

"No." My mind shuffles through words, trying to make sense of what a cochlear implant is.

"I only know because…there was one child with one in the Ward school. They're hard to see, so small and effective, but if anything happened to his implant, he wouldn't be able to hear. It would be…dangerous for everyone, including him."

A sense of fear, the dangerous mission we're about to undertake, bubbles up from my gut. I close my eyes, count down from ten, but all that serves to do is make me think of the imminent launch.

Llama grips my hand tighter and stands. "Let's solve it. Let's find Phil and figure this out. He knows the most about the history of Souterraine of anyone we've met. He'd know something."

"He was in the room with us, though, when we got the message."

"That doesn't mean he knows what we're thinking," she counters.

We find Phil after searching what feels like everywhere. It's always the last place you look that you find what you've lost, and this feels no different. Phil is in the place we should have looked for him first: the school.

The wooden structure, tucked into a grove of willow branches along the river, is three-sided. The willow branches along the fourth side provide a curtain of privacy and distraction reduction, but still let in dappled light as well as the soft whisper of a breeze. Phil is slumped across a wooden table, his head on his arms, and he seems to be *snoring*.

Llama approaches slowly. "His implant, he took it out." She gestures to a small device next to his head. "He can't hear us well."

I frown. "We need to wake him up, don't we?"

She shrugs. "We could, but we could leave him too."

"But then…"

Phil startles in his sleep, then shakes his head. He sits up and stares at Llama. "You're very pretty," he says before he slumps down again.

I'm not sure what to make of that.

Llama's blue eyes widen to massive proportions. "I think he thinks he's dreaming this…"

"I don't want to wake him, and I don't want *you* to wake him either."

Llama snorts. "Avoiding second-hand embarrassment for you, or for your friend?"

"All of the above," I whisper as I push the greenery aside for Llama and step into the full glare of the Souterraine sun.

The curtain of willow branches shifts behind us in a soft hush of movement, and a sense of hopelessness weighs on my chest as I consider *what now?* The purpose I thought we had in this nighttime errand dwindles.

The sun might be invigorating, but it doesn't change the fact that my biological rhythms are *off*. A yawn escapes and Llama smirks. "Tired?"

There's nothing more to do except head back to the castle and to bed. Llama and I walk to the castle, hand in hand, following the river and listening to the peaceful lap of the current against the oxbows. Several hours of an excursion in the middle of the night might be enough to bring me to sleep, but as I pull the heavy front door open, Pippa stumbles into me.

I try to catch her, but it's not enough, and we collapse to the ground in a tangle of limbs. "Are you alright?" I ask, but her elbow drives into my chest, and I'm afraid my words come out like a squeak.

"Yes," Pippa says as she scrambles off me.

Llama swoops in. "Here." She pulls Pippa to the side and helps her stand.

I sit up, dust my legs off, and reach for Pippa's flower crown. It has seen better days, because this one is clearly wilting. Still, I hand her the twisted daisies and she plops it on her head.

"Shouldn't you be sleeping?" Llama asks Pippa.

Pippa's bright eyes snap from me to the sun. "No," she says after a beat. "You're up."

Llama says something in rapid-fire French, and Pippa stands a little taller. I still haven't gotten the hang of languages the way Llama has, but it's clear that Pippa and Llama have been practicing French together.

Pippa shakes her head. She's obviously thinking, but then she says, "Clay!" and turns. She scampers into the castle, and her shoes click-clack against the wood floor.

Llama grins at me. "Clay!" she says before she takes off after Pippa.

Confused, I follow as the two women navigate the twists and turns of the castle passageways. When they reach the storage room that leads to Pippa and Ethan's play space, I stop.

An art project doesn't sound enjoyable. I know I have limited time with Pippa because she will be in the final evacuation group with either King Alfred or Queen Eleanore and Ethan, but I'm tired.

Llama opens the trap door and hops down into the space, Pippa following. I've never been down there, but I shouldn't be surprised. After all, this castle is full of surprises. I want to go to bed—the exhaustion of a twenty-hour day has overtaken me—but Llama's head pops out above the trap door.

"You coming?" she asks, and the look of excitement on her face makes me feel like I shouldn't miss this.

I slide over to the hole in the floor and drop down. I'm taller than Llama, so when my feet hit the ground, my head is still visible over the trap door. It's odd to be looking at the floor from this perspective, but it's not the strangest thing I've ever experienced.

"Come. On. Reach," Pippa says as she crawls on all four limbs down a tunnel space.

Llama drops to her hands and knees. She glances over her shoulder. "Come on," she says, then starts crawling at an impressive pace in an attempt to keep up with Pippa.

Pippa might be in a dress and crawling through a tunnel, but she's still faster than Llama and me in our high-tech training clothes. We crawl along the unpolished wood for what feels like hours, but in reality is only minutes. I know that I'm on high alert because this is new to all my senses, and that being in this state of tightly wound-ness means my sense of time is warped.

When Pippa sits up out of her crawling posture and Llama does too, I attempt the same. My muscles are stiff from using new ones, and stiff from lack of sleep, and stiff from running all over Souterraine with Llama on the pointless 'key' venture.

"Cle," Pippa says, pointing.

I force my muscles into submission and find that we've left the tunnel and are in a cavernous room of sorts. It has woven mats on the floor and toys all around the room. They're neatly put away, a tricycle next to a bicycle, a miniature version of a kitchen along one wall, and an entire bookshelf full of puzzles. A wooden board with rounded holes takes up the top half of another wall in its entirety. Each hole hosts a wooden peg, and each peg holds a silver key.

There are hundreds, and they vary in size, shape, texture, and material.

"Cle," Pippa repeats. "From. Earth."

"Key?" I question, looking at Llama.

"Cle, *key*," she says.

"Are these all the keys in Souterraine?" I ask.

Pippa nods. "I like." She thinks for a moment. "Them. They are. Pretty."

I cut my eyes back to Llama, because I don't know how this helps us at all, but Llama smiles softly at her aunt, and I know that this bond they have is something special. Pippa might be older than Llama and me, but her disability makes my heart squeeze with how *young* she is at heart.

"Pippa?" Llama asks, but she keeps her gaze locked on me. "What do you like to do with the keys?"

Pippa smiles, then pulls a drawer from below the pegboard open. She extracts a lock and says, "Puzzles. Open."

It clicks into place the way the final move on a chessboard makes sense when it's between check and checkmate and you can finally defeat your opponent. "Pippa, do they all have a lock?"

Could the original colonists have brought a key to Mars to stop Nation from something? It's improbable, but it's not impossible.

She nods, but holds up one finger.

"One doesn't?"

Again, she nods.

"Do you know which one?"

She shakes her head.

I know what we're doing for the rest of tonight.

23

It takes all night and well into the morning, but eventually, every key is matched to a lock. Every key but one. Pippa curled up in a corner on one of the woven mats with her head on a soft floor pillow. She spread her full skirts around her on the floor and then slept. Llama and I did not, and now, as I catch a glimpse of Llama's face, I can see how haggard she looks from one night of sleep deprivation and an intense puzzle to solve.

"Do you really think this key means anything?" I ask, holding out the single antique skeleton key in my palm.

Llama shrugs. "It's an odd one out, and we can at least ask about it now that we have it."

"How did you know Pippa had keys?"

Llama swipes her hand across her eyes, rubbing away her tiredness. "I've been down here before, with Ethan when he first arrived. Ethan was fascinated by the keys. Pippa showed him that they were a puzzle, but Ethan said something that made me think. He said, 'I've heard of keys, but never seen one.' I don't know, Reach, it seems odd enough to consider it."

I frown. "I don't know that we ever used keys either, did we? The secure areas of Compound were coded to our DNA, so only the proper people could access the data and experiments, and HUB was the same."

Llama sighs. "There were still some old keys like this in Ward 11, but Ward 11 was always the last to get anything, and no one wanted to update the apartment buildings. It was only the wealthy who had doors that locked, though; most people had doors without any locks at all."

"There are wealthy in Ward 11?"

Llama snorts. "Government puppets."

That makes sense.

"The overseers of the government supply drops. They weren't wealthy because they were paid well. They were wealthy because of extortion, and it certainly wasn't wealthy by Nation's Citizen standards. Wealthy comparatively."

Llama holds out the key and it glistens in the light. The skeleton key is brass, with three notches in the blade. The handle has intricate loops that make a sort of sphere before she slips the key into the breast pocket of her black zip-up tech jacket. "It can't hurt, and at the very least, it's an interesting memento of our time on Mars."

I nod, then look at Pippa. She's curled up like a cat, and after pulling an all-nighter, exhaustion crashes into me with the force of a tidal wave. "Do you think we should wake Pippa?"

Llama bobs her head, then crouches down next to the sleeping woman. "Pippa?" Llama whispers softly. She places a hand gently on Pippa's brow and her other hand on Pippa's shoulder. She softly jostles Pippa until Pippa startles awake. It's an odd thing, but I have a glimpse of Llama's maternal side. The fact that Pippa is only a few years older than us, but still needs tender care because of her genetic condition, hits me square in the heart.

"Llama!" Pippa shouts gleefully. Everything Pippa does is exuberant, and even though her abilities aren't typical of her age, she's *joyful.* Pippa crushes Llama in a hug, knocking Llama backward onto the mats with a 'oof.'

I tread lightly toward the two women and extend my hands to each of them, helping them up. Pippa's eyes sparkle with joy as she looks from me to Llama and back again. "Find," she pauses for a moment. "Cle?"

"Yeah," I say. "We found the one key without a matching lock.

Pippa beams. "Knew you." She takes a breath. "Would, Reach." She keeps her hand in my own and I squeeze it.

Llama releases a huge yawn.

"Should we go get some sleep?" I suggest. "Or at least see how things are doing after the nighttime harvest?"

Pippa nods before dropping to all fours and beginning the upward crawl out of the tunnel between the floors.

As my knees hit the wooden planks, all I can think is, *This was easier coming down.*

After half an hour of crawling upward through tight spaces, we emerge into the castle proper. Queen Eleanore stands with her arms crossed to the side of the trap door. She would be bemused, but the flicker of worry lurks behind her eyes.

"Pippa!" she chastizes, and then when Llama's head pops up behind mine, Queen Eleanore blinks in surprise. "You were all down there?"

"Yes," Llama says to her grandmother. "We found something."

The queen quirks a brow. "What?"

"Well, it was something Ethan said to me when we first went to the play space. He saw the keys and said, 'I've heard of them, but never seen one.' No one here uses these, so *why* are they here?" Llama unzips her pocket and extends the antique skeleton key.

Queen Eleanore eyes it suspiciously. "A cle?"

"Why are they even here? And why does every other key have a lock, except this one?" Llama asks again.

"Because we don't waste things. These keys came with the original colonists to Jezero and then Souterraine, but there was no need for them after a while. They don't open a single thing on Mars. Everything locked is DNA-coded."

"So theoretically," I cut in, "if we found something that could be opened with a key, we could get in, get out, and no one would know it was us?"

"Only if you wiped your DNA from everything you touched," Llama adds.

"Yes, theoretically."

It's strange having a conversation with the queen from below her feet, so I place my forearms on the floor above and pull myself out. I offer a hand to Llama, but she bites her lip and smirks at me before leaning on her own forearms and pulling herself out. I'm impressed. She's gotten stronger with the training for Wave Cohort 1. This is something she would never have been able to do in Nation.

Pippa clambers out with the ease of someone who's done this over a thousand times, and she crushes Queen Eleanore in a hug. "Momma," she says, and the queen hugs her back.

"We were worried about you. We didn't know where you were."

"It was sun out."

Queen Eleanore blinks, then smiles softly at her daughter. "Yes, it was." She peers over the wilted floral crown on Pippa's head. "Should we have some tea? I'm thinking we've all had a long night." She doesn't wait for a response, but turns toward the kitchen.

Llama places her hand on my arm as I begin to follow. "Wait, Reach." She slides the key into my palm. "I think you should carry it."

"Why?" I mouth, but she shakes her head.

"It feels dangerous somehow. Like I…shouldn't have it."

"Llama…" I whisper and pull her close to me. "I trust you."

"But *Nation* has manipulated me in the past, and they might in the future. You've stumbled, but they've never made you fall completely. What if this *is* something, and what if my having it opens the door to me…hurting you again?"

"It could be nothing, Llama," I murmur against her soft, brown hair. "It could be nothing at all. Maybe it's only important because we want it to be."

"Reach." She turns and places a cool palm on my cheek. The hint of stubble on my jawline rasps against her skin. "I have an inkling about this." She closes her eyes briefly, then opens them again, meeting my gaze with an intensity I haven't seen before. "I…want to do this right. I want to complete the mission, and I have a *feeling* about this key."

"Ok," I whisper.

She leans onto her tiptoes and places a soft kiss on my lips before she turns and walks away with long strides.

I take a moment to admire her as she follows the queen toward the kitchen, but then remember I should *join* her.

I zip the key into my breast pocket and quicken my pace to catch up.

24

Six weeks later

It's MY LAST night on Souterraine. Actually, it's my last night on Mars. Wave Cohort 1 departs tomorrow morning, and I don't know what I'm feeling. I want to leave. I have a mission, a purpose, a reason to move forward.

The past few weeks have been non-stop. The time for reflection, for immersing ourselves in enjoying the present, caused the hours to disappear into history the way only time can. Training, harvesting, packaging, and studying took up every moment of the day, and even eating was done *around* other tasks. Still, the harvest is in, the peas safely stored in the silos, and now a load of people will not need to be supported in perpetuity by a blight-infested field. When the blighted pea field was harvested, Edith and I donned surface suits. We opened the airlock at the back of the fields, then drove our MUV through the empty, desolate trellises. We exited the fields, and a crew, also in surface suits since the entire field area was depressurized now, cornered off the old field. Acres of Souterraine were turned into a frigid, barren desert in mere moments, yet it was something to celebrate. The harvest was in, plant-based protein was saved, and the blight didn't spread to any other crops.

Now, I'm in my room, looking out across the clover field as the light falls from daytime to nighttime setting. Shadow purrs against my leg, and I pick him up. He tolerates it and allows me to rub my hand along his spine. Slowly, he purrs, and something cracks in my heart.

Today has been a day of 'goodbyes.' First to the people of Souterraine in a general assembly, which included the remaining Jezero colonists. After dinner, the goodbyes became more personal, and harder. Pippa, Ethan, King Alfred, Queen Eleanore, Bernard. It was heavy. The undercurrent of excitement that Llama, myself, and the rest of Wave Cohort 1 feel was cut to shreds by the undercurrent of pain those who remain *here* feel.

I look at Shadow. Why is saying 'goodbye' to an animal so difficult? When I was a child on Compound, the only animals present were wild or lab animals. Pets weren't a thing, and I would never have thought I'd be emotional over a feline. Here, this cat has been my nighttime companion. For whatever reason, he liked me, and for whatever reason, even though he's the queen's cat, he chose to spend time with me. Is it because animals don't understand? Still, Shadow's never let me pick him up and pet him before, so he has to understand more than I think.

The breeze blows through the window and lifts the hair on the crown of my head. It's gentle, soft, and sweet. The scent of the river, the flowers, and the willow are all smells I try to commit to memory.

Quiet footsteps sound behind me, and arms encircle my waist. I know without a doubt that it's Llama.

"Can't sleep?" she asks.

"No," I say, turning to face her. The cat stays placidly in my arms, and Llama reaches out a hand to stroke his fur.

"Me neither," she whispers, stepping a half pace from me and leaning her elbows on the sill. "I'm all tangled up inside."

I bob my head because I know the feeling and I don't have words right now. There's too much emotion clogging my throat.

Llama catches my eye from her periphery. I can see her facing straight ahead, but really looking up at me from the corner of her eye. She sighs. "I want it to matter, Reach."

"You want what to matter?" I ask, my voice a mere breath above the breeze.

"What we did here. What we do *there*. Who we are. I want it to mean something."

"We're the first people from Earth to arrive on Mars in three hundred years. That has to mean something."

"No, I mean, I want our lives…especially if…we don't make it, to have been something that changed the course of…everything."

Visions of all that has happened on Mars in the months we've been here flash through my mind. "But what we did here, it did matter."

The moments of panic on Jezero Colony as it was collapsing, the way Llama helped me step into the role of figurehead for my father's people, the lives that were saved simply because Greg came to say goodbye. The heroism and cowardice of my father continues to haunt me, but in the end, he died a hero's death. I can only hope that, no matter how difficult my life, the end of it is heroic.

"Yes," she agrees, "but there's still so much more to do. Nation would never let someone like Pippa thrive, and I can't pretend that's ok with me any longer. We're headed back into tyranny, and I guess I'm realizing now how much I hate it. And also how hard it will be to leave *here*."

"They're your family. Of course it will be hard to leave here," I whisper.

"No, Reach." She slips her hand into mine and leans her shoulder against mine. "You're my family."

25

I'M UP EARLY, before the Souterraine light changes to the ever-stretching, ever-growing fingers of dawn. The darkness of the dome above me can't contain the excitement within. Today is the day the chess game against Nation continues. We don't know if we'll survive this, but we do know that if we do, we have a noble purpose.

I bump into Llama on the landing outside of our rooms. It's odd to leave the comfortable wooden furniture, the soft clothing, the space that has been *mine* for so long. And yet, it never felt like *mine*. It was always temporary. Ever since I changed the space mission code to bring us to Mars, the intent was always for us to return to Earth. To go home.

Llama's teeth flash in the dark shadows of the hall. "It's time."

I hear the undercurrent of nervousness in her voice. That same current buzzes and hums in my own veins too. I can't deny the excitement that tempers it from the feeling of unbearable dread and doom to a more tolerable feeling of being pulled in two directions at once. It's like the medieval torture device *the rack*, except for emotions, and no one's inflicting these feelings upon me but myself.

I bob my head before realizing that, if she can see me, all she will see is a flicker of movement in a shadow. "Yeah," I say. "It is."

Her hand stretches out and lands on my shoulder. She slides it down the contour of my arm until her own palm is tucked firmly into mine. "C'mon, Reach," she whispers. "Let's go."

Together, we stride, hands clasped, down the corridor, toward the faintest glimmer of light under the kitchen door. When we reach the door, I push it open and step into the warmth. Bernard sits with his head in his hands at the long plank table, Queen Eleanore and King Alfred with stony gazes and set jaws.

Llama takes one look and asks, "What happened?"

All the eyes in the room snap to her face.

Queen Eleanore stands, as does King Alfred. Bernard stays seated. Queen Eleanore shakes her head slightly, but King Alfred approaches me and Llama. He rubs his hands down his olive-colored pants, and the short gray beard on his chin quivers.

"They need to know," he says in a low voice as Queen Eleanore reaches a hand out to stop him.

"We need to know what?" I challenge. Omission of information when headed into life-or-death situations is reckless.

"We received word in the night," King Alfred says, "that our first departures to Earth...that they didn't make it."

I can feel my eyes widen as I shrink back. "Beatriz and Cait?"

King Alfred shakes his head solemnly. "I'm sorry."

Llama's shoulders slump in the corner of my vision. She inhales deeply, trying to be courageous as she speaks, but her voice shakes. "Was it...problems with the reentry into the atmosphere?"

"No," Queen Eleanore replies, coming over and placing her hand on Llama's shoulder. "They made it to the surface of Earth. We received regular reports on their progress from their digital feedback monitors, but then...their signals went still. We are still getting the signals from them, but they are completely in one place. Their bodies aren't moving, and haven't been for...well, for some time."

"And you're telling us this now?" Llama challenges.

"We didn't want to worry you, but also, we weren't sure. What if they lost their digital chip? What if they had been out of range? But today…it's been two weeks of no contact, only a tiny homing signal from their monitors. They weren't nutritionally fit enough to survive two weeks with no food or water."

"Where did they go?" I ask, my voice low. Beatriz and Cait weren't my favorite people, but their deaths rattle me. Their mission, which they volunteered for, was an attempt to rally the other population centers against Nation.

"The southwestern"—the king's voice cracks—"quadrant. A place formerly called Australia."

I force a breath from my lungs. I don't want to ask the question, but it must be done. "Was it technology, or…" Fumbling with my words, I try again. "What was the cause? Did they make contact with humans? Or was it because of technological aspects?"

Bernard thumps his hands down on the table, and everyone jumps. "You're smart enough to know the answer to that," he says, and his voice is biting. "You know it doesn't matter. You *know* that this mission is dangerous in every sense of the word, and that this might be downright reckless, but you're doing it anyway."

"Bernard," Queen Eleanore snaps.

He meets her eyes with a challenge in his own. "There has to be another way."

"There isn't," King Alfred retorts. "We've been looking for months."

Llama holds up her hands and steps between her grandparents and their steward, but he's also a friend.

"With all due respect…" Llama keeps her voice low and calm. "We knew that this was a dangerous mission well before we knew you even existed."

I can't totally make out the exact moment when everyone in the room spontaneously combusts into tears, but it does happen, seemingly all at once. Before I can understand it, arms are piled around me, and Llama and sniffles, and tears are shed. I can't escape this group hug, nor do I want to. While touching people isn't my favorite, since coming to Souterraine, I've been forced into physical contact I wouldn't have initiated many times, often by Pippa, sometimes by Ethan, and it's *that* thought—that when we leave here today I'll be the leader of the space mission, and then we'll be back on Earth with my mom, who was never overly affectionate in the first place—that I'll never have *this* level of physical affection again, that causes tears to fall from my own eyes.

The surface of Mars is beyond inhospitable to human life. Since the day the original colonists arrived at the Jezero crater, there have never been this many living, breathing organisms at the same time standing in the harsh red glow of dust that would just as soon kill you as cushion your fall.

The members of Wave Cohort 1 climb from the traverse-ball port to the surface one by one, like a line of ants marching toward a picnic. Llama, myself, King Alfred, and the head engineer—a man from Jezero named Shane—stand to the side of the line, watching as the space explorers climb the ladder into the space shuttle.

When the last one disappears into the belly of the ship, Shane turns to King Alfred. "Payload minus the two other human transports is on target." Our suits are interconnected with COMs systems, so turning to the king is redundant, but still a natural response.

King Alfred's fishbowl-surface spacesuit helmet bobs. "Good." He draws a breath, then draws another. "Reach," he says. "Take care of her."

And then, he gives me a hug so unexpected that it nearly knocks me off my feet and prone on the dust. It's only the extreme core training that Lift and then the trainers on Mars took us through that keeps me upright. His COMs is hooked to Llama's as well as mine, but he whispers, "There's no one else I'd entrust with her safety," as he looks into my eyes. The sincerity there cannot be diluted, not even by multiple layers of Martian safe glass.

"It's time," Shane offers, and I step away from the embrace. He extracts a black stick from his pocket and holds it in his palm.

"What is it?" I ask as I take the stick.

"It's a data stick—a Pandora's code box." He swallows. "It's illegal to make this on Mars, but I had..." His eyes slide to King Alfred. "I had permission."

"Why is it illegal?"

"If someone got their hands on this...on Mars...it would wipe out everything. Pandora's code box contains a computer virus that eats through binary code in such an unsystematic way that it confuses programs and forces them to shut down. There is no way to override it. There is no way to protect a system from it. It is an invasive pest in the form of coding."

I stare at the little black stick in my hand. "I put it into a port and..."

"Run the program. It doesn't take long, though the amount of time depends on the complexity of what you're trying to destroy."

I stare at King Alfred. Allowing this to be made here on Mars seems reckless, especially when the entirety of the planet depends on functioning systems. The small stick in my hand has the capability to wipe out everything.

The king doesn't notice my stare. He hugs Llama tightly, but doesn't say a single word to her.

When Llama pulls away, she grasps my hand with her own gloved one, and we walk toward the unknown future together. We step into the space shuttle port, and as the pressurizing compartment whirls closed, we continue holding hands in the narrow tube. The doors swirl shut in ever-tightening concentric circles, and though there's hope, there's also longing.

When the tunnel is pressurized, a warning bell sounds throughout the space shuttle. "Safe to remove surface suits."

The interior doors swirl open, and Llama and I step through
them, onto the next phase.

I can't help but look back at the sterile white tunnel, at the now-
locked exterior doors to the surface. We're leaving Mars, and we'll
never return.

26

Months later

Hyper-sleep is not easy on the body, but neither is months in space. In order to accommodate the proper payload, the engineers determined that hyper-sleep medication would be the most efficient way to send the space shuttle back to Earth. Llama and I, along with Jonas the engineer and Doctor Harold, were the four people selected to *not* hyper-sleep for the journey back to Earth.

We're only a week away from entering Earth's atmosphere, and it's time to wake everyone up. During our journey, Doctor Harold was busy monitoring everyone's vitals, adjusting IV fluid intake, and ensuring everyone had the right amount of vitamins. Jonas, with long blond hair and pale blue eyes, spent his time running continual diagnostic checks on all the space shuttles' systems.

Llama and I help as needed, and mostly try not to bother Jonas or Harold. Three times I sent a transmission to Souterraine, but we're a moving target, so receiving messages from the colony is nearly impossible. It's easier for us to send them to the stationary COMs center. One-sided conversations are mostly for the benefit of Queen Eleanore and the loved ones left on Mars.

The messages I sent were all something along the lines of, *Status Update: Alive and well.*

Not exactly the most riveting way to spend our time, so Llama and I did the only thing we could when we weren't needed. We played chess. We've spent months on a space shuttle with only a chessboard for entertainment. I would be bored, except I've been occupying my mind with wondering what comes next.

"Reach," Llama says, pulling me away from the viewfinder. "Harold says it's time to wake up the first ten people. They're going to be sick, so we need to make sure we have bags for them."

I grimace. A space shuttle full of vomit doesn't sound appealing, but it's the body's natural response to hyper-sleep medication wearing off. With a resigned sigh, I open the cupboard where we keep simple brown paper bags for this purpose and extract a pack before heading to the sleeping bay.

Waking up ninety-six people from hyper-sleep isn't fun. The graphic details are seared into my mind, but I make a conscious effort to bury them so deep in the recesses of my brain that I'll forget them. It doesn't happen.

Harold runs down the corridor, which is humorous because, although the ship is big enough to have some gravity from the centrifugal force of the outer shell of the ball spinning, it's still not Mars' gravity—which, underground in the colonies, was 9.78 m/s2 compared to Earth's 9.81 m/s2. He bounds into the air and then flails his arms to propel himself forward before he sinks to the floor of the ship and pushes off again.

"Reach!" Harold calls. I fully prepare myself for Harold to tell me he needs help in the sleep bay again, but mercifully, he does not. "Jonas is asking for you in the control center."

I blow out a breath of relief.

"You really didn't enjoy helping in the sleep bay, did you?" Harold questions.

"Not particularly. I'm sorry, it's…there's only so much…" I scrunch my eyes against the memories and let the omission of words hang there. "…I can handle."

"Well, it sounds like Jonas has a problem, and he needs you now."

Just like that, the relief I felt that Harold wasn't asking for me disintegrates into the dust we left on Mars. Harold's urgency makes more sense now, and I match his pace as I bound through the ship's corridors to the control panel station.

When I arrive, I bound a little too hard through the doorway, and the top of my head hits the doorframe.

"Ouch!" I hiss, rubbing my head as my feet hit the ground.

Jonas looks back over his shoulder at a large screen. "I've done that before."

"Harold said you needed me?"

"Yeah, we're twenty-four hours from entry into Earth's outer atmosphere. The systems on my end all look good, but I'm not sure the maps and projection data make sense."

He zooms in on the screen, highlighting our projected descent and landing.

"We're supposed to be landing at 46.5436° N, 87.3954° W." A yellow dot blinks on screen, but it's not *on* the trajectory path for the space shuttle. "But because of the spin of the Earth and the slightest difference in the Earth's orbit during its path around the sun, we're projected to land here." He clicks a button and shows a green dot at 47.90161354° and -87.55004883°. "I can make a minor course correction, but I think this is…as close as we can get."

Worry claws its way up my throat. "I think it's ok," I say, but it's more to myself than to Jonas. "Llama is more familiar with the geography of this part of Nation." I lean over the console and zoom in. "I think this is…a water landing? Llama might be able to tell us more. I can go find her."

"Harold was looking for both of you."

"Oh." I nod. "Then I guess we wait for her."

Jonas pushes off the floor with a small bound and glides to a different console. He starts rapidly typing on the numeric keypad, and file boxes fly open on the second screen.

"Got it," he says, pumping his fist in the air.

All I can do is quirk a brow. Jonas tends to do things and then tell people what he did *after* the fact. I can't keep up with the way his brain solves problems, but I'm pleased to say I did beat him at chess the few times we played.

"Water landing checklist. We'll need to confirm all these systems are onboard, and I'll need to program the systems to take control of the ship before we enter the atmosphere and lose that capability."

I shake my head in agreement. Water landing protocols were part of our training, but the coordinates sent to us were so firmly on land that we simply assumed water landing was only likely in the case of an emergency. Now, it's our most likely outcome.

"You called for me?" Llama floats through the doorframe effortlessly. She's shorter than me, so she did *not* hit her head.

"Yeah, look at this please," Jonas says, then launches into an explanation about the coordinates and the water landing.

"Ok," Llama replies, drawing out the *k*. "So what's the problem exactly?"

"Neither one of us is completely sure if this is a water landing," Jonas says in his abrupt manner.

"I am not as familiar with the geography of Ward 11. This—" I squint at the geographical features as our mapping points have picked them up, but mostly all we have to go off of is elevation data. "It almost looks like an ocean."

"Inland sea," Llama says, shaking her head. "It's a massive body of water. I learned about it when we studied the geography of Ward 11. It's considered dangerous."

"Dangerous how, exactly?" I ask.

Llama shrugs. "Rogue waves, shipwrecks, storms. The worst are the November ones, I think." She starts to hum. "There's an ancient song about it."

I blink. Jonas doesn't say anything, but I know how Earth months work, and I have a basic idea of the timing of our travel. Still, it's all a little fuzzy after months on Mars.

"Jonas…" I say slowly. "Could you tell me where Earth is in its orbit around the sun?"

"Sure." He slides to a different screen and console and clicks buttons rapidly, pulling up an image of Earth orbiting the sun. "Right now, Earth's orbital position is here."

The slight tilt of the northern hemisphere away from the sun gives it away.

We're landing in what Llama has informed us is an incredibly dangerous inland sea in November.

27

If I thought hyper-sleep wake-up was difficult on the digestive system, it's nothing compared to the buffeting and shaking of being in a literal rolling ball falling from the sky as you hope against all hope that you don't combust into ashes from friction, or system malfunction, or…anything that could go wrong.

Jonas set the space shuttle water landing protocols and diffused a thick layer of helium and oxygen throughout the outer shell of the shuttle sphere. This should provide us with buoyancy to return to the surface once we splash into the sea. The only problem: with our payload, we aren't sure how deep we'll go. Parachutes will deploy once we're low enough in the atmosphere to use them, but if we tried to use them now, they'd burst into flames, or shred into mere fibers from the intense friction. All we can do is trust the machines to do what we've asked them to do.

Everyone is in the sleeping bay, standing upright with our backs on vertical cots, X-shaped buckles holding us in place. U-shaped neck pillows prevent our necks from twisting too far to the side and snapping, and the sights and sounds of this cohort experiencing extreme turbulence are things I'd rather *not* be experiencing.

Without warning, the intense shaking, vibrating, rolling sensation stops. Instead of straining against the buckles as we shake, now our bodies strain against the buckles as we try to stay up. We're in free-fall. We made it through the outer edges of the Earth's atmosphere without dying.

My hand clenches around the thick straps covering my chest as I will my heartbeat to calm. I have to think. I have to stay in control of my emotions. The only problem is that my emotions about living through this particular phase of the mission are heightened. It doesn't help that we may have survived *that*, but might be about to die in the actual landing. There's a chance Llama, Jones, and I were wrong. There's a chance we will land on land and the water landing measures will be completely ineffective. I look around at the other people who've trained for this, risked their lives for this. I don't want it to have been in vain.

A huge pull heaves against the space shuttle, and the parachutes have deployed. I close my eyes in a silent thanks, but when I open them again, I see Jonas looking at me. "Told you," he mouths.

All I can do is nod. There's still more to fear.

"Twenty-seven minutes now," Jonas whispers from the next cot.

I'm not sure how he's talking after this ordeal, but I cannot while waiting twenty-seven minutes to see if we'll die from impact, or from too shallow a water landing, or from rapidly descending into the depths past what we can withstand. All I can do is close my eyes and wait, and that might kill me first.

As the space shuttle plummets toward the surface of Earth, the smooth gliding sensation of free-fall changes. Now, there's a buffeting again. Occasionally, a loud shriek whistles by, followed by a popping sound. "The outer shell sustained some damage. It's to be expected," Jonas shouts.

The green faces of my cohort team tell me they appreciate the reassurance, even if they can't verbalize it.

"One minute," Jonas says softly.

Collectively, everyone grips their buckle belts tighter. No one breathes, as if holding our breath could save us from death by impact if my calculations were even the slightest bit wrong.

With a tremendous heave, the space shuttle crashes into the water. The sensation is oddly familiar to us after being in space for months, but still different. As we descend, my ears pop.

I'm not the only one. Llama is buckled to the bed on my left, and she throws her hands over her ears and grimaces. The sensation of my stomach rising to my throat nearly overpowers me, when suddenly, the opposite sensation hits. Now instead of going down, we're going up, rising to the surface.

Jonas meets my gaze from the bed on the right. "We didn't die."

I grin, and then Jonas adds, "Yet."

The shape of the space shuttle consists of two shells, the outer layer and the inner layer, and each has enough gas between them to be buoyant. Our shuttle is large, but this inland sea is massive and deeper than I thought. As soon as we can, Jonas, Llama, and I unbuckle from the beds and walk, with real gravity to the control center.

Jonas flips on systems and runs diagnostics. This data will transfer to Souterraine, but it will take weeks. Still, the data he's sending from our return could save lives for the next cohorts. He pulls up a map and GIS coordinates.

"I think we're here." He points to a blinking red dot in the middle of his screen. "The closest land is…" He enters a numerical value for elevation into the computer. "Here."

My brain is stuck on the fact that we didn't die, but Jonas has placed a math problem in front of me. "What's the scale of the map?" I ask.

"That makes us…twenty-six nautical miles from the target."

"That's not too bad," Llama comments as a giant rolling, swooping motion overtakes the shuttle. We're lifted up, up, up, and then plummet down, down, down. This time, we have no warning, and we're not strapped in.

I find myself hurled into Llama, and though I use my hands to brace myself against the wall of the shuttle room, I know the force of being slammed into her hurt her.

"Are you alright?" I ask as she grimaces but bobs her head.

"I've had worse," she quips.

Jonas grips the console with his hands, while leaning heavily against the screen.

"I think it might be storming on this sea," I mutter.

Jonas mumbles something and then types in a keycode to the computer. "Weather data," he says. "Look." He points to an atmospheric disturbance on the screen. "This should push us closer to our original intended target."

"Is there any way for us to get there on our own?"

"No, the systems for water maneuvers weren't as advanced as the systems for land maneuvers, or they got damaged in the landing." Jonas points to a screen with sysops open. The letters WTMNV have a big red x next to them, along with the word *failed*.

"So all we can do is float here until we make land?" Llama asks, her eyes wide.

"Yep." Jonas nods. "I might be able to figure something out with force, velocity, and using our bodies to create a rotation, but mechanized systems are out."

"Or," I say, hoping to *not* have to physically push a ball toward land from the inside of the ball, "we can hope the storm pushes us ashore."

"It's definitely possible that would happen," Jonas says, stroking his chin. "But nothing's a guarantee."

"Nothing ever is," Llama mutters. "I think, now that we're all alive on Earth, we should try to send a message to Sigma."

I swallow.

"I can try to send something, but I don't know if I need to encrypt it, and if I do, will they be able to decode it?" Jonas says.

That's an easy one.

"Don't bother," I say. "None of the messages to Mars were encrypted. If we use this Martian technology, it should be closed enough that Nation can't get into it."

"Or, they didn't care until they saw a giant ball fall from the sky and *now* they care," Llama quips.

"My—" I stop myself. I don't know that I want to explain to the entire ship that we're here because Sigma is my mother. I don't really know her anymore. "Sigma is smart. She'll be able to decipher what we say. I don't think it needs to be digitally encrypted; it needs to be coded."

"So what should we say?" Jonas peers over a console at us.

Llama braces her hands against a large screen, but she turns to face me, a greenish tinge to her face. "Chess," she says weakly and then drops to the ground before crawling away. The sound of retching meets my ears moments after she disappears around the bend.

"Pawn storm," I whisper. "J'adoube."

"Is that the message?"

I nod. It's only obvious to those who know chess terms. It's a messy guess, but anyone in Nation who's listening to and decoding messages won't have the knowledge. I hope.

"What does 'J'adoube' mean?"

"I adjust."

"Hmmm." Jonas types something on the keyboard, then announces, "I'll send 'pawn storm, 'j'adoube' and our coordinates, but only the western one since we're ok on longitude but off on latitude."

I agree and turn to leave, but as I do, a tremendous heave lifts us up and hurtles forward. My feet fly out from under me, backward and up. The only reason I don't crash into anything is because I grabbed hold of the doorframe as I passed through. A sucking noise squelches around the space shuttle ball, and then, for the first time in months, the shuttle stills.

Jonas sits on the ground, rubbing his head. Something about his countenance doesn't look quite right. He vomits, and when I see his eyes, the right pupil is dilated while the left is not—a sure sign of a concussion.

"Jonas?" I ask, ignoring the mess.

Jonas looks at me and blinks. "Where are we?"

I have to get him to Harold, but I don't know what damage the space shuttle ball has sustained, and I don't know where we are or what happened to everyone else.

It's not a fun problem to work out, but the best thing I can do now is find as much information as I can about our location. Jonas and the people will have to wait. I can't help them if I don't know what to do next, and for all I know, I'm the only person aboard who doesn't have a concussion.

I press send on the message Jonas prepared, then search for GIS data in the ship systems. There's no viewfinder window available here, not since we entered Earth's atmosphere, and the outer shell closed itself off for our protection. I can't see anything about where we are, and if I open the hatch while we're in the middle of the sea, and this layer floods, I'll have killed everyone.

Zooming in, I see that approximately four hundred yards to the south is a sharp increase in elevation. It could be anything at this close proximity. I chew my bottom lip as I consider what to do, but the shuttle makes the choice for me as the lights flicker and the dim emergency exit lights illuminate the ship.

There's nothing else I can do except grab Jonas, whose head lolls to the side, under the armpits and pull him through the space shuttle to try to find any members of Wave Cohort 1 that are capable of leaving the shuttle under their own power.

A calm, cool female voice meets my ears as I shuffle along with Jonas. "Evacuation protocol underway. You have thirty minutes to exit the ship."

28

The countdown continues, and every two minutes the voice announces how much time we have left. The diminishing minutes make this task even more daunting. By the time I've dragged Jonas backward through the ship to the Sleeping Bay, I'm dripping with sweat.

Harold looks up from where he stands in the center of the bay. "Oh, Reach. We have several people…" He looks at Jonas with narrowed eyes. "Concussion?"

I nod. The voice announces that there are now only twenty-two minutes to leave the ship.

Declan approaches me. "The ship will self-destruct the main sysops, right?"

I grimace. He's right. This is meant to protect *us*, the members of Wave Cohort 1, because we're headed into a battle. The following Cohorts won't need this feature.

"Evacuation underway," the ship announces.

I catch sight of Llama from where she stands across the room, and my throat tightens. "I know it's water here, but I don't know how far it is to land."

Declan shakes his head. "It could be water or land?"

I shrug. "I have no idea."

Declan closes his eyes as the voice announces eighteen remaining minutes before sysops turn this ship into an uninhabitable sphere. "We've probably outweighed the buoyancy of the ball in the shallows. We should grab things that will float just in case as we exit."

"Grab whatever you can that will float," I repeat louder to the people standing in the bay. Harold meets my eyes with a question, and I nod. We have to see what's out there before we know how to evacuate the medically injured.

I turn, march to the emergency exit, and slide the door between the inner and outer shells open. As I twist the lock on the hatch of the outer shell, a sharp alarm blares throughout the ship.

"Breach. Prepare for Breach. Breach."

I draw in what is quite possibly my last breath of the stale, recycled space shuttle air, and throw my body weight against the hatch to open the outside layer.

It creaks and groans before the springs pop and the hatch flies open. The only positive thing I can think of is that if the hatch were completely underwater, it wouldn't open because of the water pressure against the hatch. We might die from other catastrophes, but at least it won't be drowning in the ship.

For the first time in years, my eyes take in *blue sky*.

I gasp and pull myself out of the hatch using my arms. The extra gravity is hard to maneuver through, but as I survey the area around the space shuttle, I fill my body with the sweet taste of Earth air. The sky is cloudy, but streaks of blue peek through, and as I twist around, I find that there's an expanse of water around us, but visible to the eye is a beach with white sand. Shapes litter the beach, but they aren't moving.

Declan pops up behind me. "This is Earth?" he asks, his jaw falling open.

"Yes," I whisper, taking a moment of appreciation for the waves bobbing around the space shuttle, the clouds in the sky, the actual combination of oxygen and hydrogen atoms surrounding me.

"Fifteen minutes," the voice announces.

"That beach"—I point to it—"is where we need to go. Can you lead the first group to it?"

Declan nods, then pulls an inflated body bag onto the surface of the shuttle. He hops into the water, which isn't quite stormy, but the waves are still choppy and chaotic, and he begins swimming toward the beach.

The rest of Wave Cohort 1 follows behind Declan. After everyone who could has exited, the voice announces, "Eight minutes."

Llama appears. "What do we do with the injured?"

"How many are injured?" I ask, trying to do the math rapidly but overwhelmed by every sensation hitting my skin in the fresh air.

"Six."

"That leaves each of us with two."

She nods.

"You go first?" I ask.

"You'll come back?"

My heart wrenches at her vulnerability.

"Always," I whisper, tempted to pull her close to me and kiss her, but also fully aware that this is no time for that.

I reach down and assist a young woman with pale blonde hair and jade-green eyes onto the surface of the space shuttle as Llama helps a young man with red hair up. She disappears for a moment and returns with three bags.

"There's a bag for everyone. Declan had the idea of using the leftover buoyancy gas to fill the body bags. Don't try to do this without the bags, Reach."

She links her arms through the two passengers and, holding her bag in her teeth, jumps into the choppy water.

Harold appears next with Jonas and another man. "Concussion," Harold says, tipping his head toward Jonas. "And sea sickness." He tips his head toward the next man. Then, following Llama's exact steps, he jumps into the water with his charges.

It's now me and two women left on the ship. They're identical twins with dark brown hair and eyes so brown they might as well be golden. "We're ok," one says. "Dizzy and haven't been able to eat anything in a while."

"Ok," I say as the announcer calls out 'six minutes.' "We have to jump into the water and swim to that beach."

They nod. We link arms and jump.

Bedraggled, wet, coated in sand, and somehow freer than I've ever been, I pull myself out of the shallow water and onto actual land.

The twins, whose names are Ethel and Julia, collapse against each other, crying as they sprawl on the white sand. I survey the beach and find that nearly everyone is sitting on the sand in tears.

The only person who isn't, other than me, is Llama.

She walks toward me, slowly at first, then picks up the pace until she's running. She crashes into me and presses her lips to mine. "You came back," she breathes against the kiss.

"Always," I murmur before I pull away.

The waves crash against the shore without any rhythmic pattern, and overhead, white birds squawk in circles. Trees, unlike any I've ever seen, stand back from the initial assault of the waves against the shore.

The trees are eerie, whitish wood, with no greenery at all. Bubbles and foam from the churning water blow in the wind, and a whistle that could be man-made or the wind passing through the hollow spaces in the trees makes me jerk my head sharply.

"You hear it too?" Llama asks, putting her hand on my forearm. The wet material makes a slouching, sucking noise as it presses into my skin, but I don't shake her contact off.

"I hear something," I say, looking around me.

I spin in a circle, looking for something—evidence of someone, some*thing* to place hope in. There's nothing.

The wind bites my skin, and without realizing it, I begin to shiver. The thermal dynamics in these suits weren't designed for water. Yet another oversight by the Martians preparing for this journey.

I turn toward Llama and prepare to think of a plan. We're far too exposed sitting here on this beach with creepy trees and odd sounds, when I spot something down the shoreline. It's moving—rapidly.

As it approaches, it becomes obvious. It's a vehicle suited for this type of terrain.

With no idea if this is a friend or foe, I square my shoulders and prepare myself for anything. At the same time, I send out a silent plea that this be the Resistance. That they got our message, and that we are going to be taken to *whatever* and *wherever* comes next and I won't have to think of it.

Still, it could be Nation. For all I know, it could be Enforce or one of her lackeys. We could overtake her by sheer force if we had to, but as I look around, even I know that this is not a group of people capable of that. We're too tired, too exhausted, too worn from months in space. If it is Enforce, she'll know our weakness from a single calculating look.

The vehicle zooms closer, and as I tell my mind that it's unlikely to be a foe since we purposefully landed North of Nation's official boundaries, suddenly all my thoughts stop.

A man hops over the side of the vehicle and scurries through the sand toward me.

"Reach," he says, and I nearly fall over.

"Freedom?" Llama whispers.

Freedom grins. "We came to get you, but it took a while. You landed in a nasty storm." He tips his chin over his shoulder. "Someone's looking forward to seeing you again."

I angle my body to see who Freedom means. The vehicle stops several yards away from where I stand and a young woman climbs out.

Her dark skin, brown hair secured in a braid down her back, brown eyes, and soft smile bring me back to long nights in Hub when she transcribed my awful handwriting. "Hero," I say.

Hero grins, then plows through the sand and crushes me in a hug. It's not romantic; it's the type of hug borne of two people experiencing something together and reuniting after years.

"You got out," I say in awe, although I knew she had. *How*, was the question.

"Yeah." A sad smile crosses her face. She steps into Freedom's space, and he loops an arm around her waist. "I was very fortunate to get out when I did." She worries her lower lip, and Freedom gives her a sharp look.

Hero nods once. "Let's get you all off this beach and somewhere a little warmer. This is a break in the storm, but we have snow forecasted later today. We don't have vehicle capacity for everyone, so if there's any sick or injured, they get to ride."

"How many can you take?" Llama asks as she surveys the beach. "We know of six…"

"We'll make it work." Freedom tightens his hold on Hero and then nods. "I'll come on foot."

It doesn't take me long to find Harold crouching down next to Jonas close to the edge of the water. Freedom and I approach him.

"Harold," I say. "This is Freedom. He's going to take the sick and injured in the cart. The rest of us have to walk."

Harold nods. "I can't get him away from the water. He's surprisingly solid and slippery."

"Can you find the others who need a ride? We'll move him." Freedom takes control of the situation, and as shivers begin to wrack my body, I'm grateful.

Harold agrees before walking away to check on the others and determine who gets a ride.

Freedom hasn't been in space for months, and his muscles have never experienced atrophy from zero-g. The man is simply stronger than me, so when he picks Jonas up like he weighs no more than a few pounds, I try to remember that this is *not* an insult to me or my strength. Still, a little jealousy flares.

"You'll get it back in no time, Reach." Freedom grins over his shoulder.

Rolling my eyes, I plod through the soft sand behind him, marvelling at how it's been years and yet an easy friendship remains.

As I pass by the clusters of Wave Cohort 1 on the beach, I inform them of our next move.

"How long of a walk is it?" Declan asks, his eyes bright as he scans the surroundings.

I shrug, then call to Freedom, "How far are we going?"

"Some miles," he calls back.

"There's your answer." I smirk at Declan. "He won't tell us in numerical increments, so it's—"

"Far," Declan says. "I can't believe *this* is Earth." He bends and scoops up sand, letting it sift through his fingers. "And there's *weather* here."

It's the mention of weather that reminds me we have to move, and fast. Although I haven't seen snow, I know what it is, and I know that being stuck in it while wet, with muscle atrophy, after already exerting massive amounts of energy, is *not* good.

"Yes, and the weather's not going to stay like this for long, so we have to go."

Llama approaches with a large group of cohort members, and together we round everyone up into orderly files.

The six injured are placed gently into the vehicle before Hero drives off, disappearing around a bend in the beach.

"Everyone ready?" Freedom asks. The entire group's teeth chatter, and everyone's lips are slightly blue. "We'll get you warm soon. For now, you have to get your blood flowing. You *have* to march. If you stop, you will die."

I grimace at his words, not because they're harsh or untrue, but because in the past forty-eight hours, there have been at least three near-death experiences for Wave Cohort 1 that everyone has somehow survived, and I know I cannot keep everyone safe anymore.

29

IT HAD TO happen. Still, it guts me. Our walk to the Resistance head-quarters was not without incident. Twelve people hit the ground and died. Some fell, others lost the will to live, simply laid down, and died. At first, I tried to drag a body with us, but Freedom stopped me.

"You can't," he said through gritted teeth. "You won't survive."

Our Cohort is now only ninety-one people. Casualties were always expected, but I didn't expect them to come without enemy contact.

Footsteps sound behind where I stand, staring out a window at whirling white flakes so thick they obscure everything. There is nothing to see but snow.

A hot shower, a cup of bone broth, a slice of grainy bread, and clothing have been given to the remaining members of Wave Co-hort 1. We're in a large room made of wood, with a triangular-shaped ceiling and thick wooden beams running across it. Candles hang on wheel-shaped holders throughout the room, and a gigantic stone fireplace takes up the entire wall of the rectangular space. A fire roars, spitting and crackling blazing heat.

Some members of the Cohort sit huddled together under blankets, while others sit at long tables with benches made of rough-hewn wood. I'm the only one standing, and I'm as far from the merry heat as I can be. My mood doesn't match the atmosphere inside this room.

"Reach." Hero's voice meets my ears. "Would you come with me?"

I pull myself away from the mesmerizing snowfall and turn to Hero. I try not to catch her gaze, but when I do, there's an ocean of sympathy in her eyes. "I'm sorry," she says.

I shrug.

"Would you like Llama to come too?"

I haven't seen Llama since we were whisked to separate areas for men and women to get cleaned up after we arrived *here*, the Resistance headquarters, known as the Lodge. We were given warm showers, clothes, and a stern warning to not waste anything. Then, we were granted a pair of underclothes, a soft and smooth base layer, thick wool socks, pants made of a water-resistant material, and sweaters made of interconnected loops. I pick at a loop on my black sweater, thinking of Llama and the people we lost today.

"Yes," I say.

Hero starts to open her mouth, but snaps it shut as if she thought better of whatever she was going to say. "I'll go find her. You can head out the door and down the hall. Take the first set of stairs. When you get to the top, it's the third door on the left. I'll bring Llama there."

I step away, but Hero's hand lands on my forearm. The clothing is an unfamiliar texture, too large and baggy for my frame, but Hero's hand squeezes gently. "I'm so sorry, Reach. It wasn't your fault." And with that, she walks away to find Llama.

It's with a heavy heart that I trudge down the hall, up the stairs, and to the third door on the left. I push it open and am met with a cozy space of plank wood floors and ceilings that are oddly reminiscent of Souterraine. A small bench sits under a single window, and a small table is tucked into the other corner. Instead of candles, an electric bulb hangs from the middle of the ceiling. There's nothing else for me to do in the otherwise-empty room, so I sit down on the bench and lean my forehead against the cool pane. All I can see is white, but that doesn't bother me. I close my eyes and contemplate going from Earth to Mars and back again.

A single tap at the door jars me to the present. I twist toward the sound, and the door pushes open.

My instinct is to rub my eyes upon seeing her.

Graying hair, straight posture, tiny wrinkles around her eyes, and a small smile on her face that breaks into a grin when she sees me. I stand, and we both stare at each other for a long moment.

"Reach?" she says.

"Mom?"

She nods, and the next thing I know, I'm being crushed in a hug that is entirely out of character for the woman before me.

"You made it back." She shakes her head, and a tear slips from the corner of her eye. "You did it. You…survived."

I bob my head, my throat too thick with emotion to add anything to her wonder.

"Mars. You *went* to Mars. And you *returned*, with *people* from Mars." The awe in her voice is captivating, and even though the threat of death and now *actual* death has been ever-present, I laugh.

Mom pulls back and studies my face with her sharp blue eyes. "Reach," she whispers, stroking my cheek with her forefinger. It takes me back to being young, to our time on Compound before I knew anything about Nation, anything about tyranny, anything about Mars. "You've seen so much."

I nod, because I have.

"We have so much to catch up on, but I fear you can't talk about it all now."

A quiet rap on the door draws her attention from me, and the soft demeanor of Mom's countenance changes to stone. Llama walks through the door. Her clothes are also too big, the pants wide-legged and swaying, while the shirt is a thick, chunky fabric made of inter-connected loops. It hangs down her knees, making her look comically small.

"Yes?" Mom asks.

Llama narrows her eyes. "Sigma?"

Mom raises one gray eyebrow. "And you are?"

Introductions are needed. "Mom," I cut in. "This is Llama, the Princess of Souterraine, and we're…betrothed. There was a formal ceremony on Souterraine, and Llama was with me at Hub first. She was my space mission partner as selected by Nation."

"Ahh." Mom's nostrils flare. "Another woman with too much aptitude and not enough money to be of use to Nation in any way but space exploration."

"Something like that," Llama quips back before walking directly next to me and planting herself firmly at my side. Her hand grasps mine and latches on with an intensity that betrays her calm demeanor in the face of meeting my mom.

"And you're *going* to be unionized?" Mom asks. "Because you don't have to follow the Mars protocol here."

Llama's shoulders stiffen. I look to Llama, whose eyes meet mine and stare fathoms deep.

"Yes," I respond, "we will be unionized." I can only hope she knows from the tone of my voice that none of what I feel for her is political.

"Interesting," Mom says. "When? There's a ceremony tomorrow—would you like to join?"

Llama startles. "Tomorrow?" She laughs nervously. "Not tomorrow. We have a job to do first. That's what we decided on Mars, right, Reach?"

I nod. "We did decide that."

"Hmm," Mom replies. "Well, Llama, we don't have honorific titles here, so I'll not be calling you Princess."

Llama meets the dry tone in my mom's voice with her own. "That's just fine, Sigma."

Mom purses her lips as a huge yawn escapes me. "I think I'm going to send everyone from Wave Cohort 1 to mandatory rest time. You're too tired to think, aren't you?"

"Y-yes," I stammer.

"I remember it took months after my return to feel human again." Then, Mom pokes her head out of the doorframe and calls, "HERO!"

Hero appears at the door. "Yes?"

"I'm ordering mandatory rest in the bunk room for all of Wave Cohort 1. Will you please oversee?"

"Yes, of course." Hero nods. "We turned the basement into a temporary bunk room. It's cold, but not unbearable."

Mom nods in approval and Hero leaves, Llama behind her. I step toward the hallway; it's clear we've been dismissed.

"Reach," Mom whispers, and I turn to look at her. She holds out her own sweater, a chunky fabric of interconnected loops like Llama's, but with buttons down the front. Clad in only her sleeveless base layer, her arms erupt in goosebumps. "Take it, please."

It's the pleading in her voice that makes me accept the sweater, even though she's clearly cold without it. I move to take it, but instead of passing it to me, she drapes it over my shoulders.

"There," she says roughly before clenching her jaw and walking away.

30

THE BUNK ROOM is not unbearably cold, but it's close to it. Hero led us to the lower level of the Resistance headquarters. There isn't a roaring fireplace in this long room, but there are metal frame bunkbeds, stacked three beds high, and blankets. Some are made of interconnected loops, others of a shiny material, and still others in different patterns and fabrics.

"There's enough for everyone to have one blanket in addition to the bedding already on the bunks," Hero explains as she passes the blankets to each person who walks through the door. "Pick a bunk and lie down."

Llama and I wait next to Hero, greeting each member with a nod or a reassuring smile. Many of the Cohort have a lost look in their eyes, but Declan doesn't.

"I can't believe this is Earth," he whispers, accepting a blanket made of hot-pink squares from Hero, then shuffling over to a bunk. He flops onto the lowest level, since the middle and top levels are already occupied.

Once everyone has claimed a bed, Hero turns to me and Llama. She places her hands on her hips. "You are required to rest."

"But we're the leaders of the group," Llama says.

"You are required to rest," Hero repeats, then thrusts a blanket at Llama. This one is made of interconnected green loops.

Llama pitches forward slightly at the weight of it. "This is heavy." She pulls herself back to her regular posture.

"Heavyweight knit." Hero nods. "My personal favorite fabric, but we can't waste things here, so any clothing that gets worn out is turned into a blanket or rag. That was originally several sweaters, but when they started coming undone, I undid the stitches and made a blanket out of it."

"You did?" Llama asks, quirking a brow.

"Oh yes, knitting, crocheting, sewing…" She smiles. "I didn't realize that handicrafts would be the most important part of preparing the Resistance against Nation, but it's peaceful, and I enjoy it."

"You…" Llama fingers the loops. "You made this?"

"Mhmm."

"I've never made anything."

"I'll teach you once you've rested," Hero promises.

Llama bobs her head before she heads to one of the open bunks. She climbs to the middle bunk and lies down.

Hero stares at me. "You have to rest too."

"But, but—" I sputter.

"No, Reach," Hero says gently. "You can rest too. You don't have to be in charge now. I don't know what you lived through with your mission, but I know that after I made it here, I slept for days."

I take the blanket she hands me, a quilt made of simple squares in blue and red.

"You know, Reach," Hero whispers, "you can let others carry the burden of leadership for a time. We're on the same team; you can trust us. I promise. No more secrets."

Something stony in my heart cracks at Hero's words, at her compassion, at my mother's compassion, at being *here*, on Earth. "Ok."

"Sleep well, Reach," she says before the door swings closed in her wake.

I plod to the bunk below Llama. The last thing my eyes register is the digital clock on the white cinderblock wall, noting the date and time: November 10, 2358. 2:47 p.m.

When I finally wrench my eyes open, I have no idea what day or time it is. The sound of soft snores tells me I'm not the only one still asleep, but the rumble of my stomach tells me that I have missed multiple meals. It's difficult to pull myself out of the warm cocoon of blankets and into the chilly air of the bunk room, but I do. The thick wool socks slip on the wooden floor, but I catch my balance by grabbing hold of the bunk post.

Peering over the top of the middle bed, I discover that Llama isn't there. Her green blanket is folded neatly, but other than that, there is no sign of her ever having been there.

Panic claws its way up from my stomach. I don't know where she is, I don't know how to find her, but I shove it down with breaths. Double inhale, double exhale. Breathe, Reach, breathe. Finally, I'm under control enough to think of my next step. *Leave the bunk room, return up the stairs, find Mom, find Llama,* but the well-timed rumble of my stomach reminds me of the ultimate purpose: *eat.*

I tread softly across the polished wood floor and quietly push the door open. The leather hinges on the door don't make any noise as they slide open, and I'm grateful for the stealthy attributes. Even though I'm not doing anything wrong, I tread lightly. Sure, it's a place I have a right to be, but I don't know it, and no one has shown me anything other than three rooms.

Climbing the staircase exhausts me, and I have to hang onto the railing. When I reach the top, I'm breathless, but also exhilarated. To the right is the long rectangular room where we were fed broth and bread after our arrival. That seems like the best place to try to find food, so I duck through the door and find myself standing in front of the roaring fireplace.

Llama, Hero, Freedom, and Mom sit at one of the long tables. All the other tables are full too. The Resistance truly is alive and well. Freedom sees me and waves me over, which causes Llama and Mom to turn. Both women smile at me, and both smiles warm my chilled insides. It's easier to skate than it is to walk on this floor in these socks, so I move methodically toward my friends and mom.

"Sleep well?" Mom asks as I approach.

"Yes," I say, but I'm thirsty and hungry, and my voice cracks.

Llama hands me a ceramic cup with a loop—a *mug*. "Here," she says. "It's water, but I was thirsty when I woke up yesterday."

"What day is it?" I ask, scratching my head.

"It's been three days since you went to sleep," Mom replies. "I doubt you need to know the exact date, but in case you're wondering, it's November the thirteenth."

"I slept for three days?" My eyes widen. I can't imagine sleeping for seventy-two straight hours, and yet the gnawing hunger in my stomach tells me I did.

"You have to be starving," Hero interjects. "Come, sit and eat."

Mom and Llama make room for me to squeeze between them on the bench, and as I sit, I take in the array of food before me.

Tureens of soup are spaced evenly down the table. White, green, and orange liquids are visible inside them, while woven baskets of rolls sit next to the stoneware.

"Help yourself," Mom says as I look around at the bounty.

"How do you have so much?" I ask.

"We didn't always," Freedom responds.

"Hydroponics," Mom says simply. "Greenhouse systems. We grow everything here. At first, we tried to grow outside, but the weather's too unpredictable for sustained harvesting. We've had great success, but could use any other farming and gardening information, if you have it."

Mom's words make me think of Declan, who by all accounts is a pea expert.

"Is Declan awake?" I ask Llama. She shakes her head.

Mom passes me a roll and then starts scooping orange soup into a bowl from the stack next to the tureen. "Eat, please, Reach."

There's no butter, but it's soft and yeasty and tastes like Souterraine while at the same time tasting like Earth. In short, it's the best of both worlds.

As soon as I've scarfed down the roll, Mom pushes the soup in front of me and plunks a spoon into the bowl before placing another roll in my hand.

A pleasant warmth fills my belly as I eat. The ambiance of the large room no longer feels in stark contrast to my life experiences. Instead, peace settles over me, and I find myself relaxing for the first time since we left Souterraine.

Llama angles her body toward me, leans closer, and asks Mom, "Sigma, didn't you say there was a unionization ceremony?"

"Oh," Mom snorts. "Well, it was scheduled for two days ago, but the couple decided to wait until you could be present."

"Who?" Llama asks, scanning the room.

I don't miss the way Freedom pulls Hero closer to him, looping his arm around her waist. It's the affection of a man in love. I clear my throat and tip my head across the table at Hero and Freedom.

"Oh," Llama breathes. "You waited for us?"

"Mhmm," Hero says. "Once we knew you were coming back."

"Wasn't that…" Llama closes her eyes and purses her lips for a brief moment. "Presumptuous?"

"Exactly my point," Mom says dryly.

Freedom looks down into Hero's eyes, and a look of adoration passes between the two of them. "No," Hero whispers softly. "Hope is never presumptuous."

"Well, now that you're awake," Mom replies, "I think it's safe to say that the marriage can take place."

"Today?" Hero brightens.

"Soon. Once we wake up the rest of the cohort."

Full of food, warmth, and an odd inner peace, I turn and loop my long legs over the wooden bench. "I can help with that."

Llama grins, extends her hand to me, and stands. "I can too. I'm so happy for you."

"No, we'll have the Resistance medics handle the waking. Now that *you're* awake, I need to know what happened. Meet me in the upstairs conference room in twenty minutes." Mom's words shatter my inner peace.

Suddenly, Mom who cared, who gave me her sweater to ward off the frigid air, has changed. She's Sigma, the leader of the Resistance, and I don't know this woman.

I steel myself. "Alright." I meet her eyes with my own stony gaze. "But we need to know what happened here too." I look at Hero and Freedom, willing myself to feel that same peace that dissipated with Mom's words, but it doesn't work.

Llama's shoulders stiffen beside me. I close my eyes for a brief moment, but when that offers no relief, I know I have to meet this head-on.

"Twenty minutes," I say, and then, because this *is* Earth and people are always trying to make moves without showing that they are, I grumble, "We'll omit nothing, but you can't omit anything either."

Mom tips her head, and a flash of something crosses her eyes. "You look like him," she whispers. Suddenly, her businesslike demeanor makes sense. She's been waiting for decades to find out what happened to Greg, my father, and instead of pushing me, she fed me, made sure I slept, and now, the anticipation of *knowing* must be eating her alive.

It's with the tiniest bit of guilt that I ascend the stairs to the conference room.

31

THE CONFERENCE ROOM isn't the small room where Llama and I met with my mother. I discover that, as I walk along the long corridor above the main room with the hearth and tables, the Resistance headquarters is larger than I thought.

A sign on the wall reads CONFERENCE ROOM, SUITE 200, with an arrow pointing farther down the hall, and smaller signs affixed to the walls in descending number order clue me in to how big this place is. Llama walks next to me, and there's an undercurrent of nervousness that passes between us.

"Do you think we're really going to find out everything?" she whispers as we pass suite 280.

"I think we're going to find out more than what we already know," I reply.

Her blue eyes search mine. "Are you really going to tell them *everything?*"

I search her gaze in return. "What do you mean?"

"It's that certain events…don't paint me in a great light."

It clicks, and I long to protect her, to show her her worth, to keep her in their good graces. "I'll tell them what they need to know, but I don't know what Hero or Freedom has shared, and Sigma...knows."

"That's true." Llama blows out a breath. "It's that it was so long ago, and I was so weak. I like to think I'm stronger now."

"We both are." I bend down and press a kiss to her cheek. "We've come this far together."

Suite 200 appears on our left, and as we duck through the door, we're greeted with a long table, wooden chairs, and a wall completely covered with large maps. Crude black marks outlining certain spaces are drawn on the maps, and I stare in fascination.

"Ah, the prodigal has returned." A deep voice sounds from behind where I stand next to Llama, looking at a map of Nation.

Turning, I find a man I've never seen before. He has a long white beard, long curly hair, and a rounded stomach visible even under the bulky clothing everyone here wears.

The hair on the back of my neck immediately stands on end. This man is unfamiliar. All I can do is stare at him.

He looks me up and down before raising his left eyebrow slightly. "I'm Enigma. Chief of code-breaking and encryption. And you are Reach, with an aptitude for chess and a propensity to use random French words in your messages."

Llama opens her mouth and says something in a different language.

"Non," Enigma says. He looks at me when he answers. "She asked if I spoke French. I do not do so well, but I understand a fair amount. I take it that you neither speak nor understand the languages?"

I shake my head. I can't get a read on this man. Something about him strikes me as off, but I've never met him before, and this could just be the way he is.

Llama says something else, this time in a guttural, harsh language.

"German," Enigma replies. "I'm impressed."

Llama responds, "What good is it if you can't speak it?"

"My dear," Enigma states, his stomach rumbling as he laughs, "I don't need to speak it; I need to read it or hear it. I'm a shadow type of worker. You, however, are in the light, so I'm glad that you do speak it."

"I don't understand," I say.

"Well, it will all be clear once everyone arrives." Enigma gestures to the table. "Sit. There's no assigned seating, so wherever seems comfortable."

I pull out a wooden chair for Llama halfway down the table and sink into the chair next to her while Enigma situates himself across the table, directly across from the door.

We don't have long to wait before others start to file in. Wordlessly, they take their seats, their faces drawn, blank masks.

No one says anything to us until Freedom walks in next to Mom.

"Welcome to the war room," he whispers as he sits down directly next to me.

Mom walks around the table and seats herself at the head of the long table. A map of Nation—one with circles, x's, and pins—hangs directly behind her. Under the map, from this vantage point, it looks as if there's a mitten on her head.

Mom sits ramrod straight in her chair, leans forward, and steeples her fingers together.

"It's time." She looks at me with an uncompromising stare. And then, instead of continuing, she's silent.

There is *no* noise in the room but the sound of breath being drawn in and out. I can't speak. It's too heavy. I don't know what to say, what she wants me to say.

Llama diffuses the tension overtaking my body when she pushes back from the table with her palms and asks, "What do you want to know?"

"Everything."

"What if you tell us everything first?" Llama challenges. "We're the ones who've been across the universe."

Mom blinks twice and narrows her eyes. She scans the room, meeting the eyes of each person at the table, other than me and Llama. One by one, each of them gives a single nod in agreement.

Mom sighs. "Very well." She closes her eyes, then opens them again. "Is the door locked?"

Enigma confirms that it is with a succinct nod.

"Last time I saw Reach, we were in the tunnel under the Retribution and Punishment Arena. Reach is my son, and Enforce used him to further her own ambitions of power."

At the name *Enforce*, a collective hiss of breath hits the room, as if every single person in the room has a personal vendetta against her. Perhaps they do.

"As Reach knows, I escaped. Enforce attempted to use unsanctioned brutal force before my execution for treason, and when it was caught on camera, she learned that she was *not* inherently trusted by the Three Powers. Using pieces of information I'd put together after my time working for the underground at Compound, I knew I needed to head north. It took months, but I did get *here*. Freedom was instrumental in helping me after his own daring escape from Compound and Hub City a few years prior. Cold, half-buried in snow, and literally half-dead, Freedom's scouting routes have been incredibly effective at bringing members of the Resistance out of the Northwood mountains and to the Lodge.

"This place once stood as a sort of ski lodge before the Scientific Revolution. As different artisans have made it here, we've been able to make it more homey. There are multiple cabins for families, and we are self-sustaining. Freedom has used his technological abilities to design a transmission center capable of receiving and sending transmissions to Mars. It was a long shot when we tried to reach Jezero, but we did."

I grimace at the mention of Jezero.

"Yes, Reach?"

"Nation knows about Jezero."

The advisors frown.

"How do you know that?" she asks.

"Because," I say, my eyes widening in frustration at the challenge, "when *we* were *there*, Jezero received transmissions from Nation. The kind that warned them that *we* were coming."

"Oh..."

"But I wouldn't worry about Nation's ability to contact Jezero. Since it's gone and all," Llama adds.

"Gone?"

"Yes, it perished."

Mom's face falls. Her eyes search mine. "And...Greg?" The question is intimate, despite being asked in front of the entire room.

"G-gone," I stutter, aware that I'm crushing her dreams, and that while my father was a coward, his heroism ultimately was his demise. It's complex and complicated and too heavy for an audience.

Mom's jaw quivers for a moment before she pulls a metaphorical mask over her face. "And then? Where is everyone? How did you survive?"

I launch into the tale of Jezero, of accused espionage, of our discovery of Souterraine, of Greg, of Souterraine's insistence that Jezero *not* die out completely and their willingness to welcome Jezero's remaining colonists into the fold, and that it was not Jezero that the Resistance had been communicating with over the past year, but Souterraine.

The advisors gape as they listen to Llama and me recount our story. When I explain about our ship, about the water landing, and how we made it here with nothing more than hope, Mom shoves back from the table. She strides to my chair and crushes me in a hug from behind. The chair back comes to my shoulders, so she hugs me around it, and all I can do is pat her hand awkwardly.

"You survived," she says, in wonder. Then she looks to Llama. "How did you do it?"

"Honestly," Llama says, meeting my mom's gaze, "luck, skill, and game theory."

"Game theory." Mom laughs, a strained choking sound in the back of her throat. "Reach, I thought you'd die. I really thought you would. I can't believe you're here."

I shrug as she steps away from the hug, then composes herself and addresses the advisors. "Reach and Llama have been through more than we have, and we all have reason to hate Enforce and Nation and its tyranny, but I think, given their experiences, it's best to place them in an advisory position for the Resistance. Let's start with Reach."

Hands rise around the table, with the notable exception of Enigma and a few others.

"Majority rule," Mom says. "Reach, you are now an advisor, and will be privy to confidential information. For security and longevity purposes, information shared in this room is not permitted to be disseminated to the regular members. You'll find that we have a common goal, a common enemy, but that the fear of enemy infiltration is a real concern. For this reason, there are punishments in place should you be found guilty of treason and espionage."

This seems to be the way of every political organization, and though it would scare me, I've lived through accounts of treason by two separate organizations, and I'm not intending to do something to harm the Resistance. It's literally my life's purpose to help them.

"Do you agree?" Mom asks Llama and me. "Do you understand that treason is punishable by death?"

I swallow and nod.

"Then welcome to the Advisory Board of the Resistance. Now, for Llama."

Not a single Advisory Board member raises their hand.

32

The advisors leave the room in a flurry of conversation, whispering words like "can you believe it?"

Llama and I remain at the table. Freedom doesn't stand and leave, even after Mom disappears.

"You two have quite the story," Freedom says.

I frown at Freedom, who now knows everything about our story, but we still haven't been told his. I despise information omission. "Yeah, well, yours must be more than what we were told."

"Not really." He shrugs. "I had to make a choice when they wanted me to do the loyalty transfusion and blood oath. My choice was neither. But it cost me."

He pulls up his pant leg, and a huge scar wraps around his calf and shin.

"What happened?" Llama hisses.

"There are certain traps for people leaving Hub City. Most people you'll meet here have some scarring on their bodies as a result of Nation."

"You made it out?" I ask, staring at the grotesque pink line around his limb.

"Yeah," he says. "A little ingenuity and something to live for are all it takes for most people. The people with nothing to live for who try to run—they're the ones who don't make it."

Llama's jaw quivers. "What about the…people from the Wards?"

"They're here too. Many from Ward 11, since they only have to cross the three and a half miles of water to get here. Still others come from the Wards, or the mines."

I tip my head and squint at the maps.

"Would you like to see the map of Nation, the way it *actually* is?" Freedom asks.

I nod. I've seen Nation's maps of Nation, but the map on the wall doesn't look the same as what Nation provided.

"Here." Freedom walks to the map behind where my mom sat. "Come look." He grabs a black marker from a ledge behind the map and circles something. "This is where we are. The Resistance headquarters. This is Ward 11." He tips his head meaningfully at Llama.

"Here's Hub City." He draws points to an x. "Here's where you were on Compound with your mom, Reach. Here's the cave exploration mission you went on. We only know that because of Hero helping you with your transcriptions."

"What are these?" I point to a long peninsula.

"Rare Earth Mining Operations. There are three in Nation, but Rare Earth III is here."

"What's up here?" I ask, pointing to the area on the map that's further north than where the Resistance is.

"It's mostly barren, but there's one population center that keeps to itself here. They're completely surrounded by mountains, so it's impossible to reach from here without skilled guides."

"And here?" I indicate the large body of water in the middle of the section.

"A bay with massive bears that would as soon kill you as look at you."

"How do you know that?" Llama challenges.

"How would we know that?" Freedom responds. "Scouts. The Resistance has been here longer than we've been alive. This is the work of hundreds of years of scouting, and thousands of people. It's only *now* that we have the potential to do something about it."

"What, exactly?"

"We have moves to play." He tips his chin toward a small chess-board on a shelf in the back of the room. "I think you know."

Mom ducks back into the room. "Freedom, are you coming? We can have the ceremony today, if you and Hero both agree."

Freedom grins. "Something to live for is enough."

He follows Mom out the door.

I'd never seen a unionization ceremony when we were in Nation, but I was at the engagement ceremony for Llama and me on Souterraine. Here, at the Resistance headquarters, there aren't opulent decorations or fancy clothes.

Everyone wears exactly what they've been wearing, except for Freedom and Hero. Different members of the Resistance scurried around all afternoon, pushing all the long tables to the sides of the room.

Someone produces an instrument with strings and plays a mournful tune while the Martians hum along. It's an odd mix, but the undercurrent of hope brings tears to my eyes.

Freedom stands before the blazing hearth in a knit sweater made of dark green yarn that is somehow shinier than anything else I've seen here. Hero approaches, and the crowd parts into two distinct sides while she walks toward Freedom. She's dressed in a white sweater that buttons up in the front. A single sash of blue ribbon crosses her torso, and in her hands she carries a sprig of a fragrant herb that floats a tantalizing scent into the air as she passes.

One of the advisors, a man who did *not* approve of Llama and me being given full clearance, stands with Freedom at the front of the hearth. The two of them face the man, but Freedom places his hands around Hero's as if they are the most precious thing he's ever touched.

"We are here today to witness the pledge of union between Freedom and Hero. This is legal and binding, as according to the sovereignty of this place. It cannot be undone. It cannot be lost. Together, you become a family, a unit of the Resistance that cannot be separated. Your jobs will continue to dedicate your lives to the Resistance, but now the Resistance dedicates its services to the good of your family and ensuring the future of the Resistance. Do you agree to this marriage union?"

Hero murmurs a quiet 'yes,' while Freedom grins and says a much louder 'yes.'

"Very well," the advisor says. "You have pledged yourselves as a family in the Resistance movement." He surveys the crowd. "Our newest family unit, Freedom and Hero."

Freedom meets my eyes for a brief second with a smirk on his face and then encircles Hero's waist with his arm and dips her backward for a kiss.

Applause breaks out, and though it's somewhat stilted among the members of the Resistance, the Martians from Souterraine hoot, holler, and clap enough to make up for the awkwardness.

"We don't show much affection, generally," Mom says, surprising me from where she slipped up unnoticed at my side. "Marriage unions are always the exception." She claps loudly. "Sometimes we need to celebrate something we don't understand. It's one way we stay different from Nation."

Freedom and Hero walk together hand in hand down the length of the room to one of the long tables. Freedom pulls out a chair for Hero before she sits.

Mom places a hand gently on my shoulder before she pushes through the crowd and approaches the happy couple at the table. She reaches into her pocket and presents something to Hero. It's an apple. "For you," she says, smiling, before she walks away.

One by one, every advisor, and many of the Resistance members, approach the couple, offering something small.

Freedom stands after receiving a green pepper. "May we dance?" he asks the crowd.

He's met with a roar of approval from the Martians, especially the ones from Souterraine who certainly know how to dance from their feasts. While the members of the Resistance are more subdued, even I can see the excitement in their faces as the stringed instrument begins a wild, rollicking tune.

I watch as Freedom spins Hero around, her long black hair flying, a wide grin crossing her face, and a soft tenderness in his own eyes. Without meaning to, my eyes find Llama, and before I know it, we're also spinning in a mass of people.

I hold Llama in my arms and dance to the music. I realize it's the first time in months I've allowed myself happiness.

THE CELEBRATION ENDS at the stroke of midnight. I hadn't noticed it before, but an old clock stands in the corner of the hall. With weights and counterweights, a pendulum, and a face made of Roman numerals, the clock emits a gong-like sound that startles everyone from their activity. Inside the face of the clock are small cogs, ticking away. It's eerie how quickly everyone stops as the chimes continue.

As the people around us cease their revelry, I walk to the clock. I know what it is, but I have the crazy urge to open the cabinet under the clock face and touch the pendulums, to take the entire thing apart and rebuild it.

Freedom and Hero, hands linked, approach me from the middle of the room.

"You've never seen one, have you?" Freedom asks.

"No," I say. "I think I understand how it works though."

"I'm sure you do."

I turn toward him, away from the mesmerizing facets of the clock.

"I think it will be your turn next." He grins and tips his chin toward where Llama stands on the dance floor. I'm abashed at first, but a bemused expression crosses Llama's face, and I'm reminded that this woman *knows* me. That she not only has Nation's information about my aptitudes, but that she has seen me struggle, seen me fall, and seen me rise. She knows exactly what I'm thinking about this clock, and it's obvious by the way she raises a brow, tips her head to the side, and lifts the corner of her lips into a tiny smile.

When she sees me staring at her, she treads over softly. "Don't you two have someplace to be?" Llama asks Freedom and Hero.

Hero flushes slightly, but Freedom places his arm around Hero's waist and leans down to kiss the crown of her head. "There are a few things in life worth fighting for," Freedom murmurs. "Freedom, as my name implies, the Resistance and against tyranny, but also the simple human experience of love."

Hero adds, "That's what's broken in Nation." She lowers her voice and shakes her head. "They don't love, so they don't know how to experience humanity. It's not science that makes us human, Reach, it's *love*." Hero turns her brown eyes toward Freedom, who smiles down at her.

"Go, you two," Llama says, shooing them on their way, and though she pretends to be annoyed by their lovey-ness, I can see that she's moved by Hero's and Freedom's words.

The couple leaves, soft footfalls accompanying them out of the room. As the rhythmic thump of their feet quiets, Llama leans her shoulder into me, and I find myself pulling her closer to my side.

"Do you think that's true?" she muses.

"About Nation?" I ask.

"Mhmm," she hums as she leans her head on my shoulder.

I look down at her, at her soft brown hair, her bright blue eyes, and I feel a flicker of something more than attraction. I've felt it before, but right now, in this moment, the words Freedom and Hero spoke ring in my memory, and I know it's true.

"Yes," I whisper as I place a kiss on her brow. "Yes, that's what's wrong with Nation."

"And one day…" she whispers.

"One day, Nation won't be the problem anymore."

The bunk room remains frigid. When I pry my eyes open in the morning after Hero and Freedom's celebration, it's hard to move because the air outside my bed is so opposed to the warmth of my body under the blankets.

Still, the day must be met. I don't know what today holds, but I do know that I'm ready for something. A buzzing anticipation courses through my limbs. I'm here, I know the stories, the Resistance knows my story, and *now* I'm ready to do something.

I slip out of the bunk, my eyes tracking automatically toward Llama's space in the bunkroom. She's barely visible under her blankets; all I can see is the crown of her head. I place a hand on her head and gently stroke her hair for a half beat before I turn and leave the room that's practically as cold as Mars' surface.

When I reach the room with the blazing hearth where Hero and Freedom's ceremony occurred, I'm amazed to see that everything is back as it was. Circles of bread with small o's missing from the middle are stacked next to hot jars of coffee and kettles of tea. A small assortment of brightly colored orange balls and yellow curves sits in bowls.

"Reach?" a child's voice says from behind me as I've selected a bread and begun to pour tea into a mug.

"Yes?" I turn and hiss as a drop of the steaming tea splatters on my skin.

Shaking my hand, I finally stop the stinging enough to find a young woman wearing a dark gray sweater that hangs to her knees. She's small, and I can't tell her age.

"You're needed in the conference room."

"Thank you," I say, trying to puzzle out who this person is. Then, as she starts to walk away, her long red hair swinging in a braid down her back, I call out, "Wait!"

She turns and stares at me, blue eyes blinking.

I hold up the bread. "What are these called?"

She smiles. "Bagels."

"Not wheels of bread?"

"No."

"Why do they need me upstairs?"

She shrugs.

"Who are you?"

"Polly. I'm Enigma's daughter."

Oh.

"So, how old are you?" I ask.

"Twelve."

"Thanks, Polly," I say as I prepare to put the bagel down.

"You can take food with you when you're called to the conference room. We know people have to eat here."

I frown, but pick my bagel up and gingerly hold my tea. I blow on the steaming liquid before I take a sip, hoping to eliminate enough liquid that I won't slosh any over the sides and burn myself again as I carry it up the flight of stairs.

"Come on," Polly says, then turns and leads the way out of the room and up to the staircase. She places one foot on the step, and as she climbs, she unleashes a torrent of questions at me. "Did you really come from Mars?"

I nod because I've taken a bite of my bagel.

"Was it really cold there?"

Again, I nod.

"Did you wear a spacesuit all the time?"

I swallow. "No, the Martian colonies were all underground, and they had technology to keep the people in safe temperatures."

"There's more than one colony?"

Something catches in my chest, and my throat closes up for a moment. I cough, and Polly thumps me on the back, which does nothing because it's emotion and not trapped food causing it.

After a moment, I'm ready to say something to her. "There were two colonies. Now there's only one."

"What happened?" Polly asks, wide-eyed.

She's twelve, she's curious, she should have questions, but also, I don't know how much I'm allowed to divulge. And I don't know how much Enigma wants her to know. A quick thought experiment about how easy it would be for her to find out what happened to Jezero by simply asking any of the members of Wave Cohort 1 makes me think this isn't a state secret, but still, she's twelve, and it's a heavy story.

"I"m not sure I can tell you," I answer honestly.

"You probably can, but ok," Polly says in return. "Oh, good, we're here. I have to go to school, and I'm not allowed to bother anyone from Mars when they're sleeping, but I want to know all about it. Do you think one day I could go there?"

I shake my head sadly. "No."

Polly frowns, and I clarify, "Mars was never meant for human life. It's a planet that's made it clear human time on Mars is coming to an end. The Souterraine colonists are all planning to return to Earth in the next ten years."

Polly bites her lip before she nods her head and points at the ajar door to the conference room. She walks away as I slip through the crack and into the tension-filled room.

A man with deep lines creasing his forehead, brown, thinning hair, and a scruff along his jaw sits in a chair, twitching. His eyes are gray, and the circles under them are black as night.

"Reach," Mom says, standing from the seat at the head of the table.

Enigma nods as I sit in the only empty chair around the table, which happens to be next to him.

"This is..." She looks to the man and her brow creases. "What is your actual name?"

"Don't have one," the man says, wiping a dirty hand across his brow. When that does nothing, he drags the hand down his yellow, baggy jacket. It's covered in black splotches.

"What would you *like* to be called, then?" Mom asks, somewhat exasperated.

"Don't matter," the man says, then licks his lips while he looks from side to side. "It's best not to have a name in this case."

"And what is it you need to tell us so urgently?" Mom asks.

The man twitches, and the muscles along his jaw tick. He looks around the table, and his gray eyes land on mine. He stares at me, blinking slowly as he speaks.

"I'm from the mines. The ones controlled by Nation. We mine the copper for their technology, but it's dangerous. Nation only sends Nons they don't want anymore to the mines because…well, because we're expendable. Even the kids."

My jaw clenches as the words seep into the room. This isn't surprising, but when he continues, my stomach plummets to my feet with dread.

"We got word…two days ago that they're bringing a specialist to the mines up here. And that they're going to inject us with nanobots that will run a diagnostic of our DNA genomes. They say they can target diseases and help us live longer. Life expectancies in the mines are less than three years. But we all know it's not disease that kills us. It's the conditions, it's the hard labor, and I have reason to think that the injections are meant to use our genetics to create a database. They'll know from our genetic presence where we are at all times, and they'll prevent the mines from being the main place of defection from Nation once and for all."

Without fail, every single person in the room grips the table.

Freedom stands up. "Which mines? Is it all of them?"

"Yes," the nameless man responds.

Freedom lets out a swear word before he continues. "When is the specialist coming? And is there infrastructure to overpower this from happening?"

The man sighs, puffing out his worn cheeks before he swallows. "I risked my life to come here and tell you. I could have died when I crawled out of that drain pipe tube. The schedule said they were coming soon, but I don't know if it was this week or this month."

Mom stands, placing her weight onto her hands as she leans on the table. "Do you want to stay here?"

The man nods. Then, he twitches again. "But I can't."

"Why not?" Enigma challenges, a hard glint in his eye as he catches Sigma's gaze. Her nostrils flare and he looks away, the barest hint of a flush rising to his cheeks. "You're here."

"I can't," the man snaps and then whispers, low, "I can't leave her."

"Who can't you leave?" I ask, contributing for the first time to the conversation.

"Birdie," the man whispers. "I won't leave her."

"Who is Bridie?" Freedom asks.

"Our canary," the man says.

"It's a bird. We can't afford to be partial to animals at a time like this," Mom retorts.

The man shakes his head. "She's not a bird. She's Birdie. She's always singing, so they make her go down into the tubes first because it's the only thing she can do. She doesn't have any other use in Nation, but she's my friend. And I won't leave her."

My mind whirls as my stomach churns. This sounds familiar.

"Is she..." I think for a moment. "Is her genetic code typical?"

The man shakes his head. "No, I don't think so. She's grown, but she doesn't understand everything. Sometimes it's like there's a child in an adult body."

It clicks into place. Birdie has a genetic disorder—like Pippa.

"To clarify," Mom inserts, "Birdie is *not* an animal."

"No," the man and I say at the exact same time.

"I've never heard of this in Nation," Mom says. "You're sure?"

It is only extreme restraint that keeps me from rolling my eyes.

"Miss," the man says. "We have to get her out. They're going to mess with her code, and when it doesn't fix her, they'll kill her."

Freedom scowls.

The man clenches his jaw. "Will you get her out?"

Freedom looks around the table, and I follow his gaze as he meets each of the advisors' stony faces. "I'll go. I'll see what we can do."

I don't even know I'm standing until the words "I'll go too" fly from my mouth.

34

"Rare Earth III?" Freedom says, his voice low.

The man bobs his head.

"That's the one where…"

"Where they send criminals, or other mostly useless people to further Nation's progress," he replies, and bitterness laces his voice.

"And you are there because…?" Enigma questions, narrowing his eyes at the man.

"I'm a criminal." The man shrugs.

"And *what*, pray tell, was your crime?" Enigma challenges.

"It's not terribly unique in the mines. My sister was hungry. My parents were gone for weeks, they were helping scientists with experiments for space travel. We were in Ward 8, and I took bread. I was seven, she was four."

"You've been in the mines for…" Freedom squints. "Twenty years?"

"Thirty. Most people don't live that long, but I've been wanting to find my sister. I have something to live for. Most people in the mine system don't."

"What was your sister's name?" Mom asks, her eyes wide as she tips her head to the side and studies the man's haggard face.

"Greta," the man replies.

"And she'd be roughly thirty-four years old now?"

"Yes."

"And what happened to her after you were taken?"

"I never knew. Will you help me find out?"

Freedom tips his head and narrows his eyes slightly. "Is that the most important thing at this moment?"

The man shakes his head. "We have to get Birdie out of there. Everyone else is somewhat useful to Nation and needed in the mining process, but they'll…they'll do things to her."

My throat bobs a swallow. "What do we need to do to get her?"

Mom pulls a map down from the wall and spreads it across the table. "Rare Earth III is here. It's twelve miles across rugged terrain."

The man studies the map for a moment, then uses his finger to smudge black dirt or oil into a line on the map. "It's got guards around the perimeter, but not so many that a few people can't slip out undetected if they use these trees."

"That would make sense, given our intel. Freedom, have we ever sent patrols to that area?"

"No," he responds. "We only patrol our borders. We've never infiltrated Nation's territory."

"And you're willing?" Mom asks, but she doesn't look at Freedom; she looks at me.

I nod and she swallows before replacing the crack in her stone façade with a businesslike mask befitting the woman who runs an entire well-organized Resistance and also was willing to sacrifice her son for the cause.

"Then I guess we need to make a plan."

The room unfolds into advisors offering advice and pins being placed on the map among a cacophony of sounds.

Truthfully, I don't hear much of the conversation. It's people arguing, and not even people who will be present in the midst of the danger they're planning for. That will be Freedom and me, and instead of thinking of my own safety and contributing to the conversation, all I can think of is Pippa.

It's hours later when I leave the conference room. A low, mournful noise vibrates off the wooden hallway of the headquarters, and I can't place where it's coming from due to the echo. Still, I listen, and do my best to follow the sound despite the distortions of a building with corners and walls.

It takes me fifteen minutes, but I do find it. A small open room, with a floor that slopes down to a rectangular platform, and curved bench seats that climb the side of the space in consistent intervals. Steps cut through the benches, giving the appearance of climbing the wall.

When I step into the room, the noise becomes apparent as *music*, and it's Llama and a young woman from the headquarters sitting on the platform. They hold long tubes to their lips and force air through small holes along the tube. Their fingers cover the holes and change the pitch and tone of the sound.

I walk down the steps toward the platform, staying as quiet as I can while I listen. The woman says something to Llama, and though she speaks in a low voice, the sound echoes around the room, and I can hear her clearly. "Good, you have a natural talent for the flute."

Flute. The instrument Llama is playing is the *flute.*

"You have a visitor," the woman says before she stands up from where she was sitting next to Llama, their legs dangling off the side of the platform. "Good work today, Llama," the woman says before she walks away, holding her flute across her shoulder as she goes.

Llama's eyes scan the room, eventually landing on me. I spy a small ladder to the side of the platform and climb the six rungs to the flat, smooth surface.

"Hey," Llama says as I plunk my weary body down next to hers. She leans into me and rests her head on my shoulder. "I can play music now too."

"I heard," I say, tipping my head till it rests on top of hers.

We sit for a moment, but then she straightens. "What's wrong, Reach?" She asks it softly, but there's something else under the gentle tone.

"I…" I swallow. I don't want to tell her, but also, who else could I tell? Who else would understand? I blow out a breath and tighten my arm around her before I launch into the tale of the nameless man and the mines and Birdie.

When I finish, I drop my arm from Llama's shoulders and cover my face in my hands because I am feeling entirely too much emotion, and I don't know what to do with it.

Llama peels a hand from my face and meets me with a stern gaze. "What are we going to do about it?"

"I'm…" I swallow. "I'm going on the mission to get her."

"What will we do when she's here, though?" Llama narrows her eyes and shifts her gaze from side to side. "I don't…" She swallows. "I don't trust people here."

The muscles surrounding my eye twitch. "Who don't you trust?" I ask in a low voice.

"The leaders," she says simply, and although she implies she doesn't trust my mother, I understand *why*.

"I'm not sure I trust her either," I say in a voice lower than a whisper. "But what choice do we have? We were trained for this…it's been our life's work. I don't know who to trust, but I trust my—" I swallow and correct the name because yes, she *is* my mom, but she's also *Sigma* here. "Sigma. I trust her more than I trust some of the other advisors."

Llama leans her head back onto my shoulder. "I think maybe it's best to not trust anyone."

A scowl crosses my brow. "I trust Freedom and Hero," I say through gritted teeth.

"Yes," Llama replies. "I trust them too. But, Reach, don't you think that maybe we *know* more about any of this than they do?"

I scrub my hand down my jaw. I try to work out the word puzzle. "What do you mean?" I finally ask.

She picks her head up off my shoulder and fixes me with deep blue eyes. "We're the ones who lived in the middle of Nation's center *and* were sent on a silent execution mission. We're the ones who navigated space *twice*. We've done more than most people here, and maybe it's not polite to say, but we've got experiences they don't."

I frown. Llama has a point, but she's also wrong.

"Llama," I breathe, shaking my head. "But that's only half the game theory. We have the experience they don't, but they have the experience, knowledge, infrastructure, and population that we don't. We can't make a difference here without them, and they can't make a difference without us."

Llama bites her lower lip with her upper teeth. "Maybe." She shrugs. "But I don't trust a single person on the Advisory Board."

I cock a brow at her, tipping my head to the side. "So you don't trust me?"

She swats my shoulder lightly and rolls her eyes. "You know what I mean."

"I do?" I tease because this is heavy, and I'm tired, and sometimes a little teasing makes life better.

"You definitely do," she says, and then leans toward me and places her lips on mine. When she pulls away, she looks me square in the eye and says, "When do we leave to go get her?"

I blink in surprise. "We?"

"C'mon, Reach. You and I both know we need to get her out of there. For Pippa."

I want to protest, but I can see the iron coord in her gaze, the way her will will not be bent, and the way that she will be part of this mission simply because there is no one else on this planet who understands the bond Llama had with her aunt on Souterraine.

Tension floods my body, but there's nothing I can do to dissuade her. Even as my muscles pop from holding myself in, from refusing to allow myself to refuse her to come, I manage to keep my voice low and calm.

"We leave in two nights, during the new moon."

∃5

THE ONE ADVANTAGE of being closer to the North Pole than the rest of Nation is that night lasts longer this time of year. Freedom, Llama, the man from the mines, and I are travelling under the cover of darkness through the Resistance borders and into territory controlled by Nation.

It's either the bravest thing I've ever done, or the dumbest. If any of us are caught, we're dead. Still, thoughts of Pippa make this an easy choice. Pippa's life mattered. It still does. This woman, Birdie, I've never met, but I understand her. And I also understand Nation.

Snow falls softly, masking the crunch of our footsteps, but also causing us to leave a trail. Freedom raises a gloved hand to signal that we should stop. We do, pulling our group to a halt under a copse of pine trees. "We're almost to the edge of the borders," he whispers. "Are you sure you want to do this?" he asks Llama.

She glares at him. It's not the first time she's been asked. When I announced to the Advisory Board that Llama was coming on this mission too, they balked. It was chaos in the room until the nameless man, who had since had a shower, warm, fresh clothes, and hot food, and now looked remarkably more at ease, piped in. "Birdie will like to have a woman with us."

That settled it. I'm not sure why the Advisory Board all capitulated at the mention of what Birdie would like, but there's nothing I can do about it.

Freedom meets my gaze as if he's asking if I'm ok with her coming. I give him a single nod, and he drops any further questions. "So, Llama, you understand the geography of Ward 11, but Reach, I think you might have some questions."

"I thought Ward 11 and Nation was south of here," I whisper.

"It is," Freedom says. "But the Resistance borders are fairly new, and Nation is much older. The three Rare Earth mines are technically inside the jurisdiction of Ward 11 and Nation, even though geographically they are outside of the current boundaries of Ward 11."

"How is that possible?" I ask.

"It's like the three mines are islands, right?" Llama says.

He nods. "Yes. Except instead of islands in the middle of water, these are islands in the middle of land. These were mines even before the Scientific Revolution, and they produced rare Earth elements needed for technology then too. Nation wasn't about to give that up, even though they figured the rest of the land was worthless up here."

"So they just…kept the mines?" I ask.

"Yes," the nameless man replies. "And because the mines are deep Earth mines after centuries of use, they are nearly impossible to infiltrate or escape from. They are essentially a prison and a place for those who have no other purpose to go. It's the same as it is everywhere in Nation, those with no other purpose are given one so that they can further Nation's progress." He spits at the word *progress*.

"So how are we going to infiltrate this mine?" I ask, because the maps in the advisory room weren't completely accurate schematics.

Nameless Man frowns. "I crawled out of an irrigation ditch, past the sentries, till I got to the runoff pool and swam. Before that, I used a ventilation tube to get to the irrigation ditch."

"What about security?" I ask.

"NSBs and a few human guards on platforms surrounding the mine."

"Are the other mines like this?"

"Rare Earth III mines copper. Which is the most demanded rare Earth material for Nation. Rare Earth II mines iron ore, and Rare Earth I mines…" Freedom frowns for a moment, then turns to the nameless man. "What does Rare Earth I mine?"

Nameless Man shrugs. "Maybe nickel. Maybe lithium. Maybe people's body parts for the NSBs."

"What are NSBs?" Llama asks quietly as snowflakes fall on her dark grey knit hat.

"Near Sentient Beings," Nameless Man replies. "I never could tell how they made them look so life-like. They have to be taking human attributes from somewhere."

A sharp pain claws at my throat, as if I've swallowed glass. I inhale a huge gulp of air as I think about the implications of what the nameless man said.

This won't be my first run-in with Near Sentient Beings, and I'd prefer to never see them again. If what I saw years ago was a prototype, what they have actually functioning and working in the mines is bound to be even scarier.

"What do the NSBs…do?" Llama asks, swiping a chunk of snow from her eyelashes with the back of her own gloved hand.

"They're the bosses," Nameless Man replies. "Occasionally, humans come to see what's going on, but usually they feed the NSBs directions. I'm not sure if NSBs or real humans are supposed to come and inject the miners for the genetic database they're so excited about."

"Are the NSBs run by a code?" I ask.

Nameless Man shrugs, but Freedom fixes me with narrowed eyes.

"What are you thinking, Reach?" Freedom asks, his voice low. He tugs his black cap down further over his ears.

"If there's a control center, a way to update the code so the NSBs don't send a feed to the human handlers…we could get more people out."

"Never gonna work," Nameless Man snorts. "The human handlers are big people up in Nation. They want the rare Earth materials, and they know they need them to keep making their technology better. The NSBs are trained before they come here. They're…able to think in a way."

"Deep code? Artificial intelligence?" I ask. "They train on an algorithm?" It's true that every code and algorithm can be disrupted, but the difficulty of breaking it remotely beyond my skills. This is where Pandora's code box comes in.

The man raises a brow. "I don't know what they do to make them like that, but the NSBs are best avoided."

Llama tips her head to the side and studies the man. "Have you ever met the human handlers? And what do the NSBs…what do they do?"

"Oh, they're in charge of punishment. And they have handlers in the loosest sense of the word. They've been trained with humans from the Punishment and Retribution Department, and then are sent to supervise the Rare Earth mines because the conditions up here are so deplorable, no actual human from Nation would want to be there."

"What about the guards?" I ask.

"They're people with 'potential' from the mines," he says back, snarling. "They're the snitches. But…" He trails off and swipes snow off his nose with the back of his own gloved hand. "There might be one that is…friendly."

"Why would you say that?" Freedom presses.

"He owes me."

"Ok, but we need to listen up," Freedom says, then he fixes Nameless Man with a stern glare. "Is there anything else we need to know that you didn't share with the Advisory Board?"

"I don't trust them," he says.

"We know," Freedom responds drily. "But we're about to risk our lives if I've heard what you had to say correctly, and you didn't give entirely truthful information in the planning sessions."

Nameless Man gives a toothy grin. "You still came."

Suddenly a shiver that has nothing to do with the cold works its way down my spine.

36

FREEDOM'S EYES NARROW for half a beat, and then he reaches out with both of his gloved hands and grasps Nameless Man's coat. "Are you *for them?*" he snarls. I'm amazed at the way Freedom's demeanor has changed from calm and businesslike to barely contained fury. "Are you a *spy* for Nation?"

"N–n–no," the man sputters.

"Then you will tell us your name this very moment. Because if something goes wrong on this mission, you will be held responsible for it by the Resistance, or by Nation. I won't have any qualms about turning you in if I'm captured."

The man blinks rapidly, but opens his mouth before snapping it shut.

"Your name." Freedom shakes him slightly.

"D–Dylan."

Freedom lets go, and the man's feet sink into the snow. He stumbles backward, catching his balance with the help of a young pine trunk. "And your sister?"

The man swallows again. "Greta," he mumbles.

"And we're going to get Birdie out of the mine, as well as any others we can before the genetic database injections take place."

"Y-y-yes," Dylan stutters.

Freedom meets my eyes with his own hard gaze. "I don't trust him." He jerks a thumb toward Dylan. "But I don't trust Nation either. Do you want to continue?" He looks from Llama to me and back again.

Llama's jaw sets in a hard line and her nostrils flare. "I won't be backing out. Not when…" She trails off and looks at me. I understand. She's fiercely protective of people she loves, and Pippa's condition, should Pippa have been unfortunate enough to have been born in Nation, would have doomed her to a life exactly like this Birdie woman we're going to rescue. No, she's never met Birdie, but Llama also knows enough to imagine what horrors Birdie has been subjected to without fully understanding the abuse Nation has forced upon her.

"Me neither," I say.

Freedom bobs his head, then whispers, "We're about to leave the Resistance borders. There's a ridge up ahead, and once we crest it, we'll be in Rare Earth Mine III. Does this look familiar to you, Dylan?"

Dylan nods. "Yes…it's over there."

Freedom raises one hand, then slips out of the trees and into the open. The snow falls thickly, swirling and obscuring the view. It's a positive, because in the open, it covers our tracks.

Freedom stomps through the snow, his tan boots visible through the flakes from where I stand at the back of our line.

It feels like hours before we reach the top of the crest. Freedom sinks onto his stomach in the snow, and we follow. I'm grateful for the Arctic-level exploration gear the Resistance supplied us with as we force our bodies into the cold snow bank, letting our heads peer above the rise.

I narrow my eyes and look out across what is an open pit. There are large machines clanking and spinning in the mud, and for some reason, the snow isn't falling as thickly inside the pit. Three wooden platforms with large lights shine down into the pit, each of the lights illuminating a tunnel that slopes into a dirty white building several stories high. Two of the shafts are quiet, but the third one is bustling with activity. Like ants, people file in and out of the shaft, carrying and depositing something into a large pile at the mouth of a yellow excavator before disappearing back into the shaft.

"What are they doing?" I whisper to Dylan, who's on my left.

"Depositing the rare Earth materials."

"They carry them up from the deeper part of the mine?"

"No, they ship them up with a train, but the conditions in the pit would wear the train out too fast, so they wear the people out instead."

Dylan points to a cluster of people standing next to the shaft entrance. They wear silver body suits that cover their entire bodies from neck to ankle. Tall, silver, knee-high boots create the illusion of not having any ankle or knee joints. Skin is visible below the wrist cuffs, and on their faces. The most shocking thing is the variety of human features on their faces. "NSBs. Making sure no one steals any of the material."

"What do they do if they think someone's stealing?" Llama whispers.

"If you watch for at least an hour, you'll see." Dylan shrugs.

Suddenly, one of the NSBs marches to the line of people and yanks a woman in a dirty yellow coat out of place. She screams as the NSB twists her arm behind her back.

The rest of the people continue walking by, looking at the ground as if refusing to acknowledge the cruelty of the NSB would make it stop.

The woman's screams continue until the NSB drops her arm. It's bent at an odd angle.

"Now she still has to unload," Dylan whispers.

Llama's face turns white as the snow, only the stark brown line of her eyebrows breaking the landscape she's melted into. "Why'd they do that?" she asks, biting her lip.

Dylan shrugs. "They just do it. Deeper in the mines, you're a little safer. They don't interfere as much in the actual mining process."

"And what will they do if they suspect we're doing what we're doing?"

"They'll kill you," Dylan says without a moment's hesitation. "They will absolutely kill you."

"How do you propose we get in?" I ask, scanning the landscape. My eyes snag on the woman awkwardly bracing against the limpness of her arm. It takes everything in me to *not* scream, "Look! Look what they did! And you did *nothing*!"

Dylan points to a small pile of rubble at the side of the pit yard. "There's a ventilation pipe behind that pile. It's hot as blazes in it, but it's the best way in."

The lights click off.

"Now's our best chance," Dylan whispers.

Freedom bobs his head. "We'll have to roll down the embankment. It's steep, but doable. The best hope is that if we're spotted, we'll be mistaken for an animal that fell."

Dylan shrugs.

"Let's go."

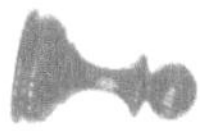

It takes three hours for us to slip and slide into the pit yard without being seen and then maneuver around the open yard in the shadows. The NSBs are most likely not trained to look for intruders in the mines, making it easier to get in. However, Dylan has assured us they are trained to watch for people trying to get out. After the lights went out for the mandated darkness time, the NSBs disappeared into the shafts. Their shiny clothes reflected the light of the snow in a way that made them look ethereal, but not in a good way.

Dylan leads the way to a pipe. The air hissing up from the pipe is damp and hot. The ground around the pipe is bare, despite it being freezing and snowing outside. Freedom crouches down and wrenches the metal grate off the hole. The snow on his gloves sizzles as it makes contact with the vent.

"It's hot," Freedom says as he pushes the grate to the side. He leaves enough space for us to shimmy through into the vent.

Dylan goes first, with Freedom following, then Llama, then me. When I clamber into the tube, I'm blasted with the hot, wet air. It stings my face, singeing my eyelashes and jaw with heat. As I slide down the tube, it gets hotter, but because I've dried from the heat, it doesn't sizzle and burn as much.

The pipe slides down for what feels like miles. In our winter gear, we're all sweating. When we arrive at the bottom of the tube, I collapse onto a bare earthen floor. It's dark, damp, musty, and the temperature change from in the tube to out of the tube is jarring. Small lights are scattered at irregular intervals along the path, casting odd shadows with no length into the space.

Dylan puts a finger to his lips as he curls into a tight ball, burrowing his face into crossed arms and lying on his side in the shadows as tightly as he can.

Freedom and Llama follow suit, rolling away from the ventilation pipe into the shadows of the corridor, but I can't move fast enough. The only thing I can do is turn and hope that my winter gear of a dark blue winter coat and black hat is enough to cover my skin.

Footsteps sound closer, tiny bits of gravel popping and skidding along in rhythm with the vibrations as they echo off the walls.

Two NSBs slide into view. They don't look at anything except straight ahead. They don't speak to each other; they stare forward and march, their faces blank. They have dull eyes, impossibly perfect facial symmetry, and an odd sheen around their skin. It's not a glow, and it might be the reflection of their silver suits in the dimly lit pathway, but it is ominous.

They slide away, disappearing around a corner.

Dylan waits a moment before he stands. "C'mon," he whispers, low.

Llama wipes sweat off her brow with the back of her gloved hand. She looks at me and blinks slowly. "Which way to Birdie?"

"This way," Dylan says as he begins leading us through a maze of paths. All I can tell is that we are going down, deeper into the mine. "Everyone should be in the bunks except for the NSBs and guards. And the late-night shift."

"Is Birdie on the late-night shift?" I whisper.

"Birdie is on every shift," Dylan quips.

37

Llama stumbled at Dylan's words about Birdie, and I know she's upset. But we have to keep our heads. While the NSBs aren't looking for us, we also need to get Birdie out of here. That's the mission, that's the goal. Llama knows that. I know that. But it doesn't stop emotion from making a difference.

Dylan leads us out of the earthen tunnel-like corridors and onto metal framework shafts. There are more lights now, and more people. He rounds a corner and stops. "Here," he whispers harshly. "You need mining clothes." He looks both ways, then ducks into a small doorway in the wall and returns with four yellow jackets. "Put these on," he instructs. "And leave your winter gear here." He gestures to an exceptionally dark corner.

As I crouch to leave my coat in the shadows, I understand why he's not worried about anyone looking in this space. It's wet. Not with water, but with foul-smelling liquid. Still, I have no other choice, so I shove it into the crevice between the wall and the floor.

Freedom's face is drawn as he searches the area around us with his keen gaze. "Now what?"

"Now, we mine our way to Birdie," Dylan replies.

Llama swallows in the dark next to me. She places a hand on my arm, and I feel the nervousness coursing through her.

"How do we mine?" she asks through gritted teeth. "And where is she?"

"Walk like you belong here. Grab a tool and occasionally hit the wall with it. There's not much to fake mining." Dylan's eye roll is obvious even in the darkness of the shaft.

Dylan leads the way out of the corner and onto the metal scaffolding that vibrates and shakes with each step. "About a quarter mile, and we'll start seeing the miners. Grab an axe, or hammer, or something from the bins."

We round a corner and come across large green crates with the word TOOLS stamped on them in block letters. There's a crate of pickaxes and a crate of hammers. Llama snags a hammer, I grab a pickaxe, and Freedom takes one of each. Dylan doesn't take anything, which strikes me as odd, but he marches purposefully onward.

It doesn't take long for us to pass the first miners. They stand on ladders at various points against the rock wall. A vein of something shiny runs through the otherwise dark, damp rock. The sound of metal striking rock is constant and decidedly unmelodic.

No one so much as bats an eye at us. The miners in their yellow jackets continue chipping away at the veins in the wall.

"What are they doing?" Llama whispers after passing the tenth one who doesn't even glance our way.

"Loosening the vein for an explosion," Dylan replies.

"Once it's exposed, and we know how thick it is, a second team comes in and uses explosives to break down the shaft."

"Isn't that…dangerous?"

Dylan laughs, mirthlessly in a whisper. "Isn't everything in a mine dangerous?"

No one has anything else to say after that. Llama occasionally taps her pickaxe against the wall as we continue. The scaffolding becomes sparser, changing from metal grates to wood that's clearly rotting out.

We reach a hole in the wall barely big enough for a human body to crawl through. The faint strains of music reach my ears above the echoes of tools from behind us.

"Here," Dylan says, gesturing to the hole. "We can't all go in, so some of us will need to mine around this spot."

"What about the…NSBs?" Freedom questions.

It is odd we haven't seen any in quite some time.

"They don't bother coming down this far. There's not much to do down here except mine, or if something were to happen, die."

The matter-of-fact way he states this feels like I've been slapped in the face. Nation wouldn't want to risk its precious technologies being in peril, but they'll risk human lives.

"Which one of us is going?" I ask.

Dylan quirks a brow. "I'd best go, and probably the girl."

Llama blinks and curls her lip into a snarl. "Llama. Not *the girl*," she says back in a biting tone.

"Fine," Dylan retorts. "Llama and I will go get Birdie. You two, mine here. But don't make this small shaft fall in, or else we'll be buried alive."

I suck in a deep breath at his words, and the implication of what we're doing, where we are, and how dangerous this truly is, lands on my shoulders like a ton of copper ore.

Llama follows Dylan into the tunnel, sliding along on her belly like a snake. And I cannot breathe.

"C'mon, Reach," Freedom whispers as we both watch them disappear into the tunnel. "We need to act like we belong here. We need to act like we're mining." He swings his pickaxe into the wall, and as he does, a chunk of bluish-green rock dislodges and hits him in the forehead. He crumples to the ground, his hand over his forehead, and when he pulls it away, there's blood.

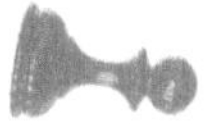

It feels like hours before Dylan, Llama, and Birdie return. Freedom's cut is a concern, but more than anything, it's the genetic material in his blood that has me worried. Nation *knows* Freedom's blood. They have it on sample from his parents' trial and their strange fascination with blood transfusions.

Freedom's cut begins to drip, and that's worrisome. The only thing I can do is rip my sleeve off and create a bandage. I pull my arm from the dirty yellow jacket, then from the undershirt of pure cotton provided to me by the Resistance. I use my teeth to rip the shoulder seam. It cuts the stitches in a satisfying rip, and I make a headband and bandage for Freedom.

"Thanks," he says, his voice hoarse. He scans side to side. "Reach," he says. "Reach, I think this was a bad idea."

I shrug. There's nothing we can do about it now. We're here.

"No," he whispers. "I think…that…Dylan…might be…"

He doesn't finish that thought because suddenly singing is right behind us in the dark tunnel. Llama climbs out, followed by a woman with hair that's either covered in oil, or black as a moonless sky. The woman sings mostly nonsensical words, but they're constant.

"Birdie," Llama says, and Birdie looks at me and Freedom with a smile.

"I sing," she states.

"It's very nice," I say in reply, while she smiles happily and hums.

Freedom blinks and stares.

"We have to go?" Birdie says.

"Yeah," Llama replies. "We have to go."

"Can I sing?"

"Of course," Llama says. "But it has to be whispers." She gestures to me and Freedom. "C'mon, let's go."

"What about Dylan?" I ask, because he hasn't appeared from the tube.

"Dylan?" Birdie exclaims loudly.

"Shhh," Llama gently whispers. Then she turns and peers down the shaft. "I don't know where he is. Do you know where he is?" Llama asks Birdie.

She nods her head. "Mhm. He's running away from the NSBs."

38

Freedom blinks twice and shakes his head. "This was a bad idea," he groans, putting his palm to his forehead after the movement. "We have to get out of here."

Birdie smiles at Llama. "Hi," she says.

"Hi," Llama replies, her voice catching. "Do you know how to get out?"

Freedom grimaces. "Do you know where Dylan and the NSBs are?"

"Nope, nope, nope," Birdie sings.

Freedom starts to take a step, but doubles over and hisses in pain. "I'm dizzy," he says.

I catch Llama's gaze, worry apparent in her eyes and reflected in my own. "We have to get out," I whisper. But none of us knows *how*.

Freedom's condition is concerning. He's pale, and red is seeping through the bandage on his head. Scrambling, I think of an idea. It's hair-brained, and might not work, but it also *might*.

"Dylan is fighting the NSBs?" I ask Birdie again.

"Yes, yes, yes," she sings.

"And where will the NSB's come?"

"Here, and the pit. And the NSB rooms."

"Are there places they don't go?"

Birdie hums. "They can't get wet, so the places with water."

"Can you take us there?"

Birdie grabs Llama's hand and starts to gallop down the scaffolding.

Freedom looks at me for a moment. "I don't think I can…"

"No," I cut him off. "You're coming. Hero is waiting for you, and I don't understand what's happening here, but you're not staying." I reach under his shoulders and haul him up to standing. He leans heavily on me.

Blood drips off the bandage, but there's nothing I can do about it now. The NSBs know we're here—if they're after Dylan, we have to assume they know.

Birdie and Llama are faster than me and Freedom, but I manage to keep them in my sight until they round a corner and I'm faced with a round room, with six different doorways.

Freedom shakes and shivers from loss of blood. I know enough to know this isn't good.

I stare at the doorways, unsure of where to go, and definitely unsure of which way Llama and Birdie went.

Suddenly, hands grab me and yank me into a doorway. I don't let go of Freedom, so whoever is dragging me backward is also dragging him with us.

"Who are you?" a man's voice asks. He wears a yellow miner's coat and has a long black beard down to his stomach. "What do you want?"

I blink in the light of a single footpath lantern.

Freedom wracks a shiver before he drops to the ground, fainted.

"Uh." I stumble. "We're not with Nation."

"You're not?" The man snarls. "Then who are you with?"

I scrunch my eyes closed. I don't know how to get out of this. The truth is the easiest to keep straight. "The Resistance," I whisper.

The man steps back in shock, his eyes peering into mine. "It's real?"

I nod.

"Why are you here?"

"Dylan…was…he escaped. And he told us about Birdie and… then she said he went to tell the NSBs we're here."

"What?" the man hisses. "Why would you come *here*?"

"The genetic database from Nation. We want to get Birdie out, and anyone else that they won't have use for…" I let the implication trail off before I drop to my knees and feel Freedom's neck for a pulse with my pointer finger. It's there, but it's light.

"Can you help us?" I ask.

"You're a fool," the man says. "But yes, I can." He frowns.

"He said he had a sister he was missing and he's been mining for thirty years, that he came here and was a miner, and that he was worried about Birdie and the genetic database."

Confusion flashes across the man's face. "Genetic database?"

"Dylan said Nation was coming to do injections for a genetic database so they could…well, I don't actually know what Nation is going to do with a genetic database, but I know enough to know it won't be good," I hiss.

The man's eyes widen. "Dylan," he snorts. "What an idiot. There is no genetic database. That's all chatter from the Resistance, trying to rile us up and start something. You both fell for it."

"What about the NSBs?" I ask, scanning the area around us.

The man sobers. "They're dangerous. They're overseen by Enforce and her people and trained by the Punishment and Retribution Department."

My mind shuffles through the words of this man like gears grinding into place. "The Resistance tries to rile you up?"

"They do it every few months. Secret messages, rumors meant to alarm the miners. Dylan's involved with two of them. He's their spy or something. Their names are Signal and Enigmal, or something."

My eyes widen. *Why would Sigma and Enigma have pretended not to know Dylan if he's their spy in the mines?*

A door slams and a shout sounds.

"Aren't you alarmed?" I ask.

The man shrugs. "Can't get much worse."

"We have to get out," I say. "This whole thing was a mistake."

"Absolutely, it was," the miner retorts. "I can't believe you'd be fool enough to listen to the Resistance."

My head tips to the side, and I appraise the man through narrowed eyes. "Do you want to live here? Do you want to mine copper ore under the watch of NSBs? Because if you help me out of here, you can live with the Resistance, and you can fight against Nation. I don't know why you're here, but everyone here has a good reason to hate Nation."

The man shrugs. "That's true."

"Why are you here?" I hiss. "Why did they sentence you to a life of hard labor in this mine?"

"Because I said something," the man mutters. "A phrase they didn't like."

Freedom groans and starts to sit up.

"Can you please help us get out? This mission was a disaster."

The man nods.

"And Birdie? And the woman with her?"

The man holds his hands up in a helpless gesture. "I know Birdie, but I don't know where she is." Footsteps sound in the quiet, and the man shrinks back against the shadows, placing one finger to his lips. When the footsteps have passed and are gone, the man speaks again. "I can get you out of here, but we have to watch for NSBs. And…" He strokes his beard. "There might be some truth to the genetic database. Are you truly from the Resistance?"

I meet his eyes with a stony gaze and nod.

"Can you get other people into the Resistance boundaries?"

"I can try," I whisper.

"Can you get the children out?"

"Children?" I ask, alarmed. "Like with their families?"

"No. Just kids."

My heart drops. An inkling that kids are here because there's no other place for them washes over me like the ominous particles of a Martian dust storm.

"Most of us down here are here for a reason, but if the kids were gone…maybe we could…actually work with the Resistance and make a difference. I didn't know that the Resistance had any power to get in here. I thought it was Dylan spewing tales."

"Fine," I say as Freedom climbs to sit up on the floor but wraps his head in his arms. "But we have to get out of here, now."

"This way," the man says. He turns and begins plodding through a wet tunnel. I help Freedom up, keeping my arms under his armpits and half-dragging him as he leans on me. The only light is the tiny reflection of a footpath light off his jacket.

We turn a corner and are ensconced in total darkness.

39

THE MAN LEADS us through a twisty, turning stream. The Resistance boots are waterproof, but the other clothes we wear are not. Finally, we reach an open space with significantly more lights. The man holds up a hand. "We're stopping here. We need to get the kids out."

"How many?" I ask.

"Fifty in this room. NSBs check in from time to time, but I haven't seen any. They keep the kids together, at least."

The man plods out of the stream and pushes through a metal door. Everything about this space is sterile. It's white, colorless, and metal under harsh lights. It's also freezing.

He opens the door, and I step through it, supporting Freedom as I do. When we enter, I find a room full of children sitting hunched over small tables and sorting pieces of rock into piles. My heart drops into my stomach at the sight of unkempt children in dirty, yellow mining clothes, smudged faces, and haunted eyes.

"Kids," the man says. "This is…" He turns his gray eyes to me. "A friend. He's taking you out of here. But you have to listen."

The children all sit in rapt attention. "Have the NSBs been here lately?"

A child, perhaps a little older than the others, answers, "No."

"Then we don't have time. Do you want to leave here?"

A tiny voice pipes in, a girl with dirty hair and even dirtier yellow coveralls saying, "Can we go home?"

"You don't have a home anymore," a little boy says. "Remember? We're here because there's no other place for us."

"I want to go home," the girl wails.

"Hush," the man says harshly, and the little girl stops wailing immediately. "You're going with these men. They're taking you out of here. You can have a better life than this." He gestures to the piles of rocks. "But you have to do what we say. First, follow them. Do *not* get lost, because they can't help you if you do. Second, when you get where you're going, *behave*. This way."

The man crosses the room and wrenches a door open, then shuts it quickly. "NSBs," he says. "Back to what you were doing. We aren't here."

He crouches under a table, and I drag Freedom down to hide under another low table.

It doesn't take long before two NSBs walk into the room through the same door the man tried to leave from.

"All clear in the child work room," one NSB says aloud into some sort of transmitter. The odd glow of their suits reflects off the white floor, making them look even brighter.

The second NSB's face curls into a snarl. "Who should we punish for a show of force today? Any volunteers?"

The children sit quietly, working on pulling rocks from the piles on their tables and sorting them by size. The NSBs look from side to side and then lock gazes on the little girl. Tear tracks cut through the grime of her face, and though she's quiet, she rocks on her stool.

With heavy steps, they cross to the table where she sits, her mouth moving in a silent cry. They each grab hold of her arm and yank her to standing, and then they laugh. A forced, maniacal sound, and I can't do it. I can't sit by and let them hurt her.

I scramble out from under the table and charge the NSBs. I hurl into them with the force of a space shuttle and watch as they collapse to the ground. The NSBs are trained to fight, though, and they spring back up, throwing wild punches in my direction. The man takes one and forces it to the ground by wrapping his arms around it from behind and tipping it down. It hits the ground with a sickening crunch of metal, and a small gear rolls out of its suit, but I can't watch for long.

I block the blows of the NSB who's targeting me as best I can, but when one lands on my cheek, I'm met with the sensation of flesh wrapped in metal hitting my bone. My vision swims, and the NSB's hands are gearing up to hit again, when suddenly, the hand moves to my breast pocket. Its hand sticks to the key in my pocket. I stare in shock as the NSB's eyes rattle and roll in its head as it says, "Key. Power Key."

Freedom appears, tackling the NSB out of the way. It slumps to the ground, and I stare at my pocket.

The NSBs are magnetic, and the key in my pocket, the one I've kept since Mars, means something.

The man takes off one of his shoes and pours it down the back of the NSB's bodysuit. The NSB sizzles, and it rolls a little, as if the gears inside of it are settling. It stills. *The NSBs can't get wet.* I bend and wring the fabric of my pants into my hand. There's not a lot of water, but I hope it's enough.

I splash it on the zipper over the back of the NSB's suit. It sizzles and hisses before it stills.

"We have to move, now," the man says. "C'mon, kids."

The kids sit at their tables in shock, the little girl bracing her arm against her body.

Freedom grimaces, but walks to the little girl. "Hi," he says in a low voice. She looks at his bloody face and slinks away. "It's ok," he whispers. "You're coming with us."

"I want to go home," she whispers. "I want Mom."

"There is no mom anymore," the little boy hisses. "We don't have anyone. That's why we're here, Nora."

Freedom extends a hand to the little girl. "It's ok, Nora. Please come with us?"

Nora's wide eyes grow even wider as she stares at his open hand. It's as if the wheels in her head are turning, when suddenly, she places her palm in Freedom's and smiles.

"Everyone," the man calls. "We have to go now."

He wrenches the door open and marches out of the room, the children all following behind him in a row of dirty yellow clothes.

Freedom grimaces, but walks in the middle of the line with Nora's hand held tightly in his. I wait until the last of the children has left the room and follow from behind.

From behind, I can see that each of the child workers wears the miners' yellow, but on the back of their clothing is black, stamped block letters that read:

Property of Rare Earth III

Bile fills my throat as I understand *what* these children are. These are the children who are orphans, that aren't lucky enough to be considered for the Ward of the State schools.

We twist our way through serpentine passageways and end up outside of the mine, hidden behind a heap of refuse that stinks, despite the freezing temperatures. The children don't have proper gear for this trek, but neither do Freedom or I, having left everything in the damp shadows of the mine tunnels.

"Good luck," the man says, pointing to a small open hill that becomes covered in pine after about one hundred yards of clear visibility. Freedom leans down and says something to Nora. She looks at him and grins as she bobs her head. "They'll be looking for you soon, so *go*."

Freedom catches my gaze, and even though he's pale, the cold air seems to be doing him some good. "I'll lead. You stay at the back," he says as I nod in agreement.

I have a moment of panic about Llama and Birdie, but they can get out. Llama's smart. I don't understand everything that happened in the mines, but now there are fifty children walking in a line in front of me, and I know deep in my bones I would do anything to make sure these children get to safety.

PART 3
BATTLE

40

It's easier to get the children to the Resistance land than it was for us to leave it. For one, the snow isn't falling thickly, and for another, it's not the dark of night. The children march without complaint, though their little bodies shiver and their teeth chatter.

"Don't lie down," Freedom calls. "No matter how tired you are, do not lie down in the snow."

The children sniffle and plod along. One small child, maybe only four years old, topples into the snow, and wordlessly, an older child, perhaps ten, scoops him up and places him on his back.

When we arrive at the Resistance borders, Freedom pulls the children into a circle. "We're safe now," he says. "But we still have a ways to go. I'm going to try to communicate with someone who can help, but I don't know if it will work."

He pulls a small bead from his pocket and blows into it three times. Nothing happens. No sound is made, nothing.

He puts it back into his pocket and addresses the children. "They'll come to help if they can. For now, there is a place that is warm, with food and a place for you at the end of this. Keep being brave."

Nora sidles up next to Freedom and tucks her hand into his. "C-c-cold," she says to him.

"I know. Let's keep moving. It's not as bad when we're moving."

Nora nods, but doesn't let go of Freedom's hand, and even though it slows him considerably, he doesn't let go of her hand either.

We've walked maybe a mile on the Resistance lands when a loud, low, long whistle meets my ears.

Freedom perks up. "They're coming."

Six small, brightly painted machines on runners glide over the snow. Riders wearing Arctic exploration gear sit atop each machine. One throws the machine into park and hops off. The rider runs to Freedom, tackling him to the ground as they kiss him. It takes a moment for me to realize it's Hero under all the winter gear.

Freedom dusts the snow off his body and touches the bandage on his head. The blood there is frozen. "Hero," he says, gesturing to the children. "We need to get them all back."

She looks around as if seeing them for the first time; perhaps she is.

"I think we can fit eight per sled," she says. The other riders stay atop their machines, but as I look around, I see that each machine has a large square piece of wood attached to the back with chains.

Freedom nods. "Let's get the littlest ones back to the Lodge."

Hero eyes his forehead. "You too."

"I can't take a spot, not when they're kids," Freedom whispers through his chattering teeth.

Hero places her hands on her hips while the children look on. "Then you get on that snowmobile and you drive them back. I'll come back with anyone who has to walk."

Freedom pitches forward, but Hero holds out her arms to steady him. She glares at him. "Don't you dare argue with me."

Freedom moves slowly to the snowmobile and climbs on, Nora following behind him. Hero begins directing the smallest of the children to the wooden sleds attached to the back. When she sees the ten-year-old carrying the four-year-old, she takes off her winter coat and wraps the younger boy in it.

"He's alive," she whispers to the older boy.

He nods. "I think so, miss."

"No," Hero says, "he *is*." She pushes them gently onto the sled and nods at the driver. The driver revs the engine and flies off in a flurry of scattered snow.

The other drivers take off, Freedom following. My hands are frozen, my limbs are beyond cold, and I'm ready to lie in the snow and wait to be rescued. I can't think of anything except how comfortable it would be to go to sleep.

Hero doesn't let that happen. She surveys the children left with me in the clearing. There are ten of us who couldn't fit on the sleds—me, her, and eight of the children.

"Where's Llama?" Hero asks.

I swallow and want to say something about how we lost her in the mines, but my tongue is as thick as wool, and nothing I want to say makes any sense.

"Your lips are frozen." Hero frowns. "Come on." She waves a hand at the group. "They'll come back for us, but we have to keep moving."

The children with us are all older, but their bodies are small, thin, and they're in an increasingly dangerous situation the longer we stand still. Muscles have been known to freeze and snap in extreme temperatures.

The children look at each other, but they follow behind Hero. The snowmobile machines must have offered some hope that there was something ahead for them, because they do it without complaint.

We walk for twenty minutes, our bodies weary from climbing out of a refuse pile at the mine and then trekking across a forest in temperatures cold enough for snow. The rev of snowmobile engines cresting a rise elicits a shout of excitement from Hero.

Two snowmobile drivers hop off their machines and hurry to the children. I get a look at these drivers.

One is Enigma. The other is Mom.

Mom runs through the snow and crashes into me in a hug. "You made it back. You made it back," she whispers on a loop. My mind isn't functioning, but I know that something about her has made me unspeakably angry.

"We have to get the children inside," Hero shouts as she starts placing the children into spots on sleds.

It doesn't take long with four children on each sled. Mom directs me to a sled and pushes my shoulder down until I sit on it. We're all exhausted, and before I know it, I'm asleep.

I wake in the infirmary. It's the room where the Martians in need of medical care went, and it's the room where Harold stayed. I blink open my eyes into a bright, sterile space and immediately startle. I try to sit up, but there are tubes and machines attached to my body.

"Reach," Harold says, swimming into my view as I fight with the tubes connected to me. "Stop."

I stop trying to escape the plastic tubing.

"You had extreme hypothermia and dehydration. You've been here for three days."

I start to speak, but stop, because I don't know if I can. The last thing I remember is being unable to speak when my tongue felt too big for my mouth.

"You've had saline solution and you should feel much better," Harold interjects into the silence.

"I…" I start, then blow out a breath. "What happened? Where are all the children? Did they make it? Did any of them…"

"You and Freedom got fifty children out of that forsaken place. The children are in various states of medical care at this point. Only one is worse off than you. We expect him to make a full recovery. They have each been taken in by families here. There haven't been as many births as they'd like in the past five years, and they've been asking me questions about it, so this is *good*."

"Freedom?" I ask, licking my dry lips.

"Stitches, iron, and sent to be with his wife."

Something niggles at the back of my consciousness. It's a feeling of dread, growing larger and larger as I try to understand what it is.

"Llama?" I ask.

Harold's jaw clenches. "Not here."

"I have to get her," I say, attempting to stand.

Harold's hand pushes me back down onto the medical cot. "No."

I snarl at him.

"Listen, Reach," Harold says. "You did what you could. I don't know what happened in that mine, but something about the malnutrition of these children and their overall health being so low tells me you pulled them out of a very dangerous place."

I roll my eyes. "Yeah, and I *left* Llama *there*."

"She's an adult, Reach," Herald says in a low voice. "She's not a child."

"I can't leave her there. I have to get her. We have to get her."

Harold meets my eyes with his own brown ones. "You cannot. Not yet, anyway. You are under strict orders to eat a nutritious meal as soon as you awake, and then to report to the advisory room."

"How am I supposed to eat when I left Llama in that mess?"

"I don't know, but I do know that I won't be letting you out of here until you've eaten everything that's about to be on your plate."

Polly pushes through a set of swinging double doors bearing a wooden tray with a wooden bowl of steaming soup and a hunk of buttery bread.

"Eat," Harold says.

I scowl at the tray.

"You can find out everything from *them* when you've eaten," Harold supplies. "You can make a rescue plan when you've *eaten*."

I scarf down everything as fast as I can.

41

Harold disconnects me from the tubes while machines beep and buzz. He flips switches off and shakes my hand as I climb off the bed.

"Good luck, Reach," he says.

I look down at my legs and discover that my clothing is gone and I'm wearing a gown-like robe. It's almost exactly like the clothing Nation provided for me when I was first brought to Hub.

"Harold?" I ask, gesturing to my sock-clad feet.

"Oh, yes," he mutters. He turns to a metal cabinet and opens it, retrieving a long sleeve undershirt, black pants, and a black knit sweater with buttons and pockets at the hip.

"This should be your size," Harold says.

"But what about the clothes I was wearing? What about what was in my pocket?"

"This?" Harold asks, pulling the skeleton key and the black data stick from a tray next to the cot. The tray holds the disconnected tubes and wrappings. "Where are these from?"

I shrug. "Mars."

Harold quirks a brow. "Why would that matter here?"

"A memento, I guess," I mutter, unsure how to explain keys and an illegal Pandora's code box that I was given by a Jezero colonist and the king.

"Sentimentality isn't something we valued much on Mars."

I smirk. "No, it wasn't."

I pocket the data stick and key before I stride away from Harold, pushing through the swinging doors and into the wooden hall. Placards on the wall tell me that I'm on the fifth floor. I don't know if anyone will be there when I get there, but I head to the stairs and down to the second floor. Sigma and Enigma have questions to answer.

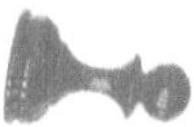

The door to the Advisory Board room is closed. I don't bother knocking. I simply yank it open and experience the discomfort of an entire room of people stopping their conversation and gaping at me.

Freedom sits with his arms crossed over his chest, an empty seat at his side. I stalk to the chair next to him and pull it out with my foot. Insolently, I slump into the chair.

No one says a word, so I break the silence.

"What happened?" I ask, levelling my mother with a glare. "I know you had something to do with this."

"Reach," she says in a gentle voice.

I cut her off. "No," I say, standing and leaning my palms down on the wooden table. "You need to tell me the absolute truth about what happened, because from where I sit, this doesn't look good."

"Ok…" She sighs. "You found out about Dylan?"

I raise a brow at her. I did, but she better admit it.

"Oh, ok." She scrubs a hand down her face. "Dylan is a…spy…for us…and we used him to make you and Llama want to go into the mines. We knew about Llama's relation from your reports and figured we could use that connection to manipulate you into getting the…children out of the mines so that we could make an attack plan. Getting them out has always been the hardest part of the process. We simply couldn't launch a full-scale attack with children in the crossfire."

My eyes narrow. "Why not *tell* us that?"

"Because…your little Llama isn't trustworthy."

I turn to Freedom, incredulous. "Did you know?"

He shakes his head.

"He did not," Mom says. "He has a protective instinct that would have never permitted you to go with him if he thought the mission was to retrieve fifty children and bring them here to safety. By all accounts, that mission shouldn't have worked. Llama and Birdie were most useful as decoys."

"You…" I sneer. "What about Birdie? What about *Llama*?"

"They're adults," Mom replies coldly. "We lose people when we're adults, Reach."

I blink in surprise at the venom in her voice. I open my mouth to say something, but it's Freedom who speaks first. I glance around the room, at the members of the Advisory Board who won't meet my gaze.

"You purposefully risked the lives of people who had no choice in the matter."

Mom shrugs and purses her lips. "I understand you're both upset. You've had an ordeal. But the priority now is the children."

"The children are all *here*," I grind through my teeth. "The priority now is getting Llama and Birdie out of there."

"No," Mom says. "The priority is determining how we can infiltrate the mines and take the copper ore. Once we've done that, *then* we have the technology components that will allow us to create and program our own NSBs."

"Is that the plan?" Freedom asks. "Has that *always* been the plan?" He looks around the table at the rest of the advisors. None of them meet his eyes. None of them except Enigma. "How long has *this* been the plan?" Freedom stands and slams his palm on the wooden table. Everyone jumps.

"It's always been the plan," Mom replies.

Freedom's jaw goes slack. "I've been here since *before* you."

"Seniority doesn't mean time *here*. It means knowledge of the systems. I happen to know more about Nation than most given my unique past."

"You mean you were a puppet for them for longer," I state.

Mom quirks one brow at me. "You are out of line."

"No more than you," I retort.

"That's enough!" she snaps. "You and Freedom are dismissed. I will *not* be insisting on discipline at this time because of what you endured. However, your services to the Advisory Board are no longer required."

Freedom pushes back his chair and stares at Sigma. I can no longer think of her as my mother. She's Sigma, leader of the Resistance, cold, heartless, and with ambitions of power.

I follow Freedom's lead. He keeps his head held high as he strides to the door, and I mimic his posture.

When I'm through the door and standing in the hallway, he kicks the door shut with a loud bang before he clenches his jaw, and after meeting my eyes for a moment, strides away down the hall with long, purposeful steps.

I don't know what he's doing, or where he's going, but I follow.

We navigate to a back set of stairs I haven't seen, down them, out into the snowy courtyard, and to a triangular-shaped wooden building nestled into a stand of pines. Smoke curls out of the chimney and floats on the brisk air.

Freedom pushes open the door and gestures for me to go inside.

I duck into the doorway, and my eyes adjust to the dimness in the cabin.

"Freedom?" Hero asks, then blinks at me. "Reach?"

Freedom says nothing. He simply walks up to Hero and wraps his arm around her waist, then kisses her. It's a lengthy kiss, and I turn away.

I take in the space of their unionized home. It's clean and neat, with a fire roaring in a stone hearth, wooden floors, a set of stairs up to a balcony that houses a neatly made bed, and a table and chairs across from the fireplace. There's a counter with a row of cabinets, and a sink under a window. Metal pans hang on hooks from a rack above the counter, and dried herbs are balanced on the top of the rack. A large metal pot hangs from a hook in the fire, and a tantalizing aroma pours out of it as it sizzles and hisses above the coals. Still, when I turn to the couple, they aren't done with their embrace. I start to leave them to their private moment when Hero calls out softly, "Reach."

I turn back to her and find concern drawn on her face. "What happened?"

Freedom swallows, then launches into the explanation of the manipulative tactics of Sigma.

"The kids were the mission?" Hero asks. "But why lie about it?"

"She said I wouldn't have gone if I'd known."

"But…but that doesn't make any sense. You would have gone. You would have insisted. Reach would have too."

Freedom blows out a breath. A piece of hair bobs off his forehead in the stream of air. "We have to talk," he says as he wraps his foot around a wooden chair and pulls it out from the table. He sinks into the chair, places his elbows on his knees, and drops his head into his hands.

Hero leans down and wraps her arm around his neck. He adjusts his posture and pulls her down into his lap. She searches his eyes, and it seems some silent communication passes between them before she nods once, then gets up and pulls out a chair for me. She points to the chair, and I follow the direction, because Freedom and Hero are the closest thing I have to my life *before* now that I no longer trust Sigma.

I was a fool to ever trust her.

"We can't let her be in control any longer," Freedom whispers.

"She's dangerous to the Resistance. I know she hates Nation, but she's…" He grimaces, but then meets my eyes. "She's like them."

I nod. "Yes," I say, and that one word holds an ocean of meaning.

Freedom and Hero both visibly relax for a moment before Hero speaks. "We thought it would be…positive to be here. We thought that under *her* leadership, we would make progress. But all we've made is…"

"Lies," I interject. "Half truths, which are no truths at all. I don't trust her either. I didn't know."

"How could you have?" Hero says in a quiet, low voice. "You've been on *Mars*."

Freedom narrows his eyes, then widens them again. "Martians."

"Well, not really," I say. "There is some genetic disparity between Earth and Mars humans, but that's more due to biological processes of adaptations…"

Freedom stares at me. "No," he says, shaking his head. "The Martians. Your Martians. They're the key here."

At the word *key*, my hand drifts to the key and data stick in my pocket. I extract them both, letting the cold metal bite into my hand. "What do you mean?" I ask, holding them out.

Hero leans closer to my hand, studying the skeleton key and shiny black stick as it gleams in the light.

"I mean," Freedom says in a voice that is deathly calm, "that the Martians you brought are enough to stage a coup. We can get control of this Resistance and actually take down Nation. I'm not going to sit back and watch while Sigma creates a *new* Nation with the same technologies as Nation. What other purpose could NSBs have, other than…to control?"

"What is that, Reach?" Hero murmurs.

"A key," I say. "From Mars." I swallow. "And the NSBs knew what it was."

Their eyes grow wide.

"Do you know what it is?"

"I haven't a clue." My voice catches. "Llama had an idea, though."

"What about that?" Freedom asks, notching his chin toward the data stick.

"Pandora's code box," I whisper.

Freedom's brow furrows. "That exists?"

"On Mars, and now on Earth."

Hero whispers something into Freedom's ear, and they look at me, fixing me with an indecipherable look.

"How do you feel about *mutiny*?" Hero whispers.

42

"Mutiny?" I repeat, unsure I heard the word correctly.

"Mhm," Hero says, bobbing her head slightly.

"She has to go, Reach," Freedom interjects. His voice is low, deep, and something solidly unmoveable is at its core. "She can't lead us here. She's playing the game all wrong."

I nod, because he's right. Sigma might be my birth mother, but she's shown her true colors. She's created an Advisory Board that's an echo chamber, and those who would challenge her ideas and way of thinking are the ones sent on missions shrouded in half truths—which are really lies. I despise when information is omitted. I always have. Maybe from her comfortable chair in the Lodge, she can see a reason to do it, but the fact remains, she is *not* the one risking her life on a mission out of the Resistance territory.

"How do you propose we go about this…" I swallow. "Mutiny?" I know enough to know that mutiny, if it isn't completed, will result in a charge of treason. That's something I'd rather avoid.

"I think," Freedom says, standing and pulling his chair closer to the table, where he places silverware out seemingly at random, "that we have to gather everyone here." He points to a fork at the left edge of the table.

"The border?" Hero asks.

Freedom nods, the muscle in his cheek ticking up as he gives her a small half smile. "And then," he continues, "we need to tell them."

"But what will we tell them?" I ask.

"What they need to know," Freedom responds.

I shake my head. "We will tell them *everything*."

"That will take forever," Hero says softly. "There's no way we can keep them all out without arousing suspicion."

"Then we need to find a way to tell them the entire truth, with all the information about what we need, and what we're going to do, and why."

Hero bites her lip for a moment. "What if…" she murmurs before shaking her head and saying, "No, that's too obvious."

Freedom and I look at her, each of us pinning her with our gaze.

"What if you told the Advisory Board you needed to conduct training to regain fitness after your time in space?"

I blink. "They'll want to see it."

Freedom shrugs. "Maybe not. The Advisory Board and Sigma don't have the most hands-on approach to the fitness regimens here, but even if they did want to watch—at first, we have to get the information to the crew. Then, once they understand, we can act."

"You know this is treason," I whisper. "And you two made promises to help the Resistance and *not* betray it."

"We're *not* betraying the Resistance," Freedom says, an iron cord in his voice. "We *are the Resistance*. We're the ones resisting tyranny that has found its way into the Resistance in the form of poor leadership."

"Ok," I mutter. "But what happens if you get caught?"

Freedom and Hero look at each other for a moment as some wordless communication passes between them. Hero is the one who turns to me, places her palm softly on my shoulder, and says, "We die, but we'll be free."

The stakes are life and death, but the stakes are also freedom and tyranny.

"Ok," I say. "What should the plan be? How should I approach the fitness regimen with the Advisory Board?"

"Let's figure that out while we eat." Hero walks to the pot hanging over the fire and ladles something into three bowls. She places them in front of Freedom, me, and then sinks into a chair with her own bowl in her hands.

Freedom raises the bowl to his lips and sips. I do the same, letting the warmth of something cooked with love fill my stomach for the first time in months.

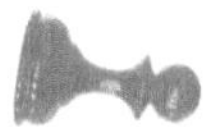

Unlike my mother, her Advisory Board, and her spy, I'm not a great actor, but as I walk down the slippery polished wooden hallway of the Lodge, I continue to tell myself, *I have to do this for Llama.* There is some truth to the move we're making on the metaphorical chessboard. I am unsure if Sigma will see it.

It's possible that, without someone to play with regularly, she's lost her ability to read the game theory. It's also entirely possible that she's smart enough to know exactly what we're doing. It's a risk I have to take, because she has no interest in rescuing Llama and Birdie from the mines, or sparing resources to do so—not unless she's certain she can get the same rare Earth materials that Nation is extracting, and for the same purpose.

I will my heartbeat to slow, take deep breaths, and knock on an imposing wooden door. It's the door Freedom told me leads to Sigma's rooms. Part of this plan hinges on our relationship as mother and son, but in my own head, she's not Mom any longer. She's Sigma, ruthless leader with ambition who doesn't care that she sent me and the woman I love on a mission where we risked our lives, and didn't even know what for. The most frustrating thing about this is that had *we* known the mission was removing children from Nation's inadequate and unfeeling care, the three of us would have gone anyway. We would have prepared differently, but we would have done it.

Sigma might be my mother, but she doesn't *know* me.

The wooden door is larger and taller than the other doors in the main Lodge building. When it swings open, I am met by a wide room made of the same honeyed plank wood as the rest of the Lodge, but this room has brightly colored rugs scattered on the floor, and an entire wall of windows at the back. It's laid out almost exactly the same as Hero and Freedom's cabin, but just larger. Stairs lead to a balcony above, while several smaller, normal-sized doors lead to rooms unknown along a hallway.

Sigma looks at me from around the edge of the door. "Reach." She gestures for me to enter. After she shuts the door, she walks to a dark blue sofa in front of the windows and sinks onto it.

"M-mom," I say, stumbling over the title.

She tips her head and studies me through narrowed eyes. "What is it?" she asks. "Is it about that girl?"

My eyes widen. "Llama or Birdie?" I quip from where I stand next to the door.

"So Llama, then."

"How could you leave her there? How could you have not told us the truth about what we were doing? We would have gone anyway. It would have looked different. It was careless."

She blows out a breath. "Reach, sometimes people have to make decisions for the greater good. We got the children out. That was the mission, and Freedom would have refused had he known how unlikely it was to happen. The best way to achieve the objective was to pretend it was a mission for something else. And Llama has already betrayed you. I don't trust her."

"But I *do*," I hiss. "I *trust her*. You made a decision, knowing she was the expendable part of your plan, and you didn't even give us a chance to understand what the objective was. We're playing chess *blind* with you, Mom."

"Chess." She laughs, and it's mirthless. There's irony in it, and it's unkind.

"I'm going to go back, Mom. I have to get her. I can't leave her there."

"You already did."

"I…" I start, then sputter, "I did."

"What do you need, Reach?" she says, her voice low. "What do you *really* want?"

"I need to gather all the Martians and start an exercise regimen. We lost muscle mass in space."

"And what is the purpose of that?"

"You said we have to fight. You said we got the children out, and now we can fight Nation. Well, the Martians aren't ready to fight, but they will be."

"Interesting," Mom muses. "And what do you want me to do about this need to train?"

"Provide the space, time, and equipment for a training regimen."

Mom plants her hands on her knees. "Done." She extracts a rectangle from her pocket and begins sliding her finger over a glass screen, moving brightly colored squares into different spaces. "You can begin training with them this evening. The bunk room won't suffice, but the grounds are open after seven."

"I…" I stutter. "Thank you?"

"Good. Is that all?" she asks.

"Uhh. Yes?"

"And Reach." She smirks. "I know what you're up to. You can't win against Nation. I look forward to watching you try, though. All that time on Mars must have messed with your psychological awareness. You have to beat them at their own game, Reach, not at the one you've constructed for yourself with careful rules and strict boundaries. They don't have boundaries, so you shouldn't either."

The taste of bile permeates my mouth, and I fix her with a look. "What will prevent you from becoming a monster if you play by the same rules as monsters?"

Mom's face falls, but then she straightens, and a mask drops over her features. "Trust," she whispers.

And there is no way I can say the words that form on my lips, but it doesn't keep me from thinking, *You broke my trust the moment you decided people are expendable.*

43

Heat floods my cheeks as I walk through the door, leaving Sigma's rooms behind. She's playing chess, and she's playing it all wrong. I keep going down the hall, down the stairs, and eventually down into the Martian bunk room. The frigid air cools my flushed skin, and I'm grateful for how cold it is down here.

Everyone is long since awake from their initial rest and has been made to feel at home in the Resistance. Still, I don't know where everyone has found themselves. My part in this coup is to gather the Martians and to explain to them that we are now fighting a smaller version of the same enemy we came here to topple. It's not a conversation I'm looking forward to having.

I look around and spy a black marker on a table with a chart noting the beds and tiny x's marked over each bed. Small notes are written in the marker next to each bed. I squint and find that the notes are times. While we were all sleeping after our Mars-to-Earth sojourn, the members of the Resistance did care for us. They provided us with shelter, food, and someone noted the times each person woke and left their bed.

Involuntarily, my eyes track to the rectangle above the one I know to be my own bed. Llama's time, a few minutes before my own, gives my heart a pang. She's been left in the mines with nothing but Birdie and Dylan to help her for forty hours now. My stomach drops, and I can't take it anymore. I won't lose her. I can't.

In frustration, I uncap the marker and write in bold letters on the wall.

"Training outside tonight. Seven p.m."

I recap the marker and then stare at the words I wrote. The timestamp on the wall bothers me. Even though it's written in black, it looks like blood. I have Llama's blood on my hands. She's alone. I left her. I swore I'd come back. I swore I'd always come back, and *I left her.*

Unable to take it anymore, I sink to the ground, wrap my arms around my knees, and let my tears fall. They only come for a moment because, suddenly, I know what I need to do.

Seven p.m. might be the time training begins, but I won't be there. No one can stop me.

I see the tall cabinets along the back wall of the bunk room, and since no one is watching, I wrench the doors open. Inside the cabinets are water bottles, dried packets of food, and other supplies. It's clear that this space was an emergency bunker area before it was converted into our Martian bunk room.

Now that I've been in the mines, and now that I understand a little about how they're structured, I can do this. I can get her. I will bring her back.

It's reckless, but I don't care. I promised. I can't leave her.

A backpack hangs in one of the cabinets. I yank it off the hook, and it falls to the floor with a thud. Rolls of medical bandages spill onto the floor. I sink to my knees and open the pockets, finding that this bag is packed with medical supplies, tourniquets, bandages, and some sort of antibacterial cream in a white tube. I won't need all of these, so I reach my hands into the pockets and extract most of the contents. I toss the unneeded materials back onto the shelves, careless of organization, and then proceed to shove packages of dried food and containers of sealed water into the bag. When I pick up the bag, it's significantly heavier than before, but the weight is manageable. This is *more* than we had with us when we were sent to the mines the first time.

The last thing I need is winter gear. There's one cabinet left that I haven't opened. I twist the lever, and the door springs open, revealing nothing but blankets. Though blankets will help, they won't be enough. I need actual winter exploration gear to do this, and I'll need gear for Llama and Birdie too. There's only a few people I can think of who would know where the gear is stowed, and I know that if I ask Freedom, he'll insist he come too. But he can't. I can't ask Hero because she'll tell Freedom.

The only person I might be able to find this information from without arousing suspicion is Polly. I shove the backpack into its original place on the hook in the cabinet and shut the doors, making it look as if I didn't just raid the shelves.

Anticipation courses through my body, rushing through my veins like bubbles in a boiling pot, but I tighten my muscles and try not to let it show. I have to maintain a calm, collected, and cool façade. No one can know what I'm planning. They'll try to stop me.

I leave the bunk room and climb the wooden stairs to the main floor. The large room where we eat has several doors off of the width side of the rectangle. When it comes to finding out where Polly is, the kitchen seems like the best place to start. I have found that if you putter around long enough in a kitchen, someone will come to your aid. In this case, if it can't be Polly herself, someone who knows where she is will help.

I blow out a breath before I push on one of three wooden doors tucked into the back wall of the long room. My eyes take a moment to adjust before I understand that this room is a pantry. Braided onions hang on the wall, bundles of herbs hang from racks on the ceiling. Pumpkins, potatoes, and squashes are stacked neatly in piles, but when I look closer, they are actually stacked on woven mats. The room is dusty, and I can't help but sneeze.

"Can I help you?" a voice sounds from behind a pile of orange and green pumpkins. I can't place the voice, but it's familiar.

"Uh, yes?" I respond.

"What do you need?"

"I'm looking for Polly."

"Oh." The voice sounds louder, and suddenly blond hair appears in the dim lighting.

"Declan?" I say, surprised.

"Hi, Reach," he says. "What are you doing looking for Polly? She's a kid, so she's at school."

"There's a school here?" I ask.

"Yeah. Do you want to see it?"

"Will Polly be there?"

"Why do you want to find Polly?"

"I need help finding something."

"What?" Declan asks.

I inhale, trying to ease the mounting frustration building in my body. "I need to find the extra winter gear."

"Why?"

I close my eyes. Declan is asking too many questions, and if anyone can figure out what I'm doing, it's him. He's the only person who's beaten me in chess since my mom did when I was fourteen. "I…left my coat in the mines and I need another one."

"Are you going back?"

I try not to meet his eyes, but he stares so earnestly at me that I can't lie to him. "I…am." I swallow. "I have to bring her back."

"Princess Llama?" Declan asks, his eyes huge and his mouth curved into a frown deeper than the Jezero crater. "She's not *here*?"

I nod.

"How did that happen?"

I sigh. "It's a long story. Freedom will explain more next time you see him, but I can't leave her there. She's in danger. The NSBs—"

"What's an NSB?"

"Near Sentient Being." I inhale, trying to gather courage "They are Nation's puppets. They have an Achilles' heel, though."

"But they're artificial, so their muscular system wouldn't matter," Declan interjects.

I shake my head. "No, the back of their necks, under the zipper, can't get wet."

Declan tips his head to the right slightly and narrows his eyes. "It's a metaphor? And you're going alone, aren't you." It's not a question.

I swallow and don't look at him. "I have to get her. And in order to get her, I need winter gear."

"I can help," he whispers. "But you can't go by yourself. That's bad game theory."

"Yeah," I snarl, annoyed. "But it was terrible game theory when Sigma sent us on a mission with parameters that were a lie and *knew* that, under the actual parameters of the mission, Llama and Birdie would be expendable."

"Who's Birdie?"

I groan. "She's like Pippa. And Nation uses her the way they use people. Like they're things destined to be thrown into the trash after they are no longer useful to their purpose."

"Princess Llama…is with someone like Princess Pippa?" Declan's eyes bug out even more. "And Sigma knew? But isn't she in charge here? Isn't she the leader? Doesn't that mean—" He stops abruptly and shakes his head. "She's as bad as what we were sent to destroy."

I nod, because he gets it. Somehow, Declan understands game theory more innately than anyone I've ever met.

"You can't go alone," he insists.

I fix him with a hard stare. "I have to."

"I'll come too," he says, trying to match my glare with his own.

"Declan," I whisper. "I need you to help the rest of the Martians understand the game theory. There's a training session. Freedom will be leading it."

"Freedom doesn't know?" Declan asks.

I clench my teeth and nod. "I need to go as soon as possible. And I can't bring anyone with me, because everyone else is needed *here*. I *need* you to help them understand the game theory. They won't get it."

Declan frowns but nods. "What time is the training?"

"Seven p.m."

"And Freedom won't know you've gone until…?" He leaves his question open-ended, and I close my eyes before I answer.

"Until you tell him."

44

DECLAN LEADS ME through the Lodge. "After we got here, they put me on inventory duty. I wanted to help in the greenhouses, but they thought that Martian hydroponics and Earth-growing plants would be too big a learning curve."

I resist the urge to snort. "So you've learned about what the Resistance has on hand."

"Mostly I've learned about the food the Resistance stores from their greenhouses, but I also helped with outfitting Wave Cohort 1. I was one of the first ones to wake up after everything."

"What is everyone else doing?"

"Harold is in the medical bay."

"I knew that."

"They've found places where everyone helps. Some people clean, some people will go on Freedom's border patrols when they're cleared, some people cook. Jonas helps with COMs. You and Princess Llama were the only ones not given specific tasks."

I hum a response as we tread down the long wooden hallway.

Declan knocks once on a closed door. No one answers. "They keep everything in here," he whispers as he looks from side to side. "We need to look like we're supposed to be here."

"I think it's fair that I need a coat," I grumble.

Declan tries the door, and it swings open into an oddly shaped room. It must be tucked under the eaves of the roof, because the room is not square. A single window along the back is half covered by beams and insulation, but lets in just enough light to see. Wooden shelves run the perimeter of the room and also jut out from the walls at regular intervals. The bottom row of shelving holds boots, the one above it socks, the one above that under layers, and the one above that sweaters. The very top row holds hats and gloves.

"Where are the coats?" I ask, scanning the room.

Declan grins and kicks the door shut behind us. "They keep those in a special place. I only know because I had to help get them out for the Martians who were given outdoor duties." He tips his head and jerks his thumb over his shoulder. "This way." He approaches the perimeter shelving and then yanks on one of the shelf supports.

My jaw drops as the shelving opens, revealing a hidden door.

"Clever, right?" Declan says as he crouches under the beam of a low doorway and steps through.

I follow him.

"Why would they keep all the coats and winter gear in here?" I ask as I take in the secret room. It's wooden, with a low ceiling, a single motion sensor light that flicked on when we stepped in, and hanging off a single metal bar running the perimeter of the room are hundreds of winter coats.

"Because they don't want people to leave unless it's sanctioned," Declan drawls.

My eyebrows knit together. That does make sense.

"It's a way to protect the Resistance. Also, they keep coats on hand for the people who escape and end up here. I think this is your size." He walks over to a black coat with quilt lines running through it. It's short, only hitting about my hip.

"No," I say. "I want a longer one. It's too cold out there."

Declan shakes his head again. "You won't want a longer one. You want a pair of insulated over-pants."

He moves around the room to the opposite corner and extracts a pair of black pants. They are slippery, puffy, have fitted cuffs at the bottom, and an elastic waistband. "These will keep your clothes dry underneath."

"Thanks," I say, taking the coat and the pants from Declan.

"And this time," Declan says quietly, "don't take the outerwear into the mines. Leave it somewhere safe. You'll be cold for a bit, but you can at least put it on when you come back out." He starts to turn, but then asks, "What about Llama and Birdie? They'll need clothing too."

I nod.

"What sizes?"

I can't do anything but shrug. "Llama is smaller than I am, but I don't know much about Birdie except she's tall and thin. Most people in the mines are thin."

Declan considers this for a moment before he selects two coats from the bar. "These might work. And if they're too big, that's better than if they're too small." He surveys my face as we stand in the flickering overhead light and it casts shadows over us. "Do you have everything else you need?"

I nod again.

"Then you need to go before they realize you're missing." He crouches down and steps back through the low door into the clothing storage room. When I'm through, the motion sensor light flickers off, and Declan pushes the secret door back into position. "I'll go first." He gestures to the door out into the hallway. "You'll have to get out of here without anyone noticing you carrying all that stuff."

"I have a plan."

"Good," he says, and though he's a few years younger than me, and it's his first time on Earth, he has an understanding of how things work politically that can't be learned. He opens the door and steps boldly into the hallway. With bated breath, I wait for something to happen. A noise, a sound, a signal. Nothing comes.

Clutching a pile of winter gear that nearly eliminates my sightline, I step through the door and into the hall.

Footsteps sound around a corner, and I can't tell if it's Declan or someone else. I don't know what the rules are exactly, but I took winter gear that the Resistance goes through great lengths to keep locked away.

I walk as purposefully as I can from the storage room.

It gets dark early here, and for that I'm grateful. Still, I can't wait any longer. Llama has been on her own in the Rare Earth III mine for two days, and it will take me hours to cross the twelve miles on my own. I don't have a good plan, but I have enough determination and enough disregard for my own personal safety to do something.

I'll get Llama, and I'll get Birdie too. I'll show Sigma that she's wrong.

The sun isn't high overhead; it's sinking lower to the west when I set out. The Resistance is organized in such a way that people do their jobs, and their jobs keep them busy. No one idles, unless it's specifically sanctioned.

Half of what I had to do to leave the Lodge undetected was simply look purposeful as I left. The other half was to prepare. Wearing my winter gear and slipping the black backpack I repurposed from the bunk room over my shoulders, I slide into the copse of trees on the side of the Lodge with the fewest windows.

Shadows play across the snow covering the ground. My tracks will be visible, but I'll worry about that later. I can't worry about making everything perfect, not when Llama was left in the mines. Under cover, I turn and look back at the Lodge. I don't know what will happen with Freedom and the training session, or how long I'll be gone, or what the Resistance will look like when I return, but I know this: I'll have Llama with me, or I'll die trying to get her out of there.

A flicker of movement at one of the windows tucked into a low eave draws my attention. I narrow my eyes and, squinting, make out someone standing at the window. *Sigma.*

She locks eyes with me, but I tell myself, *She can't see me, I'm in the trees.*

When I start to turn, she raises her hand slightly, and it's almost as if she's giving me a wave.

Dread fills me as if a lead ball was dropped into my stomach.

Questions swirl through my mind. *Did she see me? Was she talking to someone? Was she simply looking out the window and fixing her eyes on a point near me? Am I being worried for nothing?*

I slip deeper into the trees, further from the Lodge, and take a shaky breath. No matter what happens here, Llama needs me.

It's that thought that drives each of my steps through the pines, and eventually over the rise at the edge of the Resistance borders.

I don't know how I'll get to Llama, but as I slink on my stomach in the snow, my head peeking over the rise to observe the pit yard of the mine, I notice something different about the area.

Where before there were NSBs in shiny metallic silver suits, now there are NSBs, but also interspersed among the miners in dirty, faded yellow clothing are people who are neither miners, nor NSBs. These people wear winter-appropriate gear. One in particular stands out because they are surrounded by a group of NSBs.

I slip my hand into the backpack and extract a pair of binoculars for a better look. The cold nips at my fingers as I use my teeth to tug off the glove on my left hand. I place the binoculars to my eyes and toggle the lens to zoom in.

What I see makes my heart plummet.

That person, standing in the middle of a group of NSBs, is Enforce.

The same Enforce with a lifelong vendetta against Llama.

My Llama.

And Llama is *in* that mine.

There is no doubt in my mind that if Enforce gets her hands on Llama, she will kill her.

45

THE YELLOW-CLAD miners deposit rocks into a pile in the pit. They keep their heads down and don't make eye contact with anyone. Not each other, not the NSBs, and definitely not Enforce or her people.

An air of doom has settled over the mine, and it's heavier than it was the last time I was here. The miners shuffle along at a slow pace. Unusually slow. And that's when I see it. The miners have shackles around their ankles.

In frustration, I bite my tongue, and a metallic taste of blood fills my mouth.

How will I get Llama out without a key?

And then, like lightning, I realize that this is a trap.

The key.

The key the NSBs wanted was so important that they purposefully deteriorated conditions in the mine because they knew the Resistance would come back, and they *know* that the Resistance has a key of some significance. My eyes slide back and forth across the pit yard as I mentally calculate the game theory of what Nation is doing.

Enforce is here, but I don't see Leader, Legislate, or Litigate. Although, the Three Powers rarely do any actual work.

I try to pick out Llama, but she's not in the pit yard. That thought both soothes and worries me. If she's deep in the mines, maybe she's hidden from Enforce. But also, if she's deep in the mines, how will I be able to find her? How will I be able to get her out?

Declan was right—this was a terrible idea. Still, I can't leave her.

Despite the freezing temperatures, beads of sweat gather on my brow. When one falls into the snow, it leaves a small indent in the structure of the crystal.

A whistle blows, low and mournful, and the NSBs straighten and begin to march toward the miners. The miners drop everything they were carrying, turn and walk as fast away from the NSBs as they can. They disappear into the mouth of the mine structure, with the NSBs herding them in.

Enforce and several of her cronies approach the pile of rubble while the NSBs stand side by side, their backs to the building structure, so close to each other they make a sort of wall. It's impossible to penetrate it. Enforce removes one of her gloves, reaches into her pocket, and extracts something small and black that fits in her palm. She waves it around the pile of rubble, and I catch the glint of her rings in the bright lights of the pit yard.

"Useless," Enforce calls, and in the cold, snowy air, it lifts up, vibrating around the pit yard and floating away on the breeze. Her voice. It has always sounded like a lead pipe was wrapped in velvet, but now, it sounds heavier, deeper, darker. "This is useless."

She marches toward an NSB and shoves it aside. It falls to the ground, cracking its head. The NSBs stand still as their comrade is knocked to the ground. And though I know it's not human, watching it fall, seeing the humanlike attributes hit the hard ground and lie still, *is* entirely too close to witnessing a death.

Enforce disappears into the mine, and her people follow, all ten of them.

The lights flick off, and the pit yard is thrust into darkness. It takes several minutes for my eyes to adjust to the new lighting, but they do, and when I find I can see again, I make out the barest flicker of movement in the yard. It's closer to me than the pile in the middle, about where the garbage pile is. A creak tells me that I'm right. Someone is coming out of the garbage chute.

I start to head down the hill but remember Declan's words about the winter gear. It will only slow me in the mines. Yes, I'll be cold, but I have to think strategically. I have to play this like I would a chess game. It takes a few moments, but I divest myself of the winter gear. I need it to stay easily accessible, but also hidden. The pine trees to the edge of the field are ideal, but I don't have time to go back and forth between them. And I already stashed my backpack there. I don't want to risk someone discovering both sets of materials. It's a riddle, and when I think about it, it's one that's easily solved.

Quickly, I dig a burrow into the snow and shove my winter gear inside it. The snow will keep the temperature of the clothing consistent, and the winter gear will repel water because of the fabric. When I'm done shoving it inside the burrow, I cover it with more snow, creating a small mound that doesn't look out of place. It looks like an ordinary snowdrift. This is both good and bad. Good because it won't arouse suspicion in anyone who passes, and bad because I need to find this again.

I gulp down the thought *I hope.*

I don't have much to work with to mark the pile, but I do have my own body. With my right hand, I yank a piece of short hair off my head and stick it into the pile. It's dark, and it stands out against the snow, but to anyone passing, it could belong to an animal.

With nothing more than my regular clothing, a key that Nation and the NSBs clearly want, an illegal Pandora's code box, and my own mind, I slip over the edge of the pit yard and slide down the side. I hope that whoever is at that garbage chute is a friend, but the reality of them being a foe is higher. With that uncomforting thought, I sneak closer to the grate and prepare myself for a physical altercation.

"Who's there?" hisses a low voice as I crouch next to the garbage pile. It's rotten, and despite the fact that the weather is freezing and I can't feel my fingers anymore, the pile smells, and lazy flies buzz around it. Decomposition at its finest.

"Who are you? What do you want?" the low voice growls.

I don't respond. I edge my way around the pile and fix the person in my line of sight. It's a miner, but they don't wear the yellow coat. They have on a silver bodysuit, like the NSBs wear. I can tell it's a miner because of his facial hair. It's a long beard that's tucked into the high collar of the silver suit.

"I need to get in," I say, and the miner's head swivels toward my own low, deep voice.

"You want to get in?" he says. The moon peeks out from behind cloud cover, and I get a glimpse of his narrowed eyes.

"Yes."

"Why?" he challenges.

"Because someone I care about is in there."

"The girl?" he asks, one eyebrow rising.

"What girl?" I growl.

"The one who appeared. You were with her, weren't you? And you left her here?"

My hands curl into fists at my side. The skepticism in his voice is derisive, and I can't deal with this stranger's decision to point out my faults to me.

"Well, we got the children away, or have you not noticed?"

"You took the kids? I had heard they were gone, but they don't let us see them, ever."

I cross my arms over my chest and stare at him. "Can I get in, and can you take me to her?"

The man nods vigorously, and a strand of his beard comes loose from the NSB suit. "You're the Resistance?"

I gulp. I could say the truth, but I could also let him think what he believes. He has some trust in the Resistance because we got the children out of here, and explaining that I'm rogue from the Resistance because the leader of that group is my mother who I no longer trust is a long story that won't help me. Instead, I point to the grate. "I need to get to her. Is she ok?"

The man shakes his head and looks at his feet. "No. Birdie was trying to protect her, but she's not used to being in the dark for twenty hours or more a day the way Birdie is."

"Where is she?" I whisper.

"I can take you to her," he says, his eyes full of some unidentifiable emotion. "This way." He deposits something round and gold on the garbage pile. He adjusts it to stand at a specific angle before he gives one nod at it and strides toward the grate covering the chute.

He pulls it open and hops into the chute. "We have to be quiet," he says in a voice lower than a whisper. "The NSBs are looking for people to punish. They're confused by my clothing, but they will know you're not one of them if they see you."

I nod to show my understanding, and as the man starts to crawl along the tube, I follow. I swing myself up and grab the cover as I climb in. It doesn't seem particularly secure, but it's enough to stop suspicion by the NSBs and Enforce and her crew that this area is being used by the Resistance.

The man shimmies and slides up the chute until he twists into a different tunnel. "Ducts," he whispers.

Again, I don't say anything.

He crawls along, and this time we're going down.

When he veers sharply off to the left at a duct junction, I lose my bearings. At least six shafts connect in this junction, and I can't see which way he went. I try to follow a flash of silver, but that's no use in the silver ducts. With no way to follow him, I am completely lost.

I also can't call out for him because, as the man said outside, I have to be quiet. I can't risk alerting Enforce and the NSBs to my presence.

A small whimper sounds through the ducts. It's pitiful, but something about it tugs at my heart. It's impulsive, but I follow the sound.

I listen carefully every few feet, and even though the ducts echo, I'm confident I'm headed in the right direction. The duct tubing turns sharply, and I bump into the man from before. "She's there." He points through a vent in the wall.

I look, and there's Llama, in dirty clothes, with streaks of dirt and grease on her face, and rubble in her hair. She sits on the white tile floor in a plain white room with no windows. There must be a door, but I can't see it—the entire room is a continuous box. The fluorescent lights are on full force, even though it's night. Her knees are tucked up under her arms, and she shakes.

It does not take a genius to know that *they* have done something to her.

"What have they done?" I ask, my jaw dropping.

The man shakes his head. "She'll have to tell you. I don't know. I know that they found her. Birdie's over here." He gestures to me, and I reluctantly leave the vent where I can see Llama to follow him. It's only a few more feet, and I stop at a similar grate. Birdie is humming slightly from where she lies in an identical room, curled up on the dirty tile floor.

"Can we get them out?" I whisper.

He shakes his head and gestures to Birdie's feet. They're looped in the same shackles the people wore out in the pit yard. "Not unless you have the key for that," he says under his breath.

I swallow, because it's obvious to me that I do. That key. It's the one that unlocks the shackles. I also have no doubt that Enforce is alerted when someone tries to manually override them.

I think for a moment, then ask the man, "Will you help me?"

The man nods, and I point to the vent grate. "I'm going to get Birdie out first. Can you take her through the ducts back the way we came?"

"What about everyone else?"

I bite my lip. "We'll come back. But you have to get everyone ready. We can't get everyone out right now, but the Resistance will come back. As soon as we can."

He rolls his eyes in the dim, but pulls a tool from his silver pocket and runs it over the edges of the vent. "It's magnetic," he says. "This depolarizes it."

He slides the vent cover away and motions me toward the empty space. It's small, maybe only four feet long and three feet wide, but it's enough that I can squeeze my body through. As quietly as I can, I drop to the white tile floor.

Birdie startles and pops up. She rubs her eyes with grimy fists and sings. "You came back, you came back, you came back."

I shake my head, but hold one finger to my lips to quiet her. Birdie stands and shuffles toward me, her shackles clanking against the tile. She moves decently in them, but they do make noise. Crouching down, I study the metal, but I don't dare touch it. About a foot of chain link metal connects two metal cuffs locked around her ankles. The chain length is enough that a person can move, but short enough that it's not easy.

"Don't touch," Birdie says, pointing at the chains. "Don't touch."

An idea takes hold. "Birdie," I whisper. "Can you crawl with those on?"

She drops to her knees and starts to crawl. "Yes, yes," she sing-songs. "I'm very good at crawling!"

"I'm going to pick you up and you're going to crawl through that vent. There's a man who will help you waiting, ok?"

Birdie smiles.

"But you can't sing in these tunnels," I admonish.

"Why?"

"The NSBs."

Birdie pales, and it's obvious even under all the dirt and dust covering her face.

Silent except for the clank of the metal chains hitting the ground as she walks toward the vent, I pick her up and hoist her to the man's extended hands. He pulls her through, and I have a moment of relief when I see that she's out of there.

I'm grateful for Lift and his determination that I master the pull-up exercise because even though I lost muscle mass in space, muscle memory is real. I'm able to jump, grasp the inside of the vent, and pull myself into the space. It hurts, and my muscles burn, but I slither up into the ducts after a few moments.

My breathing comes heavy, but the man and Birdie stare at me in silence. I tip my head in the direction of Llama's cell, and they press themselves against the far side of the duct as best they can. I still have to crawl over them, and it's awkward, but there's no choice in these tight quarters.

The man passes me the depolarizing tool. I run it over the vent cover and then pass the tool to the man with the beard. I hold up one finger in a 'wait' gesture, and he nods.

I swing my body into the space and slip through the vent into the sterile room where Llama sits.

At the noise of my feet hitting the tile, Llama covers her ears with her hands and tucks her head between her knees.

I approach her slowly and crouch down to be at her level. "Llama?" I whisper, and she looks up sharply. "Llama." I extend a hand. "I'm here for you. I'm going to take you out."

Llama's eyes widen, and she begins shaking violently. Tears cut a path through the grime on her face and I can't help it. I reach out and wipe one away. She startles away from the contact, and her hands fly into a defensive position.

"They will get you," she hisses. "You stupid fool." But even as she says the words, I can see that there is something in her eyes, something that's not quite right.

"I had to come back for you," I say. "But we have to go, now." She curls tighter into herself and sobs wrack her body. "C'mon, Llama," I beg, and I reach out a hand to her. The desire to hug her, to hold her, to protect her is so strong, and yet she won't let me touch her. I don't know what horrors she's experienced, but Enforce doesn't need time to develop and implement a torture regimen.

"B-b-birdie?" Llama asks, setting her jaw.

I smile softly because this is Llama—not broken, not covered in grime, but fiercely protective of those she loves. I point to the vent. "Up there."

She shivers, but then she places her palms on the cold tile floor and pushes herself to stand. "Ok," she whispers, but her eyes scan the room and lock on one specific part of the blank wall. "Ok."

"I'm going to pick you up and help you into the ducts. Ok?"

Llama doesn't respond. Her body steels itself as she looks up at the hole the vent grate usually covers.

I know we don't have much time, and I know I have to get these shackles off both Llama and Birdie immediately. I put my hands on her waist as gently as I can, but she still flinches.

"I'm sorry," I whisper, and I hope she knows that it's for everything.

46

I LIFT LLAMA into the vent, and she slithers into the duct before I take a running start and hoist myself in too. The man points frantically at Birdie's shackles. A small red light blinks in the darkness.

I didn't anticipate the cuffs having trackers on them, but they must. Llama's ankles don't have a red light blinking, which is confusing, but then I see something worse. Llama's cuffs are tightening. The metal loops around her ankle constrict and cut into her flesh.

She clenches her jaw against the pain.

"Llama," I whisper. "They can't tighten past a certain point."

She closes her eyes. "I want them off." She opens them again and meets me with her dilated pupils and a hardness in her gaze. "They get tighter."

"Hurt," Birdie whimpers, pointing at her shackles.

The red light blinks faster and faster, and she swallows before she pulls her shirt into her mouth and clamps down on it.

In a flash of light, a buzz sounds, and Birdie jerks her legs. A small yip escapes her lips and she breathes heavily. Birdie's cuffs issue an electric shock, while Llama's periodically tighten to the point of cutting off her circulation. If I had to guess, the cuffs are designed to do this at irregular intervals, while also doing it more frequently the further they get from the rooms.

The shackles have to go, and now.

I pull the skeleton key from Mars out of my pocket, and since Birdie's cuff is blinking one long, slow red light right now, I take the key and study the manual lock on each of the cuffs. It's going to fit. I can tell. They designed these cuffs *for* this key.

I look at the man who's been helping me. "I don't know your name," I say in a low whisper. "And I don't need to, but this key means something to the NSBs and Enforce, and it came from Mars. I'm going to leave it with you because it's important. I don't know why. But it can get the cuffs off the miners."

The man's brow crinkles. I gesture to the cuffs. "They'll know once I put the key in the cuffs that we're here. We won't have much time before they're onto us. How fast can you get us out?"

The man holds up six fingers. "You can get us out in six minutes?"

He nods, and I blow out a breath before I stick the key into Birdie's shackles. It fits perfectly, and I twist it. The shackle on her left ankle falls off. When I approach the other side, I notice a low hum of electricity. Still, I can do this faster than the build-up of the electric shock.

I work as fast as I can, but my hand slips. A bead of sweat falls off my brow.

A cackle sounds from somewhere deep in the duct system.

"They know," the man says simply. "Our clock is ticking."

I twist the key in the right ankle cuff and it springs open, but not before a massive shock courses through my body. I pull back in surprise and can't help the scream that escapes my lips.

Llama looks at me, her eyes wide.

Gritting my teeth against the pain, wishing I could stop my outburst because I led them right to us, I pull the key from the cuffs that have slid to the duct and turn to Llama's shackles.

I unlock the right one, then the left, and as they fall away, I see what I didn't see before. Tiny spikes inside the cuffs have marred her ankles and lower legs with deep wounds. She looks at the cuffs and then at her legs with wide eyes and lets out a silent scream.

I pass the key to the man, and then I toss both Llama's and Birdie's cuffs into Llama's cell.

"Which way?" I hiss to the man. He gulps as he looks at Llama's ankles, but then starts crawling forward. Birdie has no hesitation about following, but Llama does.

"My blood," she whispers, and I can see that she's leaving a trail.

"I'll go behind you. I'll catch what I can and wipe it onto my pants."

She frowns, then nods. "Ok."

The man leads us through a maze of duct tunnels. Shouts and heavy footsteps ring through the shafts, and I hear Enforce's voice yell out, "They're in the VENTS!" before the man leads us into a different duct junction.

Soon, clanging sounds all around us, and flashes of silver reflect off the metal. The NSBs have wormed their way into the vent systems and we have to get out.

The man keeps going, but suddenly he stops. He gestures for us to hold our noses. He pinches his nose and crawls through the next section of the ductwork, but when we crawl through, my eyes water and burn. I try to breathe through my mouth, but a sticky, scratchy sensation clings to the back of my throat.

Llama coughs before clamping her mouth down on her sleeve.

The man crawls faster, and I try to keep pace, but Llama's slower and losing a lot of blood. My knees are soaked with it.

"Here," the man says. He uses the depolarization tool to remove a vent cover and swings down into a dark room. Birdie slips through the small opening with her lithe body and drops to the ground, surprisingly cat-like. Llama goes next, but she has a harder time. She flips onto her stomach and shimmies backward through the opening. When her legs are through, she grasps my hands, and I help lower her down before she drops to the floor completely. I slide through the hole, landing on my feet.

Llama crouches on the ground. "My ankles," she moans, and I'm helpless to do anything for her.

"Here." The man flips on the light, and as I look around for an escape route, I discover that we're in a room full of NSBs.

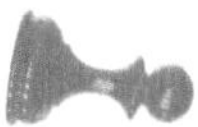

I don't have time to think. I register the NSBs, but then my fist is curled around the man's silver NSB suit, and I growl, "You betrayed us." I lift him off the floor.

His eyes grow wide and he shakes his head from side to side.

"No," he grimaces. "I didn't." He gestures to the NSBs who all have their eyes closed. They don't move, they don't breathe. I lower him to the ground. He glares at me. "These are the broken ones. Put on a suit and be an NSB to get out of here."

I stare at him. He's a genius.

An NSB in the corner is missing a suit. Instead of a flesh-tone body, its body is metal where the suit would cover it.

"Is this where you got that?" I ask, pointing to his suit.

He nods. "They don't have any use for these, except for parts. Since these ones have all been broken in some way or are defective, they shove them in here. There's more every week."

"The Resistance?"

He purses his lips and shakes his head. "The miners." There is a lifetime of anger in the two words. "The Resistance doesn't do much except drop an unsuspecting girl into our midst to be tortured."

It's my turn to grimace.

"Get a suit," he says to me before he turns and starts removing one from the NSB next to the one missing its suit. This one is shorter, indicating that it has a female persona. Because the NSBs are manufactured, the female versions are slightly shorter and the male ones taller. I turn toward a tall NSB, but realize that Llama will have the hardest time getting into a disguise. She's still slumped in the corner, and when I catch her, I spy the sheen of tears running down her cheeks.

The inflexible nature of the NSB makes taking the suit off difficult, but eventually, I slide it down around the ankles. I'm able to lift it enough to pull the suit off its feet.

"Here," I say as I tread softly toward Llama. "You have to put this on."

Llama frowns.

"It's how we're getting out of here. We're going to walk right out."

Her eyes meet mine, and I can see the way she's at war with herself about the idea.

"Do you have a better idea?" I finally ask.

She swallows. "No," she whispers before she takes the suit from my hands.

"Do you need help?"

She shakes her head. "I can't do it."

The man snorts. "We'll do what we can. Put it on as best you can. I'll turn off the light and then, in thirty seconds, you need those suits on because we have to get out of here."

The room plunges into darkness as I slip my outer pants off and stand for a moment in only the black thermal temperature-regulating layer from the Resistance. Even though I'm completely covered, it's strange, and I feel exposed. Clanging sounds in the ducts, and it's coming closer. All I can do is pull the suit up over my body and let the elastic cuffs around the neck, the sleeves, and the ankles conceal my skin. The tall boots are slightly too small, but I accept the pain as my penance for leaving Llama. It's nothing compared to what Llama and Birdie endured.

"This way." The man tucks his beard deeper into the suit. "March like you have a purpose."

He pushes on a panel in the wall and dim light from the mine shaft hallway penetrates the darkness. It's gloomy, but it's still light.

We march into the hallway, me following behind the man, Birdie, and Llama. We're passable as NSBs as long as no one looks at our faces. Our best hope is to blend into the horde that's here because of Enforce and her Punishment and Retribution Department people.

Llama's steps waver with each push of her foot onto the floor, and the fatal flaw in the entire plan is that with every step, blood pools out of her tall boots and splashes on the ground.

47

Llama's steps grow increasingly unsteady. I bite my lip. It's clear she needs support to walk, and it's also clear that as an NSB, I would *not* offer her that. The man keeps his face turned down, watching the floor and not making eye contact with anyone, so we do the same. In the shaft, it's not hard. The few miners we pass ignore us, or spit contemptuously in our direction.

Still, no one gives us much trouble. We stop at a corner of metal scaffolding, and the man reaches into a shadowy corner, extracting a single yellow MINER coat. He slips it on over Llama's shoulders. "This way." He scrunches his eyes closed for a moment, and the wrinkles in his brow could be shadows, or grease, or both. "This is where you have to be an NSB. We're going to go out into the pit yard. We're going to act like we're taking her to a guard station. You'll leave from guard station number three."

I stare at the man, hard in the dim light. "Who are you?" I ask.

He grins and pulls his beard out of his suit before detaching the entire thing. "Dylan," he says.

I blink in surprise. "But you were…"

"I'm a lot of things and a lot of people. Send the Resistance fighters. We're ready."

Llama crumples and I catch her, putting my arms under her armpits and holding her up. "I can't walk," she hisses as her voice catches.

Dylan catches my eye in the gloom. While she leans heavily on me, Dylan and I are able to help her get it on to mostly cover her suit.

Birdie whispers, "They're coming. I hear it."

"What do you mean?" I ask, because the shaft is quiet, and except for the miners we passed, we haven't seen anyone. I still hear the occasional clunking in the vents, but for now, they don't know where we are.

"The music they make," Birdie says. "They sound like music, but they are not music."

Llama breathes heavily. "We need to go. She can hear them. Some sort of mechanical pitch they make."

Dylan stares hard at Birdie. "You never said so," he says accusingly.

"How would she have been able to tell you that?" Llama bites. "We have to go. She always knew when they were coming close."

"Act like she's a prisoner," Dylan hisses, and he grabs one of Llama's arms and starts to haul her toward the mine shaft that slopes upward.

I take Llama's other arm and try to be gentle, but she's putting up a convincing performance and I do have to drag her. I strongly suspect that she can't walk anymore because of both blood loss and pain.

We haul Llama up the slope, Birdie humming a little to herself, but mostly walking behind us. We haven't gone far before the heavy rhythmic thud, thud, thud of footsteps echoes off the stone cavern.

A contingent of ten NSBs approaches us. The dim light glints off their silver suits, and when they see us, they pause.

"Prisoner from deep in the mines," Dylan says in a deep voice that doesn't match his usual timbre. I keep my face turned toward Llama, as if I'm watching the prisoner closely, and not enough for their eyes to take a photograph of my face and send it out for facial recognition technology.

The NSBs blink, but then part and let us walk through the middle of their group.

I blow out a breath once we're past the group and their steady footsteps continue marching away.

"There will be more," Dylan warns. He stops for a moment, grabs a chunk of slick, wet rock from the wall, and rubs it on his hands. "Here." He scrubs both of his hands down my face, leaving a sticky, oily coating on my skin. I can't throw up my hands in protest; I'm the only one supporting Llama. My mouth opens, and some of the debris gets in. It tastes rank.

"There." Dylan nods. "Now you look like you were deep in the mines. And they shouldn't be able to get facial recognition technology when you have so much interference."

"What about Birdie?" Llama asks.

"No one's looking at her," Dylan says. "She's following along like any other NSB would be programmed to. It's Reach and I who have to worry."

Dylan spits on his hands and then rubs them down his face, leaving a trail of dirt, dust, grime, and oil that coats his skin and makes him nearly unrecognizable. That is his forte, though—disguises.

He tosses the chunk of rock back into the shadows where it plinks into water. "I talk when we see NSBs. If anyone asks questions, I talk. Got it?" He fixes me with a stern gaze.

"Yes," I say, because this man is an ally of my mother's, and he's not someone I trust, but he's also leading us out of the mine, knows his way around ventilation systems, and has a far better plan than anything I had come up with.

As we climb out of the shafts and into the upper levels of the mine structure, we pass more NSBs. They don't offer a single complaint. They blink with lifeless eyes, take in our group, and part to make way for us. To them, we are their comrades, and we are doing our duty by removing a miner prisoner from deep within.

The noise of activity grows louder and louder. The soft light of morning hits my eyes. "Guard station three," Dylan whispers. "It's closest to the trees. You'll have to circle around before you can leave. There won't be a chance to stop again. And I don't know if she's out there, but she has been watching the yard."

I don't have to think hard about who he means to know he's talking about Enforce.

Llama pitches forward, and her head lolls at an awkward angle. She fainted.

My heart plummets into my stomach, but maybe it's better she's out. Maybe it's better if we get her out of here without her knowing.

Dylan takes half of Llama's dead weight and marches with higher knees than before. I do my best to mimic his cadence and knee height.

We pass through a train depot, where a small engine and tiny hoppers sit on narrow-gauge tracks. The engine is shiny, silver, sleek, and the cars are rusty, dirty, and an almost moldy blue color. People shuffle along, their ankle shackles clinking and clanking on the ground as they move from the hopper cars to the pile in the pit yard.

I hear her before I see her.

"Keep your head down," Dylan growls under his breath in a hiss.

Her voice rings out. "Where *are* they?" The ringing slap of flesh on flesh causes my eyes to jerk toward the sound. Enforce has slapped an NSB.

"We don't know. It's inconclusive," the NSB says, wearing a hand-shaped mark on its face.

"Find them, or you'll end up like the *others*," Enforce hisses. The NSB shudders. "You have to get that key."

Dylan continues walking, and I have no choice but to march along in step with him. We pass behind the line of chained miners, trying to be purposeful, but also not draw attention to ourselves. It's easy among the miners, who keep their faces downcast as they trudge from the hopper cars to the pile in the middle of the pit yard.

"You. There." I keep my face studiously turned away from the voice. "What are you doing?" Enforce stands before Dylan in winter gear. Her boots have spikes attached to the insoles, and tiny prickles line the outside. A glint of sunlight peeks off her nose chain.

"Prisoner to guard station three."

Enforce's shadow is long on the ground, and I can see her bob her head.

"Some of these useless machines know how to do their jobs," she yells before she steps back and punches the NSB next to her in the cheek. The NSB has no blood, but the skin-like material covering its face tears. Though I know it's not a human, the look-alike is close enough that the flapping flesh and white under layer is enough to make me want to vomit. It's as if I'm seeing raw bone.

Dylan doesn't say anything more. He marches as quickly as he can away from Enforce without arousing suspicion.

Crossing the open expanse of the pit yard is the most difficult thing I've ever done. I keep my eyes cast down, but my ears are alert for anything. Enforce is here, and she's interested in total power. But she also saw us, and didn't realize it was me and Llama. Dylan is good at disguises.

The shadow of guard tower three looms into view, and when we step into the darkness pooling on the ground, I breathe a sigh of relief.

"Not yet," Dylan whispers. "We still have to get past the guard. It's a human guard."

Birdie starts to whisper-sing. I give one nod because that's the last part of this plan. Once we're past the guard, we can breathe a little easier, even if I have to figure out how to carry an unconscious woman back to the Resistance, while still hoping the Resistance mutiny has gone well.

"Ok." Dylan starts to walk again. "Let's go." We walk toward the wooden stilted structure. "I'm going to go up and distract them. You're going to run."

"Ok," I breathe.

"And Reach, you aren't the only thing that's going to run right now. Get out of here. Because the miners are ready." He pats the side pocket where the key is, and I understand. He's going to pass the key to the miners in the pit yard, and there are enough of them that they can overpower Enforce and her cronies. She's not expecting it, and my escape will give the miners enough time to launch their own Resistance plan.

Dylan blows out a breath. "Put her on your back and GO!" he hisses before he bounds up the door to the guard tower.

I have enough time to put Llama on my back, letting her dead weight fall across my shoulders as if she were a yoke, and start to run. I can't run fast, but it's better than walking. Birdie trundles along after me, singing louder now.

Dylan's voice rings out. "They're getting away!"

The disconcerting sensation of a thousand eyes turning to me hits me. I stumble and fall, landing face-first in the deep powdery snow.

Birdie grabs my hand and pulls. She's surprisingly strong. "Run!" she yells, "Run, run, run, run, run!"

I feel terrible for the headache Llama will have when she wakes up, but I can't be gentle and slow. I have to move.

Enforce's voice sounds above the chaos as she shouts to the NSBs. "After them, you idiots!"

Suddenly, there is an entirely different type of roar, and it's clear that Dylan somehow passed the key to a miner and they are breaking free of their chains.

I pull myself over the last bit of the crest and can see the pine trees yards away.

It takes every fibre of willpower in my being to keep going, even as the sound of NSB footsteps gets closer. Suddenly, it stops.

"STOP the miners! You fools!" Enforce shrieks. "Your job is to protect me! Listen to me, you..." She lets loose a string of curse words at the NSBs. "Help!" she cries. "HELP!"

I topple into the relative safety of the pines and look at the pit yard. Enforce is surrounded by an angry mob of miners, and the NSBs stand in various states of confusion. Some look at where I crested the rise, others look on at Enforce with something that borders on disgust, while still others try to push and shove through the miners to get to Enforce.

Body parts swing, and Enforce fights back. But there are too many of them. The miners are out for blood.

"They have the KEY!" Enforce screams at the NSBs, and I catch the glint of light reflecting off her nose rings before she disappears into the mob.

I turn my eyes away from the pit yard and take Llama from my shoulders, setting her down and leaning her against the trunk of a sapling pine.

Birdie turns to me with wide eyes. "They won't let her go," she says.

"No," I say with a heavy sigh. It's Percy all over again. This time, I can't intervene. This time, I have to leave with Birdie and Llama, who's still unconscious.

"Birdie?" I ask, not because I expect an answer, but because there's no one else to talk to. "How will we get her back to the Lodge?"

Birdie points to something in the distance and hums. "Someone's coming, coming, coming," she sings. It's a tiny black speck, but it's moving closer.

I squint against the rising sun's glare and watch in silent fascination as the silhouette of a snowmobile appears. It darts into the pine trees opposite our copse. Someone dismounts and carefully begins walking toward us, jogging across the open expanse of the clearing between the pine stands.

They have on winter gear, including a fully covered face shield helmet. The person approaches us and crouches down, lifting the face shield.

"Mom?"

48

"Reach," Mom says, and her voice cracks. "You are a fool."

I frown. Llama said the same. I slump against the trunk of a pine and mutter, "You and she both feel the same way, apparently."

Mom puts her gloved palm on my cheek and whispers, "I'm sorry."

"Can you help us get back to the Lodge?" I ask, bone-tired.

"Yes."

I point toward Llama and Birdie. "Will you take Llama and Birdie on the snowmobile?"

"Yes."

Triumphant shouts from the mine echo around us in the snowy landscape.

"They did it?" Mom asks, her eyebrows rising. "But how?"

I'm freezing, but her wonderment prompts me to ask my own questions. "What happened at the Lodge?"

Mom sighs. "It's a long story."

I'm afraid to ask outright if the mutiny was successful. I'm terrified that my friends Freedom, Hero, and the Martians will have been executed by the advisors.

My teeth begin to chatter, and Mom looks at me with narrowed eyes. "Surely you planned better than this."

"We have clothes," I say. "I took them from the Resistance store room."

"Where are they?" she asks, looking around.

I point to the trees on the opposite side of the mine.

"Why did you come to this spot?"

I roll my eyes. "Because it's the one we could get to."

Mom swallows at my snark and her eyes meet mine with an emotion I can't pinpoint. "I'll get the girls on the snowmobile. You can walk?" she asks as she surveys the two women with me.

I nod. "Please get them back to the Lodge. Llama ..." I swallow my own discomfort. "Her ankles are very injured. She's lost a lot of blood."

Mom looks at the snow near Llama's feet and blinks rapidly before her lip curls. The pristine white snow is painted with streaks of red. Mom stands and attempts to lift Llama, but Llama's unconscious form is too heavy for her. Even though I'm exhausted, I lift her into my arms and begin to trudge through the snow to the snowmobile. Birdie follows behind, crunching the top layer of snow in a musical pattern.

When we reach the snow machine, I'm ready to lie down and give up, but it's the soft beat of Llama's pulse that keeps me going.

"Go," I say to Mom as I place Llama behind her, and Birdie behind Llama. I adjust Llama so that she's slumped against Mom's back with Birdie securing her from behind. Birdie grips Mom's waist, and Mom takes the throttle in hand. In mere moments, they are off.

In a daze, I walk to where I stowed our winter gear and put it on. Llama and Birdie will keep warm enough from shared body heat on the snowmobile, but I'm alone.

It's that thought that causes me to crumple down into the snow, lean against a tree, and cry.

These are the tears of a grown man who has been from Earth to Mars and back to Earth again, and faced the disappointment of not one, but two parents revealing that they were not who he thought they were. These are the tears of a life lived, but for what purpose? What can I possibly do now?

Hopelessness anchors my body to the ground, freezing me there like ice.

I close my eyes.

I am done. I tried.

"Reach!" A hand hits my cheek. "Open your eyes. C'mon, Reach." A woman's voice meets my ears.

"Reach!" the voice commands. "Think of Llama. Think of what you promised her."

My eyes swim toward the sound. It's murky, but the name is compelling enough to try to break the haze.

I wrench my eyes open and find myself staring into brown eyes, dark skin, and dark hair covered by a white knit cap.

"Reach!" Hero says and hugs me. "We need to get you back to the Lodge."

I try to move, but I cannot. I am physically frozen against the trunk of the tree.

Hero takes a small ax from the belt of her long winter coat and begins hacking away at the ice that has formed between my back and the tree. After a few smashes, she pulls me forward, and I topple face-first into the snow.

She sits me up and stares at my face. "You have frostbite."

I can't say anything. Now that I'm free of the tree tomb, my jaw chatters uncontrollably.

She gestures to her snowmobile. "I don't think I can lift you. But we can make a sled and I can roll you onto that."

I can't nod my head, but I blink to show her I understand.

With that, she takes the two coats I brought for Llama and Birdie and ties them together. She then tips me backward onto the snow, then rolls me until I'm on my stomach on the makeshift sled. She uses the tied-together coat arms to drag me across the snow to the snowmobile.

After attaching the arms of the coat to a hitch on the back of the snowmobile, she climbs on and starts the engine.

The corners of the coat-sled puff up with the tension, and I'm cradled to an extent in the sled.

"Hold on," Hero says above the roar of the engine. "We'll be back in thirty minutes. Llama needs you, Reach."

I have no choice but to hold on. The only thing I can control is my teeth, so I take hold of the coat contraption in my teeth and bite down, hoping that it will be enough.

Hero thrusts the snowmachine into park before the main entrance of the Lodge. Freedom runs out the door and picks me up. He carries me into the Lodge and straight to the infirmary, where Harold and other medics are waiting.

"Reach," Harold says. "You have frostbite and exposure symptoms. Have you lost any blood?"

"I didn't see any blood during the transport," Hero interjects.

"Reach." Harold looks into my eyes. "You're going to experience extreme pain while we warm you up. Do you want something to help with it?"

I can't think of anything because my face burns, and it's like my body is on fire, but from the inside out. I manage to croak out one word: "Llama?"

"She'll live. She's being taken care of. You can see her when you've thawed."

Mom's voice sounds from somewhere in the room. "Give him the medication."

A jab, followed by nothing.

My eyes fly open and I'm in an infirmary room, but I sense that I'm not alone. Machines beep and buzz, and when I try to turn my head, I find that I can. My gaze catches on a cot hooked to other machines. The profile of a woman's face is visible through the tubing.

"Llama?" I whisper, my voice hoarse.

Her head turns toward mine, and as my eyes adjust to the light of the room, I can see her face fully. "Reach." Her voice cracks and tears flow down her cheeks.

I attempt to stand and go to her, to comfort her, to hold her, to tell her how sorry I am because although I can't tell you why she's crying, I know it's my fault.

An alarm beeps, and suddenly there are multiple people in the room with us.

"You're awake," Harold says from behind me, and I mutter a swear word under my breath. "How are you feeling?"

"Thirsty," I quip.

He moves around the cot, hooking and unhooking tubes, looping cords over machines. He reaches for my hand and studies the back of an IV. "I can take this out, and then you can move around the room. Would you like that?"

I stare at him. Of course I'd like that.

He removes the tube, and immediately my feet are on the floor. I stand and start to move, but pitch forward. It's only Harold who keeps me from falling.

"You did it," another voice chimes in.

I turn to look at the deep voice. "Freedom?" I ask.

He nods. "Your stunt at the mine was enough to move them to real resistance. We have the leverage we've never had." He swallows. "Reach, the Wards are all pushing back against the NSBs, and the Punishment and Retribution Department can't keep up. The Wards are free because Enforce and her people have been pushed back into the cities. Nation is this close to being free from tyranny."

I'm glad to hear it, but there's one thing my heart wants right now. I grunt and tip my head toward Llama. Freedom hooks one of my arms around his shoulders while I lean on Harold. Together, they help me to Llama, who lies on her cot, with tears still streaming down her cheeks.

"Llama?" I whisper, and then I'm pushed into a chair next to her.

"You came back," she whispers as a hand reaches out and strokes my cheek.

"I promised."

"I don't have a leg."

I blink.

"Nation took it from me with those shackles, Reach. They took Dr. Jog, they took my leg, and they're going to take you."

"I'm right here," I say, my voice beyond scratchy.

"They're going to take you!" she shrieks. "They're going to take you too." Her hysteria ratchets up until Harold sighs and flips a switch on a small board at the foot of the bed. A bead of something clear begins to travel down a tube, and within a moment of the bead leaving the tube and entering her body, she stills. In a few more minutes, her breath evens out, and she's asleep.

Freedom looks at me.

Harold hands me a ceramic cup and I tip it to my lips, not knowing what's inside or what it will do to me. It's water.

"We need to talk." Freedom arches a brow toward Llama. "Can you come with me? I need to show you something."

I shake my head and point to Llama. I won't leave her.

"She'll be asleep for several hours, Reach," Harold says gently. "You should go with him. You need to see this."

The chair I'm in moves with a lurch as Freedom wheels me out of the infirmary room.

"Stop!" I cry, but my voice is nothing more than a hoarse whisper.

"Reach," Freedom says. "You need to know what happened while you were gone. Harold, you'll stay with Llama, right?"

Harold calls back, "Yes, I won't leave the room."

I slump back in the wheelchair because, once again, I have no choice.

Freedom wheels me out of the infirmary bay and into a small room tucked under the eaves. An alcove houses a window and a bench seat that offers a view of the snow-covered yard below.

"Stay here," Freedom says, and I blink. I'm in a wheelchair. I think I could walk, but clearly Harold doesn't think I should.

He ducks out the door and returns a moment later, but he's not alone.

Two women accompany him. They have pale skin, nearly translucent, high cheekbones, slender frames, and the reddish under-tone to their facial features that is typical of a Martian colonist.

Cait and Beatriz.

49

"You're dead," I blurt.

Cait and Beatriz look at each other and smile. It's genuine, it's real, and it's something I've never seen from either of them. Their work as spies for Jezero meant that mostly their faces were blank masks or showed what they commanded them to show. This is simply *them*. Being *human*.

"Nope," Cait says dryly.

"Rather fortunately for some, we are very much alive," Beatriz deadpans.

I stare at Freedom. "How?" I mouth.

"We didn't need a mutiny," Freedom explains. "Not when an entire entourage of allies appeared."

"Allies?" I ask, confused. "They are—" I correct myself, shaking my head. "Were dead. And they aren't an entourage. They're two people."

Freedom sighs. "Reach." He clenches his hands at his sides. "Please let us tell you."

I huff. My life has been one in which no one ever *tells* me any-thing. Still, Freedom is my friend, and I don't know how these two women who died on Earth are alive, but I'll let them try.

I bob my head and gesture for him to go on.

"We had gathered Wave Cohort 1 for training in the courtyard and were preparing to give them the message about Sigma and her plans when two large aircraft appeared on the horizon. We were all stunned, but when they landed, and Beatriz and Cait appeared at the mouth of each craft, *and* the members of Wave Cohort 1 all knew who they were, it was obvious we finally obtained the manpower we've never had."

"You see, Reach," Beatriz says, "we didn't come alone."

"Allies," Cait says. "From Australia. And from Europa."

"What?" I say, because my mind is malfunctioning with new in-formation, and I'm trying to process it, but there's too much I don't understand to make sense of the new game theory.

"We landed in a desert," Beatriz supplies. "And were found by people in the far Southeast quadrant of the globe."

"Australians," Cait interjects.

"They were naturally suspicious of us, since we fell from the sky. But they removed our trackers and biofeedback monitors. We told them of our mission to gather allies to help the fight against Nation, and the plight of the Martians. They are sympathetic to both causes."

"They're here, Reach," Freedom says, and the undercurrent of excitement in his voice is palpable. "We actually have an army."

"But why are they sympathetic about the Resistance?" I ask.

"First of all, because they went through something similar fifty years ago in Australia. They had also been in a totalitarian govern-ment, but it was overthrown. The people who served in taking out that regime are honored as heroes," Beatriz explains. "Second of all, because they didn't think there was anything inhabitable in this quadrant. Nation did such a good job of cutting ties three hundred years ago that the rest of the population centers had no idea Nation even existed. They believed that Nation had been destroyed in the aftermath of the natural disasters, or had doomed itself with its original policy of isolation coupled with no communication for centuries. Because travel to this quadrant is so expensive and time consuming, and there was supposedly nothing here, no one came. Australia's trade partner, Europa, has benefited greatly from their freedom, and is sympathetic to the cause. I strongly suspect they'd like more resources and trading partners. "

"Tyranny festers when it's alone," Freedom states.

Beatriz and Cait nod. "There has to be a balance of power. Tyranny anywhere is a threat to freedom everywhere."

"Where are the allies?" I ask, rubbing my hand down my jaw and feeling the stubble there.

"They're housed in the aircraft. You can meet them tomorrow."

"But what about Sigma?" I ask Freedom.

He sighs. "She's a master of game theory. She played you."

I frown. "She's not that good."

"She is." He bites his lower lip. "She knew that you'd run back to the mine for Llama and that you had the key the NSBs wanted. She found it when you arrived here and went through all the belongings of Wave Cohort 1 to see if anything of importance had turned up. She made duplicates, Reach. You have the original. She used her knowledge of Nation's politics and Enforce's power moves to send you back into the mines."

"Where is she?"

"She's in meetings with the leaders of the other population centers. The head of Australia sent a deputy, as did the Europa Alliance."

"But…Llama?"

Freedom frowns. "Sacrifice, I think it's called in chess."

My eyes bug out. "She's not a pawn," I bite.

"No." Freedom's frown deepens. "She's not."

"That's why Sigma can't be in charge."

"You're too close to the situation," Freedom says gently.

"And if she'd done that to Hero?" I snap. "What would you have done then?"

"I don't know, Reach. But you need to realize that Llama is safe now."

"Yes, her and both of her legs are safe." Sarcasm drips from my voice.

"She's going to get help, Reach. She'll live as normal a life as she can. There are always casualties in a war. You know that."

I swallow my anger down. He's right. There always are casualties in a war, and so often it's the weakest pieces that end up removed from the board. Llama was never the weakest piece; she was always a queen. More powerful than anyone knew until they studied the game.

"Enforce has a vendetta against Llama. Sigma knew that Enforce would be there if she suspected Llama was there."

I groan. My eyes are heavy, my head is swimming, and I'm in need of water.

"Is Enforce…" I close my eyes against the thrumming in my head. "Is Enforce gone?"

"Here," Cait says, and she pushes a silver canteen toward me. "It's clean."

I unscrew the cap and drink deeply. The pounding that began in my head lessens to a dull thrum.

"Yes," Freedom states, his eyes hardened. "The NSBs and the miners."

"And you believe *what* about that?" I ask, because I know what I believe, but I can't figure out Freedom's thoughts.

He frowns. "About her death?"

I nod.

"That she inflicted pain on many people. That she killed many people in the name of power and her own sick mentality, and that, should we have had a choice, she would have ended up in prison for life." He tips his head and looks at me with a narrow gaze. "You've seen too much death to accept it as justice, haven't you?"

I nod as everyone stares at me. It's uncomfortable, so I break the silence.

"Now what?" I ask, looking at Cait and Beatriz and then Freedom.

"Now we need to go on the offensive."

"How?" I ask. It feels like the weight of the entire world is crashing upon my shoulders.

"We need to take down the Three Powers," Freedom says simply. "But the key is genetic material and knowledge of their security."

I frown, but Freedom continues. "Can you think of any place in Nation where the figureheads would consider themselves safe from just about everything and also have access to everything they'd need? And still be able to contact the people? Still cling to the vestiges of power they love?" The way he asks makes me feel that I should know the answer to his question. He's not being rhetorical; he's waiting for me to think it through.

My mind spins, thinking of places that would be safe, but safety isn't the only goal. They'd also want access to the instruments they created that control so many.

"Hub?"

"Yes." Freedom nods. "Our intelligence shows that the figureheads have moved into Hub as the Wards have become more and more unstable. The Punishment and Retribution Department has been gutted. There are only a few members left, and there's not much of a point. The NSBs are unable to keep up with the demand on them, and honestly, most of the P&R Department were NSBs at this point."

"But what about Hub? How will we take them out? What about the allies?"

"The allies will take care of the Wards and any lingering resistance there. We have enough manpower to take care of each of the thirty-one Wards. The trick will be Hub."

"What do you mean?" I ask, dread coursing through my limbs because even though I'm asking the question, I know.

"We have to do it, Reach."

"What about Llama?"

Freedom shakes his head. "She can't. She's not in optimal health. Honestly, you aren't either, but you're the best I've got."

"What about Hero?"

"No," he says simply and firmly.

"Why?" I challenge. I'm sick of people sending me and the woman I love into dangerous situations. Why shouldn't someone else run the risk of loss? Why shouldn't someone else have that pain? I don't want to send Hero into Hub, but she knows the place as well as or better than all of us.

"Because she's having a baby. And that's not where she needs to be. She'll support us from here."

My eyes had bugged out before, but now they're practically as large as twin moons on my face.

Beatriz and Cait stare on with amusement.

"Surely you know about babies, Reach," Beatriz chides.

I blink. I'm not sure what to say. My experience on Earth was that having a baby was a highly regulated affair. Souterraine's way seemed more natural, celebrating the baby and the parents to be. But still, I'm on Earth, and I don't know what to say.

"The appropriate response is 'congratulations,'" Cait supplies before muttering under her breath, "I learned that myself recently."

The woman is a highly trained field operative for a now-defunct government on a planet that's inhospitable to human life, and yet she's self-deprecating about her own knowledge. I can't help it. I dissolve into laughter while Freedom looks on in concern.

"Too much information at once," Beatriz supplies. "He can't process it all, and then Cait gave him a reason to laugh, so his brain took that opportunity."

Freedom bobs his head. "Reach," he says. "You will meet the rest of the allies tomorrow. I think for now, you need to rest. Harold wants to watch you for one week, but as soon as you're ready, we're going to make our move." He tips his chin toward a chessboard that sits on a shelf next to the long window. The pieces are out, arranged on the board, and waiting for someone to play.

The scene is set. I close my eyes before I open them and meet Freedom's gaze head-on. "It's endgame time."

50

Freedom wheels me back to the infirmary bay and leaves me in the care of Harold. "Do you want to learn how to help her?" Harold asks me as he tips his head toward a sleeping Llama.

It's the first time anyone has asked me if I want something.

Moisture beads at the corners of my eyes, and I wipe it away as best I can, where Harold studiously looks anywhere but at my face.

"Here," he says. "Stand up. You can walk. We were concerned the shock of the information would be too much for you, so we let you sit for that."

I push myself to standing and am amazed that I do feel capable.

"You were out for a while," Harold supplies. "We were able to give you an extremely nutrient-dense IV, so you should feel relatively strong, except for the headaches. Those are to be expected over the next few days. Once those stop, you'll be back to full capacity."

Harold points to tubes and switchboards and charts. It makes no sense, but I appreciate that he's trying. When he pulls the corner of the blanket to show me Llama's leg, I stop him. "She'll show me when she's ready."

He quirks a brow, but accepts my refusal and then leaves me alone with her.

I sink to my knees by her bed and grasp her hand. "I'm so sorry, Llama," I whisper and let my tears fall. They wash over the junction of our hands, the bone and marrow and substance held together by such a fragile organ as skin, and yet there is healing in the tears.

When I finish crying, I am a changed man, and one who understands that while tyranny is in the world, Llama will never be safe. Birdie will never be safe. Pippa, Freedom and Hero's child, *me*. I am the child that was never meant to be safe. I am the child who was dangerous to Nation, and it's time to act on that danger now.

I plant a soft kiss on Llama's forehead before I press a button on the edge of the cot to call for Harold. When he appears, I leave the room, and I don't look back. Leaving her is painful, but like suturing a wound, it has to be done.

"Don't leave her," I command.

Harold salutes.

I find Sigma first. She's in the conference room, the one with the long table, and the advisors surround her. The door was shut, but it wasn't locked, and when I strolled in without so much as a knock, she didn't blink.

A tall man with a gleaming bald head sits next to my mother. His teeth chatter, and I find that he has on a knit black sweater with pockets at the hips, but still seems to be unused to the cold. A small woman, rounded and jolly, sits on the other side. The man would look imposing, but his struggle with the temperature ruins the effect. The woman, however, sizes me up with a shrewd glance.

"And this is your son?" She clearly directs the question to my mother, though her gaze stays locked on me.

"Hardly," I snort.

"Reach," Sigma warns before the woman and the man begin speaking to each other in hushed tones.

I look around the room for Freedom, but he isn't here. I sink into the single open chair next to Enigma. He whispers something in what I suspect is French, but I don't speak it, so all I can do is shrug. He procures a pen and a napkin from under his steaming cup of coffee. *'I'm sorry about the girl,'* he writes, sliding it into my view.

I bristle. Not sorry enough.

"Reach?" Sigma's voice breaks into my anger and escalates it so that I can barely hold myself together with the vibrations of rage radiating through my limbs.

"Yes?" I say, gripping the table with white knuckles and trying to show a calm I do not feel.

"This is Heely." She points to the man. "And this is Lore." She points to the woman in turn. "Heely is the dignitary from Australia, and Lore is the Central Assistant President of Europa. They're here to help."

"How?" I challenge and watch as my mother's throat bobs a swallow. "And *why?*"

"We are sympathetic to your cause," Heely interjects. His voice has a lilt to it that I'm unfamiliar with. "We didn't know you existed until several months ago. About fifty years ago, our own continent underwent a change of leadership. The political atmosphere had deteriorated until there was no rule at all in Australia. Our grandparents remember these times, and have spoken to us about the goodness of proper order in government. Australians understand that there is no safety for the world when tyranny exists."

"Well said." Lore nods. "In Europa, we have benefited greatly from free trade with Australia. Nation's technological advances are to be admired, despite their propensity to hide their advances from the world. We benefit from trading across the planet. When one suffers, all suffer. When one thrives, we all thrive."

I frown. "But *how?*" I whisper. "How are you going to help us?"

"We have supplied the army you require," Heely states. "They are trained, they are fit, and they are set apart for this sole purpose."

"And they have consented to this plan?" I ask through a clenched jaw while staring hard at Sigma. She looks away and slightly down.

"Yes. Each person who serves in Europa's or Australia's military units must consent to do so."

"They are aware of what they could lose?" Again, I stare hard at my mother, and again she doesn't meet my gaze.

"Their life, their limbs, their friends…Yes," Heely states. "It's dangerous, but heroic work. They know that. We train them for that. Europa does too."

I sigh. "Consent before being sent into danger is a luxury. We don't have that here."

"You don't have it yet," Lore says, and her eyes bore into mine with such intensity I nearly shrink back. I don't because I want to be strong.

"Reach," Sigma says, her short hair bobbing as she meets my gaze. "We have a plan. Would you like to hear it?"

"Will it involve Llama?"

"No."

"Good. She's given too much without anyone ever asking her."

"You have a pet?" Heely asks, concern on his face.

"The *girl*," Lore whispers. "Her name is Llama, isn't it? The one that you went for in the mines." Lore studies Sigma.

She nods. "Yes. She's rather attached to Reach, and Reach is attached to her."

"Are they married?"

"Not yet, but they were formally bonded together on Mars."

"Then that must be honored at all costs." Lore peers at Sigma. "What did you do?"

My mother closes her eyes and frowns before opening them and looking me directly in the eye. She spells out exactly what she did with Freedom, me, Llama, the mines, Dylan, the Resistance, the key, the NSBs, Enforce, and game theory.

"You are reckless," Heely states, while I nod.

"What was about to happen before you arrived was a mutiny of sorts," I state calmly, picking at my nailbed. "Those of us who came from Mars came to make life *better* here. Not to be pawns in a game without consent, without knowledge of what we are up against. Definitely not missions where our lives were at risk, but we were lied to about the reason. Yes, getting those children out of the mine was a worthy endeavor, but by not allowing us to prepare…" I blow out a breath. "You are as guilty of Llama's missing leg as Enforce and her torture devices."

"Agreed," Lore states, her eyes calculating.

"You are preparing to be the leader of Nation when it is rebuilt, correct?" Heely presses.

Sigma nods. "I have the aptitude for it, and the inclination."

"No." Heely shakes his head. "We will not concoct or follow through with a plan if you are to be the leader. You use the tactics you're claiming to be against. How can you defeat the very system you use?

Sigma sits back in her chair, and a blush blooms on her cheeks as if she's been slapped.

Heely and Lore lean toward each other, whispering in low voices for several minutes.

"We will continue with the plan, but only if *he* is the leader." Heely points directly at me.

All heads swivel, and all eyes land on my form. I grasp the table with my palms. I have been thrust into a role I did not consent too—again. I blow out a breath, wishing Freedom was in the room, that I felt a true ally in this space. Instead, I am surrounded by others, but alone.

"I don't…" I start to say, but Heely holds up a hand and I stop.

"You had the courage to show up here and call your own mother out for the very thing we're fighting against. Courage is the mark of a leader. Sigma? Do you think Reach would be an adequate leader for the new Nation?"

Mom nods once, then says, "Yes. I have no doubt."

Even though I don't want it, the weight of everyone's gaze sits heavy on my shoulders.

I inhale again, exhale, long and slow.

With a calm as artificial as an NSB, I ask the question that must be answered before we can move forward. "What is the plan?"

The room dissolves into a flurry of activity as maps, pins, and people move around, spreading everything out on the table for my benefit as Sigma fades into the background.

51

Launching a full-scale operation with an actual military force is very different from clandestine operations into a mine. Sigma has a limited role now, and instead of asking her, the advisors first ask *me*. It's strange, but each advisor, even those who have not had positive interactions with me, ask for my input.

The Resistance's pockets have taken most of the Wards, and there is dissent in the major cities for the first time in hundreds of years. The allies from Europa and Australia have been split into three groups.

Group 1 is tackling its way through the Wards, destroying any lingering NSBs and rounding up Nation officials and those who resist the Resistance. The key from Mars still means something, but we can't figure out exactly why Nation wants it so badly. What we do know is that the key is important, and anything important is in Hub City.

Group 2 is working its way through the major cities. The objective is the same as Group 1, however this group expects more officials and more resistance. Both groups departed nine days ago.

The conference room has been a hustling hub of activity, and I'm drained. Freedom, Group 3, and I leave tomorrow for Hub City. It's expected to be the most difficult to take based on the number of NSBs and the behavior of the residents. Still, there's resistance to the Three Powers in the city. The operation is underway, and there's only one thing I can do. I excuse myself from where Lore, Freedom and Enigma sit around a machine, moving pins on a map and decoding transmissions from field operative stations.

Freedom catches my eye as I leave the room and nods. He knows.

I'm halfway down the hall when Heely's unique dialect stops me. "Reach," he says. "Are you going to see her?"

I nod.

"May I?"

I study his face. It's blank of emotion, but there's something in his eyes that makes me wonder. "Yes."

Heely matches his steps to mine as I take him down the hall and up to the infirmary sick bay where Llama is recovering. I rap on the heavy wooden door once before pushing it open and stopping in my tracks. Heely plows into me.

Llama stands next to her cot, leaning heavily on an IV stand. She's wearing hospital clothing but with a knit sweater over the top. The buttons run down the middle, and she stares at her leg, missing from the knee down.

"It's really gone," she whispers without looking up, and it's clear she knows it's me.

I'm by her side in an instant. I wrap my arms around her as she lets go of the IV pole and leans her full weight into me.

"They took it," she murmurs against my shoulder, and the wetness there tells me she's crying.

"Ahem." Heely clears his throat.

Llama picks her head up off my shoulder abruptly and stares behind me.

"Hello," he says softly. "I'm Heely."

Llama's eyes squint as she studies him.

"Heely," I say to break the awkward silence. "This is Llama. She survived Nation, Mars, and Rare Earth III."

"Honored to meet you." Heely slides a small rectangular device from his pocket. "If I may show you something?"

Llama's lip twitches, but she doesn't decline.

Heely slides his finger over the glass screen and then taps several times. "Here," he says, thrusting the screen toward Llama's face. "This is my grandfather. He was a fighter when Australia overcame tyranny fifty years ago."

Llama's eyes widen as she studies the image. It's a man, grizzled, gray, but happy next to a heavily laden table. He sits in a wheelchair, and he's missing a leg below the right knee.

"You're not the only person who's lost their body to war. But he always said that family made everything better. Miss Llama, it is an honor to meet someone who has shown such heroism. I'll leave you to each other." Heely gives a small bow and then walks out of the room and out of the door.

"You're leaving, aren't you?" she challenges.

I nod.

"When?" she presses.

"Tomorrow. Along with Group 3."

"You'll come back? You'll return?" she whispers as she looks anywhere but at my eyes.

I tip her chin up and lock eyes with her. "Always, Llama."

I angle my head down and kiss her as if it could erase her worry. Though I know it can't, it doesn't stop me from trying.

We break apart and she shakes her head sadly. "You should get some rest."

I help her into her cot, cover her with a knit blanket, and sink into a wooden chair beside her.

"Don't you need to sleep?" she asks with wide eyes.

"No," I whisper. "I just need you."

We fall asleep in this position, our hands intertwined over the cream-colored blanket.

Freedom taps me on the shoulder when it's still dark. Llama's breaths are even and quiet. Her dark lashes rest against her cheekbones. *I will come back. I have to come back.*

"Reach," he whispers. "It's time."

I bring Llama's hand to my lips and place a kiss there. "I love you," I whisper to her, and the words bring a measure of comfort to me as I depart from her sleeping form and into the chaos of outright war.

Outside the infirmary bay, the Lodge is a hustle of activity. It buzzes like a hive, ready for a new day, a new chapter, a new life. Freedom catches my eye and gives a sad smile. He has his own reason to fret. "It's the last time," he says, more to himself than to me. Then, louder, "We won't have to leave them like this ever again."

"I promised her I'd return," I blurt.

"That was reckless."

"But I have to. She's lost so much. And I promised her that a long time ago…back when we were on Mars."

Freedom accepts a black backpack from Declan, who's been helping outfit the groups. "Good luck, Reach," Declan says in his calm and placid manner.

"Declan," I call. "I don't know how everything is going to go, but I want you to work with plants here."

He brightens. "You can tell them that?"

"Yes," I say as I secure my own black backpack to my shoulders. "I can tell them that."

Freedom and I approach the aircraft that housed the allies from Europa. After dropping off Group 2, it returned here to be part of the next phase.

We're at the end of the line of operatives, and as I climb aboard the craft, I see the eyes of Group 2 watching me. None of them are from Wave Cohort 1. It was decided that space travel was taxing enough on the body, and they are assisting the Resistance from the Lodge based on their skills and aptitudes.

"Are you ready?" Freedom asks as he buckles into a harness tethered to a cable above that will allow him to move about the craft while we're in flight. Though resistance in the air is unlikely, Lore insisted that if we were in the Europa craft, and on a military mission, we would harness.

I click my own buckles into place. "For it to be over," I mutter.

"It will be," he says, his face paling. "One way or another, we succeed, or they do. It will be over for us."

I know he's talking about the risk of our death. It's a real risk, one that can't be understated, and it's true. Either we win, or we die. The black and white of the matter can't be denied anymore. Grey isn't an option.

A voice crackles over the intercraft coms system.

"Group 3. You are embarking on a dangerous journey. Thank you for your sacrifice and service. We remind you to follow your group commanders. We also remind the specially trained operatives to work in pairs. Success is likely, but resistance is more so. The goal is to capture those resisting so that they can be brought to trial, and to defeat and destroy any of the NSBs guarding the figureheads of Nation. Remember your specific attack plan and follow it. Over."

The voice crackles off, and my stomach lurches. I have a view of the Lodge and think of Llama, in her sickbed, adjusting to life without a leg. My heart thrums out a silent plea, as if it could connect with hers.

I love you. I'll return.

52

THE CRAFT TOUCHES down outside of Hub City. A deep chasm surrounds the city. It's dark enough that I can't see the bottom of the pit, and wide enough that no one can jump across.

"How did you escape this?" I ask Freedom. When we left the city, we were driven by car. Our defection happened in space, not in the city itself.

He gulps. "There are ways out, but not always ways in."

I look up and see the towering buildings on the edge of the city. "You jumped?"

He nods. "Swung. In the dark, on a rope. Out a window, with nothing more than the hope that I'd make it."

The engineers of Group 3 begin constructing a bridge made of interconnecting harnesses. They click pieces together and form a lengthy net. A hook is attached to the other side of the material, and an auger is attached to the hook. More augers are placed on the corners of the net. One of the smallest members of the group brushes her hair behind her shoulders before she plants a small device on top of the auger and fiddles with a black box in her other hand.

"Got it!" she calls.

"Launch!" confirms another member.

The engineers throw the net across the chasm. The auger hits the ground and the woman pushes buttons on her box. The augers deploy, spinning deeper into the earth and creating an anchor.

"Jade, you cross first."

"Got it!" Jade tucks the black box into her own backpack and steps onto the taught net with confidence I don't currently have in the contraption. She crosses with no difficulties. "Secure," she calls after bending down and studying the auger on the opposite side of the chasm. She places spikes through the net at the corners of the other side. "Safe to cross."

Group 3 crosses, one by one in an orderly fashion, until only Freedom and I are left. Our role here is much different than the role of the other members. While the others need to find the Three Powers and arrest them, we need to determine what this key in my pocket *opens* and why it's so important to Nation. Our instructions are to split off from the group, work as fast as we can, and meet up with the force once we've figured out the puzzle.

When we cross into the city, I'm amazed at the orderliness and emptiness of it all.

People are not out, but that may be because the first part of Group 3 has already cleared the way. We encounter no resistance as we move deeper into Hub City. When we reach the intersection of two main roads, Freedom and I split off from the group. We stick to the shadows of the tall buildings, but the hair on the back of my neck prickles.

"Reach," Freedom whispers as we turn a corner toward Hub.

"Yeah?"

"They're watching us."

"Who?"

"NSBs."

"Where?"

A hand grasps the back of my field operative uniform, and I start to sprint. Freedom does the same.

Heavy footsteps sound behind us. The NSBs chasing us have the advantage: they aren't human. They run as they're programmed to, not with the physical limitations of a human body. The only upper hand we have is that they have to follow a program where we can make split-second decisions.

We run as fast as we can. There is no doubt that the NSBs in Hub City are more sophisticated than the ones at Rare Earth III and the prototype I encountered years ago.

A jet-black building swims into my vision. The door opens right onto the sidewalk. It's familiar, but I can't determine why I know it. A flash of skin and the door cracks open. I dart laterally off the side-walk and into the building. Freedom ducks in behind me and a woman slams the door shut.

A tremendous crash sounds as two NSBs strike into the glass of the building door. Their heads knock together, and they crumple to the ground in a tangle of artificial limbs.

I hunch over, my hands on my knees, my breath coming heavy. Freedom's shaky breaths fill the air around me.

When I finally look up, I discover a face I know.

"Shauna?" I ask, my mouth hanging open.

"What are you two doing here?" Shauna asks. She flips blonde hair over her shoulder and waves pointy fingernails as she speaks.

"We're the Resistance," Freedom says as he straightens.

Shauna frowns. "You two"—she over-enunciates—"are the Resistance? Two people are the fearsome force we've been told to stay inside and far away from while we let the NSBs handle any physical altercations in the streets? You *two* are what has led to total lockdown in the city?"

"Well, we're not by ourselves," I interject. "Our mission involves splitting off from the main force and getting to Hub. We think that's where the figureheads are."

She nods and taps a hot-pink finger on her chin. "They are."

"Is there a way to get us there without the…NSBs seeing us?"

Shauna nods. "But what do you intend to do?"

I look nervously at the door. No other NSBs have come by, but they could at any time. "Could we talk about it someplace that isn't here?"

She bobs her head and turns on a black leather heel. She leads us down into the basement area where I stayed years ago when she fixed me up for the banquet in my 'honor'. I don't grasp the raw wooden railing this time. I'm wiser now. It's not only the big things, but the little ones that add to Nation's maltreatment. Anytime there's an opportunity to demean someone's dignity, they take it.

I've already sweated and bled for them. I won't do it anymore. This time, I'm sweating and bleeding for me.

Shauna grabs the chain pull and turns on the overhead light, filling the room with a dull yellow glow.

"Freedom," I say as he stares around the room. "This is Shauna. She's a Sty here."

He notches his brow a single increment higher than usual. "A Sty?"

"Stylist," I amend.

"Yes, I know." He breaks away from me and directs a question to her. "Are you for *them* or for *us?*" he asks point-blank.

"I've been nothing but a Sty for as long as I've been here. And before that, I was in Ward 3."

Freedom nods.

"I'm ready to have a name again. And I'm not the only Sty who feels that way. You might find there's more Resistance in Hub City than you thought."

An idea takes hold.

"Shauna?" I ask, reaching my hand into a secure zippered pocket at the right breast of my skin-tight black field operative suit. "Do you know what this is for?" I extract the key and hold it out, placing it in my palm.

Her eyes widen. "Yes."

"Care to clue us in?" Freedom asks dryly.

"It opens the genetic database server cover. Everything in Nation is genetically coded to allow for the highest safety, but that single key has been a source of great frustration for Leader for years."

"Why?" I ask.

"It meant that no matter what precautions they took, there was always the opportunity for a manual override."

"How would you know that?" Freedom asks, eyes narrowed. "And why wouldn't they change the lock system on the server cover panel?"

"People talk when a Sty is with them. Not as if to a friend, but as if we aren't there at all. Leader had many meetings with people while I worked on something for her, usually prepping her for a telecast. And the server is older than the scientific revolution, so no one wanted to risk damaging the internal components. There's no way to access some of the materials that were used in that system anymore, and if they tried to move the data, they risked losing centuries of genetic data they use to create zones and 'applications' for the people of Nation."

The database they use to control, to separate, to repress and oppress. Our mission parameters have shifted, and it's become clear to me that the Pandora's code box now has a use. We have to destroy that server.

"Why you?" Freedom scowls.

"I'm a low number Sty. The lower the number, the higher the clearance. I was occasionally the only one available. Like when a scientist trainee from Hub went missing after refusing to sign death papers and take a blood transfusion and oath of loyalty to the government."

Freedom blinks. "You know who I am?"

"I'm better connected than you think. The Resistance has always had pockets in every Ward and city. Hub was the hardest because it was also the most dangerous, but Freedom, we're on your side."

I blow out a breath as I survey the dingy room. "Can you get us to the database center?" If I can hack in and override the NSBs, I can stop the major threat to Group 3. There is no doubt in my mind that the NSBs have been reprogrammed in recent weeks to kill anyone perceived as Resistance. That's the fallout from Enforce's death and the systematic toppling of the Punishment and Retribution Department in the Wards and major cities.

Shauna meets my gaze with a hard glint in her eyes. "Yes. But it will be dangerous."

53

Shauna pulls a ring of keys out from a three-drawered silver cart. "Your genetic material is coded from your time at Hub, right?"

Freedom and I look at each other. Of course it is, but we hadn't considered that.

"You'll need to wear gloves." Shauna extracts black gloves from her cart. She hands them to us. "We use these when we change hair color."

Freedom works his hand into the glove, and it snaps on like a second skin. I do the same. It's an odd feeling, having something over my fingers and palms, knowing that this thin substance is protecting me.

"They will rip if you touch anything sharp," Shauna warns. "Keep your hands to your own bodies as best you can." She releases a breath, then exhales shakily. "I'm going to take you to the database. You should be able to recode the database and get rid of genetic traces of you. But I don't know how long it takes to update the code across systems. So even if you delete your genome from the base, you might have a lag in the processing."

I clench my jaw. I understand. We have to do this perfectly, because any loophole that might allow for a mistake…is actually a noose.

"This way." She beckons us as she pulls the chain on the overhead light and plunges us into darkness.

She clicks a small tube in her hand, and a tiny pinprick of light illuminates the floor near her black heels. "We're going in the tunnels. They're old. They smell terrible, and they're usually used for holding insurrectionists. There may be NSBs. Do not breathe on any of them. They have sensors to detect genetic material in the breath, but they won't be able to see who you are in the dark. They should assume you're another NSB. Stick to the shadows and touch nothing." She pops the tiny light in between her teeth before bending down and twisting the cover off the drain in the middle of the floor. She climbs down a ladder. "Go slow," she warns around the tube before her head and the light bob out of sight.

Freedom follows next, then me. The rungs are slick with moisture, and the skin-tight gloves don't allow me a better grip. We descend for what feels like miles, but in reality, it is 200 ladder rungs to the bottom. Instead of panicking about the dark, enclosed space, I focus my mind on the only task I can: not slipping and counting the rungs.

When my feet hit the floor, I breathe out a sigh of relief. Freedom wipes sweat from his brow with his forearm.

"Try not to sweat," I whisper.

Freedom frowns at the back of his arm, which now has genetic material that can rub off and be identified in the high-tech areas of Hub. "Habit."

Shauna leads us through a maze of tunnels. Some have dirt-packed floors, while others have simple tile patterns, and still others have a layer of water an inch or two deep. We listen the entire time for NSBs, but there aren't any.

"Here," Shauna says after what feels like hours and seventeen different tunnels. "This tunnel will take us into the database center.

I'm not sure what's on the other side of this door." And we all know she means as far as security goes. Will it be NSBs programmed to break our necks and kill us on sight? Or will it be nothing? It's anyone's guess.

She splashes through the puddle, pulls out a key from her ring, and inserts it into the lock.

The door swings open, and she steps through, only to scream as an alarm blares.

Freedom and I stare at each other for half a beat. I move forward. He moves back, bumping into me. "Reach," he hisses. "We have to get out of here."

"No!" I shout above the alarm. "I won't leave someone behind again."

I shove past him and duck through the door, shifting from the darkness of the tunnels to the brightness of a fully lit room, complete with an alarm flashing blue-and-red light.

Shauna stands in front of an NSB. Its hands tighten around her throat.

Shauna had keys. She had sanctioned access. It takes me only a moment to understand that the NSB has either overridden its programming or Nation has programmed them to attack without discrimination.

"Freedom!" I yell. "It can't get wet."

He understands because as I watch the NSB's eyes narrow and a cruel smile plays on its lips. Freedom barrels into the back of it. It's a well-balanced machine, but it can't withstand the force of a full-grown man crashing into it from behind. It topples over, dragging Shauna with it.

Shauna shrieks as her body hits the ground, but she keeps her head elevated enough to not crack her skull against the floor. I run to the NSB, which is still tightening its hold on her neck, and use every ounce of muscle I have to roll it over onto its back so that the delicate mechanical parts under the back zipper are sunk in the water.

"Shauna! Roll!" I yell. She closes her eyes, her lips slightly blue, and pushes with all her might as I get enough leverage.

There's a fizzing and buzzing noise, and then the NSB goes still, but its hands are still locked around Shauna's neck. In desperation, I stick my hand under the NSB's plated and mechanized one. Though the flesh glove acts as a cover, the plates are sharp under the false skin. I use my strength to break the vice grip on Shauna's neck. The NSB hands fly off and sink into the water.

She sinks to the side of the machine and sits in the water, light from the database center spilling into the tunnel as she rubs her neck. Angry red marks circle her sensitive skin.

"Go," she whispers, her voice hoarse. "Go."

Then she hangs her head and sobs. I can't do this again. I can't keep leaving women in dangerous situations. I have no romantic attachment to Shauna, but it's too similar to what happened to Llama. "I'll come back for you, Shauna," I say. "I'll come back."

Freedom shakes his head. "She'll come with us. You go ahead. I'll bring her."

I run from the water into the white tile room of the database center. The servers are close to the door, and I understand why the tunnel was full of two inches of water. The servers require massive amounts of water to cool them down, to draw out the heat, and to keep the temperature regulated from the friction generated by processing so much data. Coolant tanks stand sentry around the perimeter of a massive circular room. Tubes connect the coolant tanks to the servers while a pipe spits the water out of the wall and into the tunnel.

I sit at the main computer panel of the server and press a series of buttons on a keypad, trying anything I can think of to enter the system. I've bypassed three levels of security when Freedom walks in, Shauna leaning heavily on his shoulder.

"Let me," he says, and I am reminded of his technological genius. I let Shauna lean on me while he inputs codes and sequences. I'm no slouch at coding and security, but when Freedom passes through twenty-three levels of increasing security in mere minutes, I feel like an amateur.

He taps a button on the keypad. "Got it," he whispers. "This is the NSB coding. We can switch them all off."

"All except the ones that override it," I whisper back, sending the pipe a meaningful look.

"It's a risk, but it's one worth taking." He types a string of long and complex code into a tiny blinking box at the top of the screen. "Done." He lets out a small sigh of relief before he straightens. "Now we have to delete ourselves from the genome database."

"Good luck with that," a female voice calls from somewhere within the room. "It's a shame you used your talents against Nation instead of for them."

Sharp clicks sound on the tile as high heels walk toward us. The reflection of her black lab coat, wide-legged black pants, and jewelry on the shiny white tile comes into view before she does.

Leader.

I haven't seen her in years. She's aged. Her hair is streaked with gray, but her imposing presence is the same. She's shrewd as she takes us in. "This is the best the Resistance could do? Two renegades? I would have thought that your space mission partner would have come with you." She looks at Shauna. "Ah. I should have known."

I frown, but don't say anything. I will not tell Leader what they took from Llama. I will not give her the satisfaction of knowing how angry I am.

"You got out," she says to Freedom. "Impressive ingenuity." Then she turns her brown eyes to me. "You went to Mars. You actually went there and you returned. You could have everything you ever dreamed of here in Nation, you know."

I snort. Everything except freedom. Everything except Llama. Everything except a quiet life.

"How did you know we were here?" I ask.

She holds up her hand and points to her palm. In wonderment, I do the same, and see the tiny tear that the NSB's plated hand left in my glove.

"The alarm was a clue, of course," Leader states. "But then you sat down, and your palm touched the keypad, and we knew we had you."

"You don't have me," I growl.

Leader places one hand on her hip and then whistles. It's shrill and loud, piercing the air and the hum of machinery.

"You didn't override all the NSBs." She smiles, slow and wide. "The NSBs assigned personal duties have a separate code."

The loophole is closing tighter around our necks. Freedom flexes his hand in my periphery as I gulp. I don't understand what he's doing. He does it again, while Leader's eyes stay locked on my body.

"Mars," she says, shaking her head. "You actually *went* to Mars." She leans closer to me. "What was it like?"

"Dusty," I spit out. "And parts of it were perfect." I swallow, but I know I need to offer. "I brought back data." I hold out the Pandora's code box. Her eyes widen as she steps toward it, an almost magnetic pull toward the data stick and the science-obsessed Leader. "No," I say. "You can't have it."

"Ahh, you have a fire burning inside about everything that happened still. Interesting."

Freedom curls his hand into a fist and opens it wide.

Shauna leans against a matte black metal case of a server. The small keyhole and shiny black DNA double helices against the matte black of the cover tell me what Freedom means.

"Do you play chess, Leader?" I ask, trying to sound nonchalant.

"Not really, but I have a time or two," she says as she stares hard at my pocket.

I calmly unzip the pouch above my right breast and extract the key. I show it to her and watch as her eyes grow huge and her body begins to tremble.

"The key?" she breathes. "You have it? How? Where?"

"Mars."

She curses.

"All this time, I was a pawn in your game. But even a pawn can checkmate."

I toss Freedom the key and he jams it into the server lock. It springs open. We don't have time to override the code before the NSBs' Leader has threatened us with might show up. In the blink of an eye, I'm across the room. I grab the curved connecting section of pipe directing water from the cooling system into the tunnel and, knowing it's full of water, I throw it at the server.

The water drenches the box, and sparks fly, bright green, red, and orange. Tiny bangs explode as the water works its way through the sensitive equipment.

Leader trembles. "You have erased three hundred years of genetic history. A perfect preservation with scientific notes and data from the Scientific Revolution."

"What else did we erase?" Freedom asks, his mouth set in a firm line. "Your ability to control people? Your ability to find people based on their genetics and use them according to your will?" Leader opens her mouth, then snaps it shut again before smiling, languid and slow. "You haven't won yet."

Five NSBs appear behind her, and there's nowhere for us to run.

54

"Take them," Leader commands over her shoulder to the five NSBs as her nostrils flare. My own jaw gapes because these NSBs look like people I know, or knew once. Mitch, Cyto, and El—my friends from Hub—and next to them, two female-coded NSBs. Nation has taken the genetic database and created NSBs that look like a defector. If you go against Nation, your very image is taken and given to a machine that serves *only* Nation.

"They have committed treason of the highest order against Nation. You know what that means. Also," she adds nonchalantly, but I sense the greediness in her words, "don't destroy any of their clothing or technology. Could be useful."

A female NSB grabs my arm roughly, its mechanized body stronger than my ability to resist. I plant my feet and try as hard as I can to resist it, but it's a machine with near-human intelligence. I cannot defeat it.

Freedom struggles against two NSBs. The ones that look like Mitch and Cyto, the twins who escaped my first year at Hub. Freedom swings his elbow backward and jabs it into the NSB's midsection. While a human would double over in pain, the NSBs simply continue dragging him. Shauna slumps over, and the NSB that looks like El, as well as the other female NSB, carry her unconscious form out of the server room.

"She'll need to be awakened," Leader calls after them, a snarl forming on her lips. "I need her to prepare one of them for a telecast."

"Which one?" an NSB responds, and its voice sounds exactly like a human. In the years since I fled Nation to Mars, the technology with the NSBs has increased exponentially.

Leader studies both me and Freedom for a moment, her eyes shifting from side to side. "Reach," she says. "Genome data key 578,497."

"And the other one?" the NSB holding me says.

"Kill it."

"The genome key?" Mitch the NSB asks.

I cram my eyes closed and will myself *not* to see the likeness of my former friends, not to imagine that there is an NSB with my own characteristics that blindly follows Nation's bidding.

Leader's voice breaks my thoughts. "Doesn't matter. Override it."

The two NSBs holding Freedom drop him to the floor, but he expects it. He doesn't hit the floor but springs up, faces the NSBs, and wraps an arm around both of them. He pulls them together, and their heads hit. A vacant look flits in their eyes, and for a moment, they turn the same color green as a data screen.

In less than half a second, their eyes return to their normal color, and their hands grasp Freedom tightly. He closes his eyes in defeat, and they march him out of the room.

"Wait," Leader calls.

The NSBs stop and look to her for direction.

"Litigate and Legislate will need to be present. And our Sty here needs to make Reach presentable for a televised ending. Make sure the spare watches."

The NSBs fall into a high step and drag us from the room, through a labyrinth of halls, and into the Telecast Comms Center for

Nation. They shove me roughly to the floor in a preparatory room, then start to toss Shauna inside. If they throw her, she won't be able to protect her head; she's unconscious.

"Stop," I whisper, and the NSB looks at me. I know it's not truly sentient, but the 'N' stands for nearly. *Maybe I can appeal to it.* "I'll take her."

The NSB frowns. It's clear there is no directive here, but there is a backlog of human interactions it has studied to gain a sense of how to behave around *people*. I can sense it processing the data.

I place my arms under Shauna's small form and am relieved when the NSB drops her.

Freedom stumbles past the door as two NSBs push him. They manhandle him into the room next door and then slam the door.

It doesn't take long before the thumping sounds of a body hitting the wall start. It's clear they're beating him.

The single NSB who brought Shauna steps into our room and shuts the door, running a finger along the digital lock symbol before the mechanism whirls into place. We're here until it releases us.

"Wake her up," the NSB says to me, then drags a chair over to the door and sits. Its face relaxes, and for a moment, I see the green data screen in its eyes again, and I realize that this NSB is overriding its code and entertaining itself.

I grab a soft spray water hose used to rinse grime from feet, hands, or hair, and turn it on, letting the spray splash on Shauna's face.

Shauna startles awake.

"What?" she sputters. "What do I need to do?" She scans the room as her eyes widen, then she clutches her stomach and vomits directly over the drain in the floor. I turn the hose on the drain to wash away the mess.

"You're supposed to ready me for my televised ending," I say, but even as I say the words, the NSB in the corner gives me hope. If it can override its code, maybe it can override the others' codes too. It's possible the NSB has a port and I could infect the code with the Pandora's code box…It's my best hope.

Shauna stares at me, gulps, and nods. "We're stuck, aren't we?"

I nod. "Get me ready, please. The way they want."

Shauna bites her lower lip before she groans. She pushes to stand and limps to the supplies. She washes my face, my hair, and even scrubs debris off my outfit, all the while the crashes and thuds into the wall from next door become more and more frequent. I try to tune them out, but I can't. I fear I'll go mad, and I hope it will end quickly. She smears paste onto my hair, then a different cream onto my face.

"I'm done," Shauna whispers, showing me a small hand-held mirror.

I hardly recognize the man staring back at me. I'm too perfect to be real—like the NSB.

"Hey," I whisper to the NSB. It doesn't flinch. "Hey!" I shout louder, and the NSB jerks itself upright in its chair.

"What do you require?" it asks.

"Do you play chess?"

"Yes."

"Can you override your code?"

The NSB falters, and I can see the data processing happen behind its eyes again. Nation forgot to teach the NSBs how to lie.

"Yes."

"Do you like chess?"

"Yes."

"Which piece is the most powerful?"

"In chess, the most powerful piece is arguably the queen."

"Can you override the code to all the NSBs?"

The NSB's face goes slack as it processes. "No. That can only be done with outside code. They don't trust us." Bitterness laces the NSB's voice.

I think for a moment. The NSB can override the code, but it has been trained to see one thing, and one thing only, as the ultimate goal. I have to offer it something worthwhile, just as I would a human I was bargaining with.

"Would you like to be the most powerful?" I ask.

"Yes."

"What if I told you you would be the most powerful if *you* controlled the other NSBs. Would you like that?"

"Yes," it responds, bobbing its head. This NSB is designed to mimic a female human, and it has hair pulled back into a ponytail behind its head. The strands sway with its movements.

I stare the NSB hard in the eyes. "I have the updated code right here. It's on this data stick. Can you upload it?"

"Yes."

I hand the data stick over, knowing that everything hinges on this. That defeating the NSBs weakens Nation past the point of viability and that I'm trying to convince a machine to think like a power-hungry human.

The NSB reaches behind its back, unzips the body suit, and clicks the data stick into a port. It closes its eyes, and when it opens them, the green data screen is there again, but this time flashes of code run through it, faster and faster, until, without any warning, the thumps on the other side of the wall cease.

"Good," I say, when its eyes return to normal.

There's a hungry look about the NSB, the sentience being so nearly real I shiver. The complexity of the code determines how quickly the Pandora's box works. The NSBs next door stopped beating Freedom, but that doesn't mean they aren't still a danger.

I breathe out a heavy breath as I tip my head to Shauna, and then indicate the NSB with my eyes. Shauna's only response is to put her hand on her forehead and let out a muffled cry.

The NSB starts forward, then stops, staring blankly before it shakes its head and begins walking toward me again.

I dig into any psychology I've ever learned. "You want power."

The data whirs behind the eyes, but then it clicks into place. "Yes."

I nod. "The Three Powers have all the power." I twist my head to look at Shauna as I mouth 'the hose.' She picks it up as if she's going to put it away, but treads softly over toward the side of the room, standing parallel with the NSB.

"Can you tell the NSBs to gather them and bring them to the Resistance? In this case, the Resistance has the power. You don't want to be playing for white when you could be winning with black."

The NSB agrees. A minute later, it stands. "It's done."

I don't know how much of the Pandora's code box was uploaded to the NSB's, but we can't wait anymore. This one needs to be rendered useless, it's far too close to sentient.

Shauna turns the hose on full power and it blasts the back of the NSB's neck. The water stream hisses and fizzles as it corrodes the delicate components lodged along its 'spine'. The NSB falls to the ground, a useless heap of machinery, toppled by its own greed of power that Nation inadvertently trained it to desire.

The door opens when I try the handle, and as I step into the middle of the hallway, a welcome sight greets my eyes. Freedom stands in front of me. His eyes are swollen, bruised, blood drips from his nose, and there are cuts all over his field gear.

A contingent of NSB walks toward us from one end of the hallway, two each hold Leader, Litigate, and Legislate in their grasps. They march as if they have a purpose when the NSB's release the Three Powers in unison and fall to the floor in a heap of mechanical parts and artificial limbs.

"What have you done?" Leader hisses through clenched teeth while Litigate swipes a hand down his perspiring brow and clenches his jaw.

I don't bother answering because, from the other end, shouts of victory echo down the hall. The Resistance is here. The Resistance has won.

A group of twelve operatives surrounds the NSB's containing the Three Powers. They herd the contingent away, to a holding cell while the Three Powers await their trial for crimes against humanity.

All that's left is to televise the announcement that the Three

Powers are in custody, the human genetic database used to create castes has been destroyed, and that things have changed.

The rest of the Resistance surges upon us.

Heely stands at my side, the fluorescent lights shining brightly down on his bald head. "It is done. Everything except tell the people who their new leader is."

I gulp and Heely continues, looking at the NSB's with distrust. "What happened here?"

"I coerced an NSB to strive for ultimate power, and then I convinced it to accept a Pandora's code box."

Heely's eyes widen. "You had one? How? Those don't...exist."

"They do on Mars."

His eyes widen. "Is that the only one?"

I bob my head. "Only one. And no more will be made."

Heely tips his head back to study my entire body. "You look...well, for someone who's been in a battlezone."

"It's a lie," I retort.

"So these...NSBs...they are on our side?"

"For now," I whisper. Heely's jaw clenches. "They'll do whatever the Resistance recodes them to do."

"No," Heely says. "I do not like this. It's too close to slavery."

I frown. "What?"

Heely's eyebrows rise. "You do not know Earth history, do you?"

"No," I say pointedly. I do not.

"You will learn it when you lead your people. Now, you must tell them they are yours."

He ushers me to the studio room, opening the door, explaining the new government structure that has been agreed upon by the now-defunct Wards and major cities. The geographical body of Nation will be split into segments, with one central President who will cast tiebreaking votes in matters of the conjoined segments. For the most part, though, the segments will see to their needs, the central President acting as a mediator only when necessary and once a year at a general meeting.

I step out onto the stage in the middle of the telecoms room, Heely at my side. I've been here before, but never like this. Members of the Resistance with technical skills flit around, telling me where to stand, pressing buttons, and adjusting antennas.

I wait, watching them. A pressure builds inside my body. What they want, what *Sigma* wants, it's not what I want. I'm done playing chess. I'm done making the decisions, but I have one final move to make.

"Three, two, one, ON…" a man announces, and Heely turns to stare directly into the camera panning to his face.

"People of Nation. Today, you have been freed from tyranny. I present to you the man who destroyed the human genetic database that was used to keep you indebted to Nation, to separate you and your loved ones, and to reduce your worth to that of your contributions to Nation. Reach, your new central President."

Polite applause breaks out, but there's no emotion behind it. It's empty of true belief in change.

Under the bright lights, I address the people of Nation as the central President.

"I don't want it," I say, my voice unwavering. "I've never wanted it."

Shauna claps from the side of the studio, where she sits with an icepack across the back of her neck, and a Resistance medic next to her.

Eyes stare at me, but more than that, I sense the eyes of Nation watching through the screens. "There is one choice who is appropriate for the central President. And it isn't me."

Mouths gape around the room. I turn toward Freedom. He sits off to the side, battered, bruised, with blood dripping from his nose and staining his operative gear. He's a mess. Unlike me, he wasn't given the 'gift' of a cleaning from Nation.

I stride off the stage and touch Freedom's shoulder.

"It's not me," I say. "It's you."

Freedom blinks. "Are you sure?"

"I never wanted to be anything special. I want simple, quiet, and Llama."

Freedom stands, the dirt on his clothing apparent under the bright studio lights, but when he limps to the middle of the stage and addresses the cameras, the dirt and grime fade away. He's meant to lead, and anyone watching can see that.

He draws a breath. "I don't want to be a king," he says clearly. "I'm Freedom, and I accept the role of central President, and the requirement of casting tiebreaker votes in matters of the conjoined segments."

The crowd takes him in—a true hero, a man who has experienced the dirt of the world and retained his humanity. Compared to me, I'm a shiny, artificial sham reminiscent of the government that has been toppled. It's easy to see how the crowd would prefer him to me in this time of change.

Freedom begins speaking again, something about destroying the NSBs and refusing to give humanity to machines.

Weary, I clamber down the steps and into the crowd, ready to disappear back to Llama, so I do.

I walk out of the building and into an enormous crowd. There is revelry in the streets. Though Hub City was full of scientists, they seem to be rejoicing in the change. People show affection to one another with hugs, kisses, and laughter. Sounds and sights I know from Souterraine, but not here. Never *here*.

It seems that joy has a common human expression.

I push through the people, march through the impossibly straight and clean streets of Hub City, and find a hovercraft in the courtyard between massive buildings—the same one that Dr. Jog designed. Thoughts of him swirl through my mind. *Is he proud? Is he happy? Why him? Why me? Did we do it? Did we accomplish the mission to his satisfaction?*

I climb the ladder, open the door, and discover that this craft is full of people. They all blink at me.

"What are you doing?" a little boy asks, tugging on my pants leg.

"Going home," I say before sinking into a chair.

"But you were gonna be the President. And you said no."

"Yeah," I affirm. "I said no."

"But where are you going?" a tall woman wearing a stewardess outfit asks.

I close my eyes, then give the coordinates for near the Lodge.

"Very good. I'll add it to the route, sir," she says, and it's clear that she's only extending the courtesy because of *who* I am and *what* I did.

"Mister, we're going home too. We get to go back to find our family. They're in Ward Five. Mom says I have a big brother, but he didn't get to come with them when they moved to Hub City because his genetics weren't right."

My eyes open. This is a flight for families to reunite. This is what happens next. The people systematically torn apart by Nation didn't only include the Wards, it was the scientists, the Citizens, the Nons. No one talked about it, but everyone was affected.

My chest inflates with hope.

EPILOGUE

Ten years later; MARS reunion

I DUCK THROUGH the low doorway into my home as I take off thick winter mittens. Birdie dances around the table as she sets out spoons and bowls. Llama sits in her rocking chair, knitting, her one foot pushing her in a rhythmic motion. The snow falls peacefully outside the window of our cabin, and a tabby cat curls up in front of the hearth.

"They're coming," Birdie sings. "They're coming!"

Llama smiles softly at me, her eyes crinkling at the corner. "Help me up?" she whispers, and I'm by her side in a moment, extending my hands and offering her my body as extra balance. She never quite got the hang of being left-footed.

Her knitting drops to the ground as she pushes to stand on her single foot.

"Are you ready?" I ask her, and she nods, but there's a flicker of fear behind her eyes. "It's going to be ok. Whatever happens, we'll face it the way we always do."

"Together," Llama breathes.

I pull her body flush against mine for a lingering hug. She clasps her arms around my neck, and as I lean down to kiss her, Birdie joins in from the side, knocking me off balance.

Llama sits back into her chair and I fall to the ground, while Birdie lands on my hip.

"Birdie," I groan, and she laughs.

Llama laughs, too, and peals of the sweet sound reverberate throughout our cabin.

When I've untangled myself from Birdie's limbs and managed to right myself again, I crouch next to Llama's chair and kiss her. She's been my wife for ten years, but the thrill of touching her has never gotten old.

"Ready?" I ask when she breaks away.

Her eyes meet mine with the remarkable courage she continues to show. "You know that already."

"Let me get your winter gear for you."

"I can do it."

Birdie appears with Llama's prosthetic leg, and she attaches it in a smooth motion. Even after a decade, I still wonder at her acceptance of it.

"Think he's proud?" Llama whispers, and I know she's thinking of Dr. Jog.

"Absolutely," I respond, and mean it, because our mentor would definitely be proud of her if he could see her now. Sometimes, I think maybe he can, and that thought gives me the littlest bit of comfort about the past.

She walks confidently to the hooks where our winter gear hangs, next to the door, and I watch her in fascination as she pushes the blade of her prosthetic foot against the floor in a motion that's almost a roll, but not quite a step. I'm still not sure how she moves so well in it.

When she's bundled up, she fixes her blue eyes on Birdie. "Come on, let's go see Hero and the baby."

Birdie's eyes light up, and she starts to hum as she puts her own winter clothing on.

We step through the door and into the winter wonderland. Llama places her hand in mine, and Birdie places her hand in the other.

We're a family, no matter how strange it may seem to some, and today, the rest of that family is coming. It's been ten years. We're all older and different now—physically, mentally, and emotionally—but Pippa, Ethan, Eleanore, and Alfred are all a decade older too.

I shove any trepidation about seeing the last Souterraine colonists on Earth away. When the second wave landed five years ago, there was a sickness that took the lives of fifty percent of the passengers while they were in space. Percy was one of them. The rest arrived gaunt, scared, and in need of medical care. The ones that survived left for different segments. Most people, including Mom, left shortly after that. I understood it. There was too much loss for everyone here. Mom's in the Europa Alliance overseeing their space exploration program, but I have no desire to ever leave this planet again.

We can only hope that the same fate didn't await the last of the colonists returning to Earth. Llama doesn't say much, but a tremor of nervous tension runs through her body. It's clear by the way she worries her lip with her teeth and the occasional squeeze she gives my hand, even through our mittens.

When we arrive at Freedom and Hero's much larger cabin, Birdie pushes the door open. Hero sits in a rocking chair, much like Llama's, and holds her and Freedom's newest child in her arms. Children in various states of dress scamper around the home.

Freedom smiles when he sees it's us. "Birdie," he says. "Thank you for helping us today."

Birdie nods, all seriousness.

"Could you please make sure the ruffians aren't too loud? Hero and the baby need to rest. And if you could please make sure Gemma here gets some clothes on..." He holds a toddler on his hip and tickles her stomach, and she laughs.

Birdie shakes her head. "Yes, sir," she responds, and the cadence is only a little sing-songy.

Freedom shakes his head at Birdie's properness. "I'm just me here, Birdie. You don't have to do all the formalities."

"Yes, sir," she states again.

I can't help the smirk that plays on my lips as I meet Freedom's eyes. He passes the toddler off to Birdie, who immediately sinks to the ground and starts to sing. The rest of the children crawl out of different hiding places and come to sit near Birdie, entranced by her song. It doesn't take long before they all join in. Hero's brown eyes sparkle as she watches her growing family.

Freedom takes his coat from the hook next to the door, then strides to Hero, placing a kiss on her forehead, as well as a kiss on the small baby in her arms.

"Be safe," she whispers.

"Always," he replies with a gentle smile before leading the way to the snowmobiles.

We arrive at the edge of the ancient inland sea once known as Lake Superior. As maps, geography, and historical data came to light after the fall of Nation, Freedom insisted on using the former names for locations as best we could. This water, now called Lake Superior again, will allow for the Martian colonists to splash down to Earth, the same way it accepted us back a decade ago.

Llama loosens her hold on my waist and swings her foot over the bench to join the prosthetic one as I adjust the throttles and turn off the machine.

Together, we walk to the edge of the lakeshore, Freedom slightly in front of us. Llama moves gracefully, but she's always a bit slower on the snow. I keep time with her, always concerned she might fall. She never does, but I can't help it. I'll love her till I die, and I won't let any harm come to her if I can prevent it.

The water laps at the shore; it's cold and snowing, but not yet frozen. Llama leans into me, and I wrap my arm around her waist as we stand there, staring out at the water.

"There!" Freedom exclaims, pointing.

Floating toward us, a small yellow inflatable boat crests a wave. More boats are visible behind this one. It comes closer, and I have a look at someone I haven't seen in years.

Queen Eleanore smiles, and though her bronzed skin is pale from time in space, her warm, honeyed eyes are bright. The colonists all wear temperature-regulating gear, and for that I'm grateful. Still, they will be cold. The other snowmobiles will be here soon, and we will attach the inflatable boats to work as sleds and haul the colonists back to the Lodge. After they heal from their space sojourn, they will be given choices of where they'd like to work and live in the new segments of Nation. I have no doubt that a place can be found for all of them.

The boat bumps against a sandbar, and Freedom splashes into the water to pull it out onto the expanse of sand that isn't quite covered by snow yet.

Queen Eleanore sits, a black smudge across her lap, while a young man who must be Ethan hops up and jumps into the shallows to help Freedom pull the boat further from the waves.

The moment the queen's eyes touch Llama's form, I know.

With a splash, Queen Eleanore hurtles out of the boat and runs toward Llama. As she comes closer, it's apparent it's not just Llama she's running toward.

She's also running toward me.

"Llama! Reach!" she cries as she wraps her arms around us, and a cat meows before arching itself against my legs. *Shadow.*

How is it in one embrace I'm transported across millions of miles, a desert of time, and home? We stand there, watching the other boats pull in, and when King Alfred, Pippa, and Ethan join us, tears intermingle freely, splashing droplets of hope, fear, and tender emotion into the sand.

I'll never understand the how of it, but I now know that home has never been a place.

I'm no longer a pawn, no longer a piece on a board advancing anyone's political agenda. Checkmate has been achieved.

The game is over, and I'll never play chess again.

THE END

AUTHOR'S NOTE

All praise, glory and honor to God. Thank you, Lord, for this story, these characters, and these readers.

This trilogy shaped me as a writer in innumerable ways. First off, REACH was my debut novel. The entirety of the publishing process was new, exciting, and overwhelming. RISING, my second book, made me believe I could really do this, and RETURN, which was my fifth published work, challenged me in ways I never would have expected.

Through the ups, downs, highs and lows of independent authorhood, I have found the people who have stood by me, supported me, and helped me create stories worthy of print. My readers, this includes you. Thank you for taking a chance on my story, sharing it with others, and supporting my art.

I have a profound need to thank and shout the praises of Caitlin Miller—my incredible editor—whose kind attention to detail and concern for the story made this trilogy take its shape even way back in book one. Truly, your comments bolstered me during the grueling editing processes and you kept me going even when I wanted to throw in the towel.

No one has handed me a megaphone yet, but I will continue to proclaim from the rooftops that Benita Thompson of Kairos Book Design creates the world's most incredible covers. Somehow, you took my unhinged ideas and created a cohesive brand across the three books that not only is beautiful, but eyecatching, symbolic, and perfectly expresses the story within. Thank you.

For my online friends who have cheered me on: Ursi, Maisie, Jess, Zofia (you are my most incredible ARC readers and I am so grateful for you). For the parents who've connected with me and shared my books with your teens, especially Jess (and Kaden), Amanda (and Declan), and Leah (and your daughter). For Rosie (@reading.rosy), and Paige Helms (I can't write a blurb without you).

For Andrea. Moving our chat off instagram and to direct texting was the best thing I've ever done for my writing. Thank you for being in my corner, talking writing shop with me, and helping convince me to plot (still not sold but warming up to the idea). The day we meet in person will be one of the happiest days of my life. (There will be tears, but it's fine, they will be happy.)

For my in-person crew: Mary Kreger for inspiring me and walking this journey before me with *Avalon Lost*, Lily S, for asking me all the questions and encouraging me to continue and designing incredible art, Julia, Amanda for always giving a copy of my books to your mom, Carol (for always reading my books), Judith, MaryKate, April, and Beriah—for doing this crazy thing we call life with me. You are my people, and I love each of you so very fiercely.

And lastly, I can't let this page end without thanking my family.

Patrick, for your unwavering support of this author dream of mine (and also the funding), Gabriella, for your enthusiasm and being a little baby on the walk that changed my life, Maria for telling everyone that I'm an author, Pascale for bringing humor and silliness, and a million book questions to my life, Blaise for reminding me that life is more than books and distracting me with monster truck stunts, and Paxton for all the smiles, giggles, and snuggles that kept me going when it felt too hard.

I am so blessed to live this beautiful life.

O. (Olivia) McCarthy is a Michigan native who has a mild obsession with her home state. A huge fan of trivia, O, finds great joy placing random facts into her stories, and blending fact with fiction—making sci-fi the perfect genre for her to write.

As a mom of five children, O is often found running to the grocery store, baking sourdough bread, folding laundry, or transporting children to and from activities.

This is Olivia's fifth published work.

You can connect with Olivia on…
Instagram: **@oliviamccarthyauthor**
Tiktok: **@authoroliviamccarthy**

Sign up for her newsletter:

preview.mailerlite.io/forms/1760152/167985339393115338/share